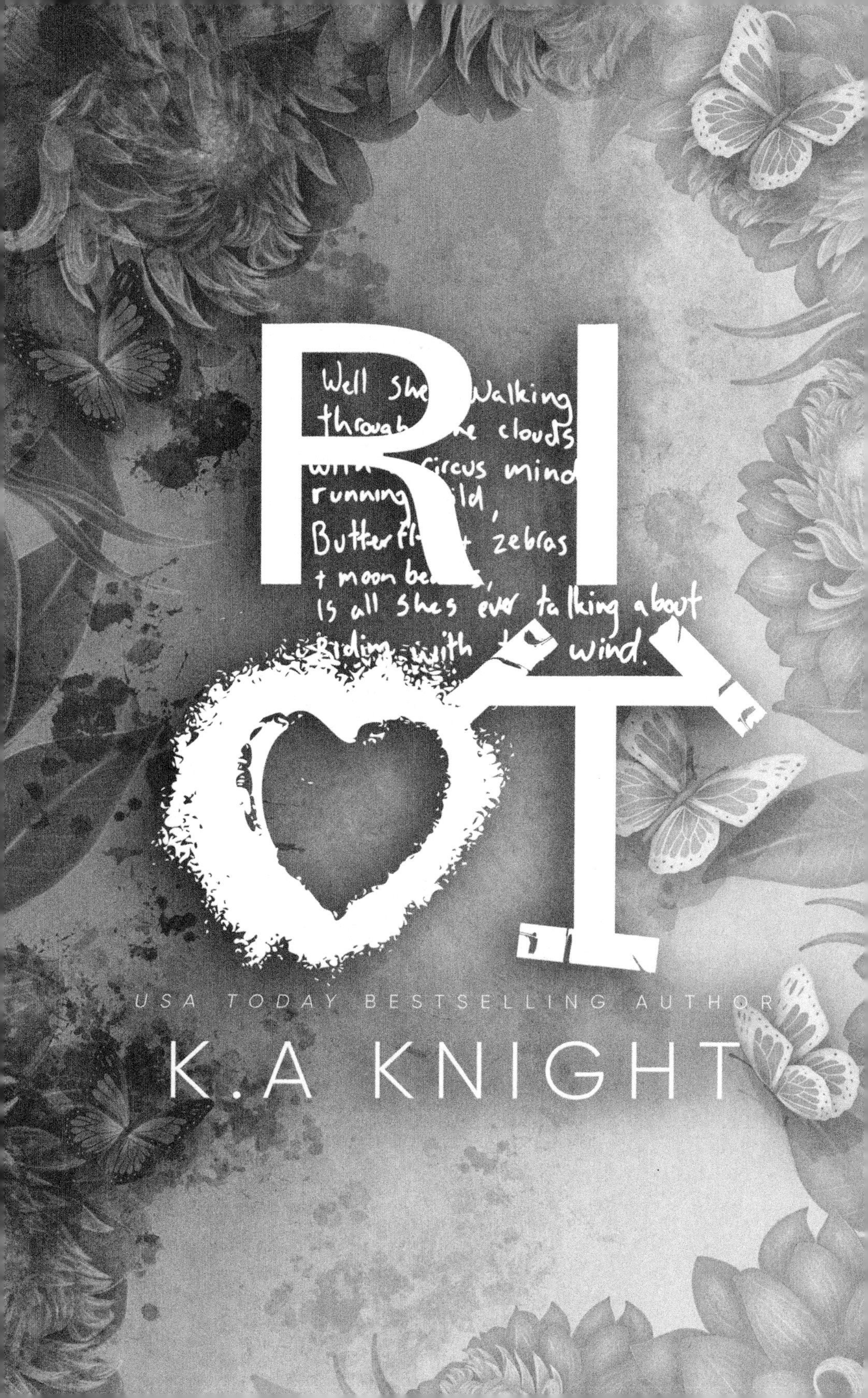
RIOT
USA TODAY BESTSELLING AUTHOR
K.A KNIGHT

Written by K.A. Knight.
Edited By Jess from Elemental Editing and Proofreading.
Proofreading by Norma's Nook.
Formatted by The Nutty Formatter.
Art by Dily Iola Designs
Cover by Moonstruck Cover Design & Photography

READER CONSIDERATIONS

This is a very dark book not meant for anybody under the ages of 18. Content includes: explicit sex, explicit violence, stalking, murder, torture, sexual assault, dubious consent, depression, PTSD, childhood abuse, drug missue, alcohol misuse and much more.

PROLOGUE

"It seems the music world has been filled with nothing but scandals in the last year or so, and tonight is no different. We have another shocking revelation for you. Fallon, the world's most beloved morbid rocker, has released a statement ahead of her upcoming book and tour—"

"The statement sent the world into shockwaves this morning as Fallon finally addresses the rumors swirling since her childhood—"

"Many are horrified at the allegations and truth coming to light about Fallon's past—"

"Many remember Fallon's father, legendary rock star Agille from the band Electric Giants, but it appears nothing was what it seemed—"

"It seems Fallon, the ice queen of rock, is ready to melt—"

I turn away from the news reports with a Cheshire cat grin.

Melt?

They have no idea.

I'm about to start a tidal wave.

I'm going to start a riot.

ONE

Fallon

More dahlias arrive, and I stare at them with a sigh. I don't know how he got my address, but he has friends in high places. Kage is an up-and-coming rock star, and for some reason, he has set his sights on me.

Fool.

Tossing them in the trash, I walk farther into my house without an ounce of regard for the beautiful flowers that have shown up every single day since I turned him down at that awards show. Maybe it should bother me that I don't feel anything anymore, but that icy numbness is better than pain.

I am simultaneously empty and too full at the same time. My entire existence is a juxtaposition. I can never quite fully breathe, yet I am numb. I sing about love and hope, yet I have never felt anything but despair and pain.

Maybe I should start at the beginning and why they call me the ice queen.

Why I can't trust the man sending the flowers . . .

Why I became the way I am . . .

A year ago . . .

I am expected to be okay, but no one cares if I'm not, so I grit my teeth and suffer alone, knowing that one day, it will be too much. They will care then, and that makes me so angry, I want to scream. I want to rip their perfect illusions to shreds, but instead, I sip the overpriced Champagne and force a smile onto my face. No one looks under the surface. My chest tightens by increments with each short, sharp breath, and the room is closing in. My clothes are too tight, and my skin is too hot.

I feel it all and nothing.

I am alive but not living.

I am just moving through life, trying to make myself as small as possible. I feel like I don't belong, as if I don't have the right to take up space in a body that doesn't feel like it fits.

Part of me hates everyone, while the other part of me begs for them to notice me.

Maybe someone will care someday, or they won't and I'll be stuck here, screaming inside, forgotten and alone where I belong.

I'll be left with the other relics of the past people chose to ignore.

I shake myself from my thoughts, and then I see him.

He shines as he walks around the tables and sits at my side. His face is familiar, and I can't remember why, but suddenly, I can breathe again. I can feel, and I just stare.

It's another awards show. I don't even know why I'm here other than it was better than being alone at home, trying to pretend everything is fine.

He grins at me as he turns to see me watching him, and it's like my eyes clear when I see the devastatingly handsome man sitting next to me. His hair is black and swept artfully back—not too short, not too long. His perfect skin covers high cheekbones and a sharp jaw. His eyes are dark and deadly looking. I see tattoos peeking from his suit, but I force myself to stop looking. There are a lot of attractive men here, and tall, dark, and handsome isn't in short supply—not with the money they spend to look that way, even if there is something different about this one.

"Hi, I'm Kage. You're Fallon."

"How astute," I retort. My cutting attitude is enough to deter most people, but his expression doesn't falter. If anything, his smile grows, his eyes twinkling as he leans in.

"I've been called many things, but that's a new one."

I offer him a tight smile and force my eyes away as the awards show begins. I want to slouch, but I remember my extensive training and force myself to sit taller, holding my Champagne like a shield and giving my hands something to do.

I feel Kage lean closer, but I don't glance his way. "Where's your boyfriend tonight?"

"Husband," I correct, peering at him. This close, he has beautiful golden flecks in his eyes, so different from my cold ones.

"That's the one." He aims a rakish, crooked smile at me.

Rolling my eyes, I turn my attention back to the stage. "He didn't want all the attention." He hates it. He hates the cameras and the fans. I loved that at first, that he hated everything as much as I did, but now it just annoys me. I might not feel much when I'm with him, but at least he was a buffer, an excuse. Now, he seems to avoid these things as much as possible. I might be a cruel bitch, but I love my job and singing, and I want to support new singers in a way I never was, so I'm here, alone, being hit on by the playboy of pop/rock.

Yes, I know who he is even if I'll never admit it, nor the fact that his woodsy scent wraps around me.

When his mouth nearly touches my ear as he leans in, my heart pounds for the first time in a very long time. "No offense, beautiful, but that's a pile of shit. You need to be showed off and have someone who shines with you, not holds you back. You shouldn't settle for someone who isn't willing to love you at your brightest."

"And what would you know about that?" I snap, growing annoyed. He isn't saying things I haven't already told myself, but it's annoying that he's seen them. Why did he notice that? How closely has this man been watching me?

"A lot. I'll show you if you'll let me." He smirks, his eyes heating as they sweep down my body.

"Are you forgetting my husband?" I point out the ring on my finger, the one I bought since he was struggling for money when we first met. That was another thing I liked, being in power and knowing he was dependent on me, not the other way around. It meant I had a hold on him. Toxic, I know, but it's a lesson learned.

"I don't see him here, but if you tell me you're really happy in your marriage, then I'll back off. I'll wait," he murmurs, his eyes only for me despite our surroundings, and I'm sucked into the aura that surrounds him despite everything.

"Wait?" I repeat.

"Wait." He nods, leaning in until his mouth is pressed against my ear. "Wait until you're done with him, tired of him, and toss him aside, and then I'll be right here, waiting."

I snort, a sound I never make, and my heart spasms at his words. He's implying I'll end my marriage, which I don't think I ever will. Despite the coolness between us now, I genuinely care for Gerald. Maybe not as deeply as one should for their husband, but still, it's more than I've ever felt before.

I might even love the man, if I were capable of that.

I should say all that, but instead, something else slips out. "What makes you think I would ever give you a shot?"

"Because, baby, I'd be so fucking good to you. I've been waiting for a chance to meet you . . . to love you."

"You're insane," I reply since we just met. "Besides, I don't do love."

"Then I'll love enough for both of us." He shrugs casually, like talking about loving me, a married stranger, is totally normal.

What is this guy's deal?

He seemed so sane online and in interviews. He's filled with life, love, and passion, everything I'm lacking.

"That will only get you a broken heart," I retort rather than ignoring the crazy bastard grinning at me like I'm the best thing he's ever seen. It's not the usual obsession I see in fans or men. He's not wondering how quickly he can get into my pants, although desire is there, and he's not reaching for my fame or my money. He's looking at me, truly looking at me, as if he sees all the way to my bitter, broken core and likes it. There is pure want in his eyes, obsession, as if nothing else in this world exists but me and my words.

It's addictive and slightly terrifying.

"Then break it," he urges, still smiling. "Fucking smash it to pieces, sweetheart. I'll thank you for it."

"You're fucking insane." I laugh, shaking my head as I clap along with everyone else.

He leans in once more, his eyes only for me. "You have no idea, Fallon, but you will."

Trying to shake Kage is like trying to avoid the paparazzi. He's everywhere I turn. During the awards show, he flirted until I made my escape, and now he's heading toward me at the after-party. I quickly make my getaway, saying goodbye to Beck Danvers, a new rock star who is genuinely kind, but on the way home, all I can think of are his eyes.

His promises, wicked looks, and lustful glances.

Despite the situation, my hand sneaks under my dress in the back seat of my car.

My head falls back as I slide my fingers across my pussy, rubbing my clit. My back arches slightly as I widen my legs.

It's wrong, and the ring on my finger catches on my panties as I slip my fingers deeper inside and stroke my cunt, feeling the wetness gathered there. His face fills my mind, along with his obsessed eyes as I gasp, circling my throbbing clit.

Lust pours through me, and I've never felt anything like it before.

My back arches in the leather seat, and my teeth dig into my lip to stifle my moan of pleasure as I dance toward my release. I see his wicked eyes watching me in my mind and imagine his hand snaking under my dress and replacing mine, demanding my pleasure.

"That's it, sweetheart. Come for me. Let me worship you."

I almost scream as I come harder than I ever have before, and when I pull my shaking fingers out of my panties, I stare down at the slickness there in embarrassment.

Shit, what's wrong with me?

"We are back, Miss Fallon." The voice comes through the divider. Fuck, did my driver hear me? Oh well, he gets paid enough.

Without a word, I slide from the car, watching the iron gates close as they seal me into my mansion once more. I don't even spare the white-and-brown exterior of my estate a glance. Most of the lights are off, but the door is unlocked.

"Good evening, Miss Fallon." I nod absentmindedly at the staff and head up one side of the staircase to the second floor. My heels click down the hall, the wooden floor that was hand-carved just for me taking the brunt of my shame and anger as I reach the open double door of my room.

I head straight to the bathroom adjacent to my room, kicking off my shoes, dress, and jewels as I go without care. I unbind my hair as I step under the spray of the shower, letting it wash away Kage's woodsy scent, which I can still taste.

I have to scrub my body twice, and when I'm done, I slip into a lace cami set and pad across the plush gray carpet toward the king-sized bed that is the main feature in the room.

One side of the bedding is made, while the other is wrapped around my sleeping husband.

I slide in next to him, turning to him in the dark, my hand tracing across his chest and lower.

He rumbles. He's awake then, not asleep.

He doesn't ask about the awards show or my night. Instead, he captures my hand and pulls it up, pressing it to his chest and holding it. "Not tonight."

That's all he says.

Not tonight.

I turn over, giving him my back as my eyes connect with the moon, which seems to shine just for me outside of my arched windows, showcasing the estate I proudly bought for its opulence. It's just another fuck you to my father.

Now, though, it feels too big and empty.

"I'd never let you go."

His words chase me into fitful dreams.

TWO

Fallon

"Well, Fallon, I only have one more question, if that's okay?" Louise, the interviewer, asks kindly. I hate interviews, but they are a necessity. I'm still tired from a restless night, and when I got up, Gerald, my husband, had already been gone. I wandered my huge, empty house, wondering when our marriage had become this cold.

Or maybe it always was.

Maybe I just didn't notice it, detached from my own reality like I always seem to be.

Apart from him, a little voice whispers.

I hate that it's right. Last night, Kage brought my detachment to a screeching halt and forced me to feel with just a flirty conversation. I don't know how or why, but it left me shaken and on edge. It doesn't bode well for the interview, and I know I've been stiffer than I should be. Maybe that's why I don't see the daggers coming until it's too late.

Usually, I'm two steps ahead.

Not today.

Today, they win.

"We were recently sent these pictures, and I thought we should ask you since we're worried."

I glance behind her to the screen they use, and my smile freezes on my face as I stare. My heart crumbles in my chest, and my entire world falls to pieces around me. I feel like I sink into the floor, but I'm still sitting here stiffly. Cameras and lights are aimed at me, and I start to sweat, my body overheating even as goose bumps rise on my flesh.

"Is everything okay in your marriage? Your husband's infidelity will be all over the news today, and I know this must be a very hard time for you both, but your fans are worried about you."

Infidelity.

The word echoes in my head as I stare at the pictures displayed there to cause as much damage as possible. They are pictures I have never seen before. There, with a bright smile on his face, brighter than he's ever given me, is my husband. A woman is locked in his embrace, and her lipstick is smeared across his face. There's one of him with his head thrown back, and another of him lifting her over his shoulder as they go into a hotel together. The last is the worst, and I can't breathe as I stare at it.

It's from a long-angled lens, and it was taken through an open window.

He's on his back, the sheet pooled around him as his back arches as the same woman, now naked, rides his cock. The date is from last week.

It was the date of our anniversary, when he was late to the dinner I had painstakingly planned since it felt like I should. He was late.

He was late because he was fucking her. I don't know which annoys me more. The fact that he dared to be late or that he dared to fuck someone else like he doesn't have the fucking catch of all catches at home. I fucking cooked for him. I never do that, I hate cooking, yet my thoughts come back to one solid musing.

My husband is cheating on me.

Maybe he has been for a while.

He cheated, and I'm left staring as they wait for my reaction.

They will use it to sell their show and their papers, all while my world splinters around me. I created the perfect life as a fuck you to my past, and now it's crumbling. The safety and sanctuary I created is gone.

Stolen.

"Fallon, are you okay?" The fake concern is cloying in her tone, and I blink, bringing her back into focus. Her eyes are narrowed. They want me to break. They want to plaster it across TV, hysterical Fallon who cries after finding her husband is cheating on her with a younger, hotter woman.

They want my anger and pain.

They won't get it.

I've spent years burying my feelings, repressing them after what I've been through. I've never given into the pain, and I spent years being camera trained by my father. The punishments if I failed were a lot worse than this now.

I don't crack, not even a little, but I know I will eventually, like a ticking time bomb.

I feel it building like a wave behind a dam, ready to splash over.

I need to get out of there now. The panic in that thought is what gets me to unhinge my jaw and speak, even when it feels like I've swallowed my tongue.

"This interview is over. Thank you for having me, Louise." I can scarcely breathe as I stand. I can't even lift my hand to wave at the fans, and in the complete, deafening silence of the studio, I calmly walk off stage when all I feel is pure agony.

Shock.

Pain.

It's more than I've felt in years, and the emotions are so strong they stagger me. I can't breathe in enough air or see as I hurry to my car, and once inside, I slam the partition closed and let the tears fall.

My hands hit the seats as I sob, the barrier silencing them so the world will never know. I scream and cry as the tears slide down my cheeks.

He cheated and destroyed our marriage. More than that, he destroyed everything I worked for, leaving me ambushed and weak, which I hate.

Maybe I didn't love Gerald, but I cry for what I lost, for the love we could have had, the friendship, the companionship, the buffer, and everything it means.

I am unlovable.

I will never be enough, just like my father said.

I know the paparazzi will be waiting for me at home, so I swallow down my pain. I bury it so deep they will never find it. I clean up my face, smooth my hair back into place, and tug on my dress until I'm perfectly put together.

I appear cold and aloof, even though I'm falling apart on the inside.

I get out of the car, waving at the cameras, and head into my house.

He cheated on me? *Fine.*

I don't need him. I don't need anyone.

He's just another person in a long list of those who let me down.

I was a fool, but I won't be again.

I didn't break down for the cameras, but inside my house, I did.

His clothes lie shredded around me. All the expensive suits and designer clothes I meticulously bought and viciously tore apart. The bottle of wine is half empty as I take a deep drink from the bottle.

He will be back soon, and he will find his suitcase outside, along with divorce papers. I want this over and done with quickly. He knew what he was doing, knew what would happen. He wanted out, and he got it. He will no longer have my money and house to fall back on. Gerald can face the wolves alone. He destroyed everything we had, and now I'm doing the same.

We were partners. Maybe there wasn't love and passion like he wanted, but we always agreed on being a united front. Not anymore.

I don't even give him the benefit of a conversation because he doesn't deserve it. Nothing he could say can change what he did, and I can never forgive him for sullying our marriage and the trust he won from me when no one else ever could.

I look at the TV, seeing the name they are calling me after my stony exit from the interview.

Ice queen.

I like it.

Cold and impenetrable.

No one will ever hurt me again if I am ice.

I give them nothing—not a post or an interview. My husband gets what he came into this marriage with and nothing else. The cars, the houses, and the money are all mine, and he can't have them. He won't take them from me, and I made sure of that with a prenup.

Without me, he's nothing, and he knows it.

I ignore my phone and the doorbell—the staff was instructed not to answer. The locks have already been changed. He worked quickly, but I was quicker. I swept every inch of him from my life as swiftly as he entered it. I don't need a reminder of another person who hurt me, and when I stand and head downstairs, I instruct the staff to clean up the remains of his clothes.

It's done. It's over.

I wander the house aimlessly, needing to keep moving until I see the flower lying on the kitchen counter. For some reason, I'm drawn to it, picking up the blue and pink dahlia before opening the black card alongside it.

For every time we have met, I will send you one as a reminder that I am not going anywhere. I told you he didn't deserve you. Give them nothing, baby. I'll be waiting for you.

Your Kage

There's a number under that. I scoff, crumpling the card even as I pick up the flower once more.

I can't bring myself to throw it out for some reason.

K♥F
Golden Love
I'll be with you.
I'll wait for you.
Golden Love
Can't you see
I'm your fool?

THREE

KAGE

I'm finally back.

I've been training and touring, but now I'm back, and she won't get away from me this time. Fallon is the love of my life; she just doesn't know it yet. It isn't just desire. It's a need to peel back the layers to the woman underneath. I bet she had no idea when I sat next to her that night a year ago that it changed my life forever. I've fought tooth and nail to get where I am just to be near her. I've been obsessed and in love with her for years.

I've sent her a flower every single day we have been apart—one flower for the number of times we have met—or so she thinks.

She doesn't have a clue how I have built my life to be her equal so I can give her everything she deserves and be her partner.

I have watched everything about her. I've seen the men she has paraded through her life—models, actors, singers, doctors, and a prince —but never more than once. I watched her ex-husband blow up his own life, and I protected her from it, not that she will ever know.

When he tried to sell stories about her to make a quick buck since he's broke, I blocked them. I also… *spoke* to him, and he disappeared from her world, leaving her without the constant reminder of betrayal.

I don't know if Fallon ever loved him or if she's ever truly loved anyone.

It doesn't matter.

I love her enough for both of us.

"Kage?" Alice, my PR manager, queries. I spare her a look and a polite smile. I am the sweet, kind pop star to most people. They don't have a clue about what hides underneath—what I hid just for her.

"Yes, agree to the events," I respond as I stand. Her eyes sweep down my body, and my smile dips in annoyance. I have made careful choices to build my team so none of them look at me that way so Fallon has nothing to be jealous about.

I know they call me the playboy king, but that was all a carefully crafted image to make me desirable so I could catch her attention, and it worked.

"See Elijah on your way out," I comment as she stands, teetering on too high heels. Her smile warms, her iPad clutched in her grip as she saunters out of the suite I am currently staying in. I'm planning to secure the house right next to Fallon's. The present inhabitants just need a little helping hand in vacating . . . and selling.

I hear Elijah enter, and I command, "Get rid of her," without looking at him, my eyes scanning the city beyond. I wonder where she is and what she's doing right now.

"Alice? Damn it, Kage, she was the best—"

"Now," I snap.

He knows better than to argue. He might not understand why I'm so strict with my staff, but he doesn't have to. We might be friends, but no one comes before Fallon and the future I'm building for us.

"I'll find another one." He sighs as he starts to leave.

"Elijah." I turn to face him. "Pull the car around, I have somewhere to be."

"We have that interview—"

I raise my eyebrow, and he groans.

"It's only the most important thing in your career, but what do I know?"

"Good boy." I grin as I turn back to the view.

I'm coming, Fallon. You better be ready.

I knock on the ornate door and wait. The house is nice and big, but it isn't what I care about. My eyes go to the house next door, separated only by a wall. If I'm lucky, I will be able to see into her windows. I might even knock the wall down.

It took me a whole year to earn enough to afford this life, to afford her and give her whatever she needs, and I'm not wasting another second. The door opens, and a butler blinks at me. "Sir?"

"I have a meeting with the Culets." I slip past him with a sweet smile.

"Oh, uh, please follow me. They are in the sitting room right now." He spares me a confused glance but leads the way, and once I'm in the sitting room, I wait for him to leave before turning to face them.

They are an older couple who come from money, but it's drying up. I know since I had a guy look into it. I might have also had their advisor invest in some bad investments and lose their money all to get them right where I want them. They blink at me in unison, looking exactly as I imagined they would.

"Who are you?" Mrs. Culet asks, her pearl necklace almost tucked into her pink blazer. Her legs are encased in a matching pink skirt, and they are crossed perfectly. There isn't a gray hair out of place, even in her own home. I spare her husband, who was reading the paper, a look. He's frowning at me, not wanting to be rude but not remembering a meeting.

He won't because there isn't one.

"You don't need to know my name. All you need to know is why I'm here. I'm here to buy your house." I smile widely. "I have the paperwork here. The price is very fair, and I have added a little extra if you are able to vacate by the end of the day."

Mrs. Culet gapes, her mouth open. "Get out this instant."

"No." I step closer, feeling my eyes go cold and lifeless.

"You need the money. We both know that. You can't afford this house or lifestyle anymore. Take the money, invest it, and say you wanted a change, move out of the city. I don't care. Sign the paperwork, I have somewhere to be."

"Who are you?" Mr. Culet asks, folding his paper.

Opening the briefcase I carry, I set it on the table before the china tea set and spread out the documents and pens, and then I pass the offer to both of them. Elijah could have done this, but I'll use any excuse to be close to Fallon, not to mention I won't take no for an answer. I watch them read it, their eyes widening as they share a look.

"More than fair." I nod. "Sign now or I will knock a few thousand off with each second I wait."

I'm already overpaying for the house, but I don't care.

"You want us out tonight?" Mr. Culet says slowly. Desperate people do desperate things. He's already been turned down by three banks. He's bankrupt and about to lose it all, then here I come like a lifeline, too good to be true.

I shrug. "Tonight. If you manage that, I will throw in an extra million."

Without a second more of hesitation, he scribbles his name and stands. His wife gasps, flying to her feet. "Herald, this is our home. It was my mother's and father's—"

"And is our saving grace. We are going to lose it either way," he hisses. "Let's take the money and move out of the city like he suggested. This is what we have been hoping for—a miracle."

She stares, looking aghast before gazing up at me. "Why are you doing this?"

"I want this house," I reply.

Nobody knows the depth of my obsession with Fallon, and they never will.

She slumps but signs, and I hand them their copies before closing the briefcase. Lifting my phone, I punch in a number. "It's done, send the money." I wait as he confirms it then hang up. "The money is being wired to you now. I will be back tonight. If you are gone, the extra funds will be wired. Mr. and Mrs. Culet, nice doing business with you. Enjoy retirement." I leave.

Outside, I pull down my shades, my eyes going to the house next door once more as Elijah joins me at my side. "Bring on a construction crew. I want that wall knocked down."

"Sir, that might not be possible."

I spare him a look, silencing him. "Make it happen," I say. "Now let's go, we have an interview to get to."

Leaning back in the chair, I direct a cocky smirk at the camera—one I know drives the fans wild, but it's all for her. Is she watching? Does she soak up every second of screentime about me like I do about her? Does she look for clues in my answers? They are right there for her. She's the reason I do this, and they have no idea.

"Rumors say you have moved here permanently." My interviewer smiles. I know it's good manners to remember her name, but I just don't care.

"The rumors would be true."

The crowd screams, females shouting and waving at me, and I blow a kiss.

"Is it closer to your music?" the interviewer asks when they calm down.

"There's something special here, something important, so that's why." I grin. My PR team tells me never to talk about relationships or mention women. Most of my fans are women, so I'm an untouchable fantasy they don't want tainted. If they only knew the truth. I will never belong to them. I'm already hers and always have been.

"Could there be someone special prompting the move? You've been making waves, and coming back home seems out of the blue. You've risen to number one on most charts, and you are the trending celebrity on every platform—"

"Now you're just flattering me." I smirk and glance at the camera. "There is someone special." I hear the crowd gasp as their hearts break, so I let my smile widen. "You guys, my fans, I'm here for you."

Liar, but I know my fans and Fallon aren't ready to hear the truth yet.

"Well, that's good. I think we would have a lot of broken hearts here today if there were someone. I've read that you have the most marriage proposals of any artist of all time." I laugh with her and ignore the question. It's common for fans to hold up signs, messages, and send emails. It's the norm, but none are from her. I check every day.

"So now that you're here, in the center of the music world and at the top, where else is there to go? What else is there for you to do?" she asks when it's clear I'm not going to answer.

Smiling shyly, I roll my lips inward, tasting the metal of my lip ring as I wait for the screams to die down once more. "There's always more to do. Music is my passion." Lie. Fallon is my passion, and music is hers so it's mine too. "I want to create as much as I can and work with some incredible artists to make that happen."

"Do you have any in mind?"

"One or two. Namely Fallon." The crowd goes even wilder then. That's right, cheer for my girl. She's fucking brilliant. "She's the top of my list for sure. Her voice and writing are incredible, and I think it would match my music." I write every song in hopes she will sing it with me.

"Didn't you meet Fallon at an awards show once? I'm sure we saw pictures of you two looking cozy." She's digging. I wait, and the pictures show on the screen. Fallon's eyes are on me, and she's so fucking beautiful, it hurts. All the attention was on me, and I was watching her. How could I not? She's fucking perfection. She's my obsession.

She's my everything.

"Ah, that was a good night." I grin. "I was awestruck when I met her. She was so charming and kind. She applauded every act no matter who it was, even when others didn't, and then congratulated them all at the after-party."

"So there was nothing else?"

"Trust me, if you had a girl like Fallon, you wouldn't be keeping it a secret, am I right?" I call, and the crowd hoots. "No, she's the type you show off and brag to the world about, so sorry, nothing to talk about."

Yet, because when I have my girl, the whole world will know about it.

I'll make sure of it.

FOUR

Fallon

Even ice queens get lonely sometimes, so I fill my houses with parties. I go to awards shows, date, and see friends. I am the it girl in public, but behind it all, I want the world to truly see me and how much I'm begging for something, *anything*, to melt this ice.

I am beautiful, and I create beautiful music. My house is filled with awards and wealth, and I never feel like I deserve any of it. I surround myself with the most gorgeous things in life, and it's all a lie to cover the truth. On the inside, I am ugly and unlovable, and it often feels like they know that.

I smile as I sip my Champagne—another party, another set of lies. People are desperate to feel anything other than the aching loneliness we are all born with. I'm no different. I pose for pictures, laugh, and drink with them. On the outside, I'm everything they think I am—cold, beautiful, and untouchable.

The truth is, I think I'm destined to be alone forever. There is something unlovable about me and they always see it, which is why they leave and hurt me. Now I usually leave first because I don't want to give them that power. I made myself heartless so they couldn't break it. It's easy to be unlovable without a heart.

Some people change their weight, their looks, their interests, or even their lives in search of love, but I can't change who I am. I can't change this thing deep inside me. No matter how much I change my appearance or my life, I'm the reason no one could ever love me.

"I think we should break up." The voice is soft, low, and angry, coming from my left. I'm in the back of the party, hiding with what's his name.

Todd?

Tim?

Shit, I'm sure it begins with a T. We've been on a few dates, and we've fucked and had some fun. He got pictures from the paparazzi out of it, showing the world he's hot enough to be with me, and it will carry him higher in the acting world he's part of. He'll get the recognition because of my name, and for a few days, I didn't have to be alone. It's also a nice bonus to have a hot guy to show everyone who hurt me.

Lifting my glass, I scan the party for familiar faces as I take a sip. "Okay."

"You are just so cold and—"

I turn my frosty gaze on him for a moment. "I said okay." When he just stares at me, I sigh in annoyance. "You can go now."

"Fucking bitch," he spits as he rips himself from the seat and storms away. I watch him go.

What do you do when you keep getting hurt? You stop letting people in and shut out the world to protect yourself, but in doing so, you miss so much. I don't experience the bad, but I also don't experience the good. I just exist like a phantom moving through a world that doesn't quite feel real, and when I'm gone, there will be no one to mourn me. I will just be gone, like a passing wisp of wind, here for a moment and then absent.

"Shit, Fallon, did you just dump Tez?" Amanda, the one whose party I'm at, hurries over, throwing herself next to me. She's beautiful—we all are here. She became a supermodel at eighteen, and I know she worries she's getting too old and they will cast her aside, hence the lavish parties to show she's still relevant.

Tez, I knew it began with a T. What a stupid fucking name.

I shrug, and she laughs, tossing her long, toned legs over my lap. "You're a hard bitch to crack," she remarks, but it doesn't sound like an insult. "I get it." Her eyes go back to the party. "I don't let them close either. They always want something—money, fame, a name—it's never just because they want me." She blinks, bringing her bright blue eyes back to mine and smiling wickedly. "So break every heart you can, Fallon. I'm sure they will thank you for it when you're done." She winks as she gets up, answering the cheering of her name.

Unlike me, Amanda is the life of the party. She's loud and so eager to please people, she does everything for them.

She's life, while I'm ice.

Maybe that's why we are friends.

I grow bored after a while, and when I'm bored, dangerous thoughts whirl in my mind. To block them off, I numb them, downing my drink as I search the crowd until I find what I'm looking for.

He's watching me, leaning back against the bar. He's younger than me, but not by much, and he's either an actor or a model. I don't care. His blond hair is swept back from his chiseled face, and his body is muscular and draped in the finest new clothes money can buy. He sips his drink, watching me make my way through the crowd until I stop before him. I see anticipation in his gaze, and also a cocky understanding that I want him.

I can work with that. He seems like the type to fuck and not call, and that's exactly what I need right now—no attachments, just numbing pleasure.

"Hi, do you want a drink?" he starts, undoubtedly beginning his usual routine. I don't have time for that. I can feel the spiral coming, the thoughts wrapping around me like barbed wire, their sharp edges ready to tear me apart until they taste blood.

"Leave your drink," I tell him as I turn away, and when I glance back, he's frowning. "Are you coming or not?"

He hurries after me as I head to my car and slips in the other side. I reel off a hotel address I know is close but also discreet, and he grins over at me. "My name is—"

"I don't care." For a moment, he looks offended, so I grab his chin and pull him close enough that his eyes drop to my lips, insult forgotten as he realizes he's about to have me. "I don't need your name or your life story, and you don't need mine. I plan to fuck your brains out and then leave before you wake up. You can order room service and lounge around knowing it's paid for and you've been well fucked. Do you have a problem with that?"

"Not at all." He smirks before he grips the back of my head and closes the distance, his lips crashing onto mine.

Good, this is what I need to forget.

We make it to the hotel in record time, and I head in through the back door. I have a standing room here for this. No one comes home with me. That's my place. Here, they get me for a few hours and that's it.

He follows eagerly, like a little puppy, and we barely make it to the room before his hands are on my body. I press mine to his muscular chest and push him through the door. He stumbles back, and I smirk, kicking it shut as I step around him and shed my dress and heels. "On the bed," I order him.

He strips and lies down, stretching out every tan muscle for me. He really is pretty and perfect for what I need—a palate cleanser. Sliding up the bed, I lick the bobbing tip of his cock, and his head falls back with a groan, his fists gripping the white bedding.

I move farther up his body, biting his nipple as he gasps, and then I stop when I'm over him. His eyes blink open, his pretty mouth parted. Unchecked desire burns in his expression. What is it like to feel that much? I lean down to taste it on his lips and feel alive for just a moment.

"Fall—"

I cover his mouth with my hand. "I don't need your voice, so let's put that mouth to better use since you can't seem to follow rules."

Slinging my leg over his shoulders, I press my hands against the headboard and sit on his face. His hands grip my hips as he gets the point and pulls me closer. I don't care if he doesn't like to eat pussy. He's eating mine.

If he wants inside me, then he has to earn it. He doesn't get to come unless I've gotten to at least once. Otherwise, men are too selfish to care about my pleasure, and then what's the point of them? I could have more fun with a dildo.

Luckily, he's not half bad with his tongue. I ignore his slapping hands when it becomes too much and grind into his mouth. I set my own rhythm, using him until I come all over his mouth. I slip down his body, his chin and lips glistening with my release. His cock leaks for me. It's a nice size, so I reach into the nightstand and pull out a condom, rolling it down his length as he watches me.

"Please," he whispers.

Good boy, he learned.

He's realized he isn't here to use me. I'm here to use him, and he wants it.

His bronzed chest heaves as I perch on his hips, my hand working his length, and he groans for me, his back arching. I torture him a little until neither of us can stand it, then I lift my hips, press him to my entrance, and slam down on his length, impaling myself as we both cry out.

There's no other sound apart from the slapping of our hips and heavy breathing as we fuck each other's brains out. His hips lift to meet mine, setting a hard, fast rhythm. My hands grip my breasts, tweaking my nipples to build my pleasure before sliding down my stomach to flick my clit.

He watches me with narrowed eyes, his jaw jumping at the sight, and I feel him jerk inside me.

"Don't you dare." I slap his chest. "You don't get to come until I do."

He lifts his hands to pull my head down for a kiss, so I smack them away, pinning them with my hands as I roll my hips, riding him as he groans loudly. I close my eyes. He's a beautiful sight stretched out below me, but I need more, and for some fucking reason, his blond hair changes to black, and his bright eyes turn dark and obsessive.

I wish I could say it was the cock inside me that gets me off, but it's the whispered "sweetheart" in my ear that has me crying out on the model's cock. He bellows his release, and before he's even finished, I'm climbing off him and heading to the minibar.

"Wait, are you going?" he asks, his voice hoarse and thick with heavy breathing.

I can feel my cream sliding down my thighs, and when I glance back, his eyes are locked on my ass as he sits up in bed, trying to recover. "No, I'm getting a drink to give you time to recover for the next round."

"Fuck, you might actually kill me." He slumps back into the bed as I pour myself straight vodka and shoot it back as I turn to him.

"But what a way to go, right?"

The grin he gives me is dirty and delicious, and after another drink, I walk back over to the bed, ready to lose myself in him again and the pleasure I can find in his body.

At least I don't think of anything else in the meantime.

By the time I make it home, it's early morning. I leave my car in the driveway, knowing it will be put away, but the usual early morning peace is disrupted by a cascade of voices. Frowning, I glance next door to the usually very quiet old couple's house and see moving vans as well as a whole bunch of people carrying boxes inside.

Did they move?

Shit, they were the perfect neighbors, quiet and unobtrusive and too stuck up to want to speak.

I hope the new ones are just as nice. Shaking my head, I walk inside to crash into a dreamless sleep, thanks to alcohol and sex.

FIVE

KAGE

The kitchen isn't exactly my style, but it can be redone. In the meantime, I sit at the oak dining table meant for at least twelve people and scroll on the tablet before me. My coffee is cooling in my left hand, and there's a spread big enough for an army across the table since my new chef seems to want to overfeed me. That's fine by me. He'll be cooking for two soon enough anyway.

My eyes catch on a familiar face in the news, and I frown at the fact my alert didn't go off. Navigating to the story, I skim it, glancing at the pictures to see her.

Fallon looks so beautiful, wearing a short red dress and dripping in diamonds. There are multiple selfies of her and her friends at a party. I don't know any of their names, but they must be singers or models. My eyes are only for her, but don't they see it? She stands out in every single picture. No one can even compare. There's one farther down of her heading to her car with a guy in tow, and I smirk as I sip my coffee.

He doesn't matter, none of them do, and they never last. She has a different one each time she's spotted, as if she's making a statement. It doesn't matter because they'll never fully have her or know her. No one will except me.

Fallon needs someone to consume her so she can't ice them out, and that's exactly who I am.

I will never give up on her. She can have her one-night stands because I'm the forever kind. I'm here now, and I'm never letting her go.

I gave her time and space to heal from her messy divorce.

I built my name and my brand to be her equal, and now it's time she knows it. It's time she remembers that promise I made.

Putting the tablet down, I drain my coffee as I stand without sparing a look at my frazzled manager, Elijah, who's working hard farther down the table.

Shrugging into my leather jacket, I glance down at the outfit I carefully picked out—loose black jeans with a chain belt, a white shirt, and my jacket. My black hair is styled perfectly, and I look chic and the completely opposite of her sleek, old-money style and the pretty boys she picks.

I won't be another man to her. I'll be the only man.

I dress like a rock star, and I intend to fuck her like one—dirty, hard, and never-ending.

"Where are you going?" Elijah asks without lifting his eyes from the screen.

"I think it's time to introduce myself to my new neighbor, don't you?" I wink as he turns a confused gaze onto me. "You're always telling me to be friendly."

"Yes, but you never are," he retorts. "That's what's freaking me out. No offense, Kage, but you only care about one person in this world, you—"

"Yes, and she's next door," I finish for him. "Be a good boy and eat the food. You look tired." I head out, ignoring him as he calls after me.

No one will stand in my way, not my manager and certainly not Fallon. I've been waiting for this day for a year. Three hundred and sixty-five days since I have seen her with my own eyes, smelled her, and touched her. It's been far too long. I don't plan to be apart after today.

Ignoring the workmen who are busy changing the house to my

specifications, I head outside and straight to the left to the wall. It will be torn down eventually, but until then, I grasp the top and haul myself over, landing on her property.

Whistling to myself, flower in hand, I head to her front door. My eyes land on the impressive car collection parked to the right. My girl is a collector of fine things, and I'll be one of them soon enough.

I rap my knuckles on the huge door and wait. I expect one of her staff, but instead, she opens the door. Her hair is mussed and loose, and she's in nothing but a silk robe. I almost swallow my tongue. Her dark eyes narrow in annoyance before flaring as she gawks at me, her pretty pink lips parting.

"Hi, sweetheart, it's been too long." Using her stunned shock to my advantage, I step past her, making sure to drag myself along her body despite the big doorway. I almost groan when I inhale her scent. I want to drown in it, but instead, I invade her house. Hers is a little different than mine, done in all beiges, grays, and blacks. It's modern, traditional, beautiful, and also ice cold, just like her.

I love it.

I stop in the kitchen, smirking at the flowers lined up on the windowsill—my flowers. I wondered what she did with them.

"What—" She hurries after me, and I turn. Her eyes are narrowed in anger and her hands are propped on her hips, parting the robe to reveal delicious, pale skin. I cut off her rant by thrusting the flower at her. "Two a day now," I inform her, "since we are meeting again. Trust me, sweetheart, you are going to need some bigger bouquets for how much I plan to see you."

"What the fuck are you doing here, Kage? You can't just barge into my house!" She snatches the flower, throwing it to the side. The fury in her gaze turns me on.

"You remembered my name, good." It makes me insanely happy to know that. I sign it on every card. I know my girl has a tendency to ignore names, so the fact that she memorized mine? Yes, I'm almost gloating.

"It's hard to forget it when these flowers turn up every day and now you. What's your problem?" she hisses.

"I told you . . ." I step closer, and she doesn't back down, even as she tips her head back to meet my gaze. My boots touch her bare toes, and I notice they are fucking cute as shit. She even has a little flower toe ring that makes my cock way too hard. ". . . I'll wait. Well, I'm done waiting. Your husband is an ex, and I gave you a year to get over it."

"Oh wow, thank you, a whole year to get over my husband cheating—"

I grip her chin, and she freezes, her eyes widening. I'm betting no one manhandles Fallon and lives to tell about it. Shit, her neck would look so good with my bruises. "A year to forget the idiot who let you go—one you never truly loved. I was more than generous."

"You really are insane," she whispers. Hearing those words on her delicious lips makes my heart skip a beat, like she just whispered dirty nothings to me.

"You make me that way," I murmur, dragging my thumb over her plump bottom lip, obsessed with its fullness.

"Ms. Fallon, shall I call security?" a worried voice interrupts.

Her nostrils flare. "No, I can handle this."

"That's right, sweetheart. You can handle me." My hand drifts up, and I wrap a stray lock of her shiny black hair around my thick finger. She slaps it away, but I just grin.

"Get out of my house, Kage," she demands, seeming to remember herself.

"Okay, I just came to see if you needed a plus one to the red-carpet event tonight."

She points at the front door, and I walk by her side. My eyes sweep over her, drinking her in since the pictures I have from online and my PI don't do her justice. "It's for the new movie *Friction*, right?"

She frowns. "How do you know?"

"I was invited too, mainly because I asked, but I'd rather go as your plus one. It's your night and your songs." I grin as I step closer again, brushing her hair behind her ear, letting the silk run through my rough fingers when I want to fist it. "Let me know. I can be ready in a moment. I'll be waiting."

"I have a date," she snaps as I turn and step outside.

"Sure, don't worry, sweetheart. I'm just next door if you need me."

"Wait, what?" she calls from the open door.

I feel her gaze on me as I casually hop her wall and wave from my front door.

I hear her door slam and grin.

Game on, sweetheart.

I wait all day. I shave and shower, and I style my hair and debate on my scent before remembering the way her eyes dilated at the awards show, so I go with the same one. I bought it in bulk just in case. I slip into a nontraditional suit. She might want the perfect arm candy, or so she thinks, but deep down, I know she doesn't.

My ice queen wants someone to shake her up. She wants someone to defy her.

The black jacket I have on ends just before my waist, one side higher than the other. Two gold buttons are perfectly placed in the deep V. The other side is longer, hanging down to just above my crotch, and more of the fabric wraps across my chest with a golden buckle at my side. The sleeves are wide but expose my tattooed hands. My slacks are decorated with gold buckles all down the sides and they flare wide. Since I know she's wearing gold, I wanted to match. I don't wear a shirt underneath, adding my flower necklace—the same flower I give her every day.

Now, all I have to do is wait.

Like clockwork, the black car arrives in her driveway where I'm waiting. I watch the door open, and a muscular blond actor climbs out. He wears a cocky smile on his lips as he glances at the house, and he takes a quick picture in front of it.

Rolling my eyes, I walk out of the shadows.

He frowns and steps back as I approach before he blinks, his eyes widening and smile growing. "Holy shit, you're Kage. I'm a big fan, man." He holds his hand out, and I just stare at it with an arched brow until it drops. "Um, are you here for—"

"Fallon," I finish for him since his voice is irritating. "She changed her mind. She's going with me."

His brow furrows as he glances at the house, and I step into his vision to block it. "She texted me like an hour ago."

"Well, things change. You can go now," I reply, dismissing him.

"I'll just ask her . . ."

I press my hand against his side and push him back.

He stumbles, his cheeks heating in indignation. "Dude, what the hell is your problem?"

Pulling out a wad of cash and a signed autograph, I throw them at him. "There, that will get you some of the fame you clearly want. You can go now." When he continues to stand there, I step closer. "I suggest you take the offer while it's still a nice one. Next time, it will be an order, and you won't like what happens."

"Fuck this, she isn't worth it." He grabs the cash and dives back into his car, taking off.

Grinning, I turn to the house and head up the steps, hitting the doorbell and waiting.

She doesn't keep me waiting long, and when she opens the door, I stare.

Her hair is styled back from her stunning face, her eyes darkened and glittering with gold. Her neck is encircled by a huge gold necklace, and bracelets line her arm while rings adorn her perfectly manicured hands. The dress makes my cock jerk because she looks fucking stunning.

It's a deep, glossy gold, with sleeves sliding down the top of her biceps. The fabric flows like water into a heart-shaped neckline with piles of glistening fabric. There's a deep V between her breasts, leading into a wide band around her waist, and then the dress flares out, cascading down to her feet. The front has a huge slit, showing her long, perfect legs and black heels.

I swear there's a fucking halo behind her head.

She looks like an angel, one I want to do terrible things to. I have the insane urge to mess up a small section of her hair to prove to myself she's real.

"You look utterly perfect, Fallon," I whisper, possessively dragging my gaze down her. "Like a fucking goddess ready to step into our world."

She just stares at me, and I grin. "Kage." She blinks, clearly confused.

I keep one hand in my pocket and offer her my other arm, knowing my eyes are blazing as I stare at my goddess. "Shall we, sweetheart?"

"Where's—" She frowns, clearly trying to remember his name, and settles on saying, "My date?"

"Right before you. The other guy bailed, but I'll gladly be your arm candy for the night."

She frowns in annoyance. "No, I don't like to be outshined."

I take it as a compliment. "Trust me, Fallon, in that dress? No one could outshine you. Now let's go before you're late. I know you despise tardiness."

She's fighting her need to ignore me and her desire to be on time, and eventually, time wins. She barges past me, heading straight to the car I called for us. I hurry to keep up, still smiling, and open her door. Her nostrils flare as I offer her my hand. Grinding her teeth, she lays hers in mine, and I kiss the back of it, my dark eyes on her.

Both of us are caught in the moment, but then she swallows and looks away, climbing into the car. I bend down, making sure her dress is in before carefully shutting the door and walking around to my side.

Her gaze is on me, sweeping across my outfit. "Like it?" I ask, leaning back to show it off.

"It's different," she replies. "Not necessarily bad."

"So sweet, my heart." I wink as I take her hand. She tries to free herself from my grip, yanking on it, so I slide closer, placing our joined hands on her bare thigh.

She stiffens and glares at me, but I just grin.

"Seriously, what's your problem? Do you want fame, money, or an inside story?" she demands.

"I have fame and more than enough money to spoil you for the rest of our lives. I want all your stories, but not to sell. I want to consume them," I tell her as I lean in, inhaling her scent that drives me wild. "I want every part of you I can get, Fallon."

"Why? What is this obsession with me? You met me once, and you're suddenly here. Why?" she asks. My girl has to pick everything apart to understand it. I like that. She can rip me open until she finds the answers.

"Because I can't seem to breathe without you. I have been yours since the very first moment I met you. You own me, and I'm tired of staying away, so I'm not anymore. I'll be here every day, even when you don't want me to. I'm not going anywhere."

"Why? For sex?"

"I want your body, I won't lie, but I want your heart even more. I want your life, your soul . . . I want every inch of you I can get."

She stares for a moment. "People don't talk like that, Kage."

"I say exactly what I mean. Choose to believe it or not, but my actions will prove my words are true." I lean back, my eyes on her as we speed through the city. The dark confines of the car have me imagining all sorts of dirty thoughts, mostly involving her lips.

"I don't understand you. I feel like I should be scared of you," she mutters, but there are no traces of fear in her voice, only confusion.

Gripping her chin, I rub my thumb over her painted lips, memorizing them as she inhales. "You don't have anything to fear from me. Everyone else? Yes, but not you. I would never hurt you. I would rip out my own heart before I did, so just relax, sweetheart, and let's have a good night."

"Why me, Kage?" she asks. "Why me?"

"Why not you, Fallon?" I murmur as I lean in, almost tasting her lips. "Why not you?"

SIX

Fallon

I hold his gaze, curious and slightly scared.

This man is a few years younger than anyone I usually date, but he watches me like he knows exactly what he wants—me—and he plans to get it by any means necessary. There's obsession in his eyes, burning with his desire as he waits for me to speak. I just stare, unsure what to say. Usually, I'm in control. I hunt my partners and use them, but I have a feeling Kage won't make it easy.

No, I should stay far away. Getting involved with him would be complicated. He sees and wants too much. Crossing that line, though delicious, would be like waving a red flag at a bull.

"Nothing to say, sweetheart?" His lips curve with a grin, and I swallow hard.

He really does look incredible tonight, not just in a three-piece suit way, but in a made an effort way. His clothes make a statement. Not only do they match mine with tiny elements that shouldn't make me happy, but he wears the shit out of them. They mold to his body, and the outfit, which would look outrageous on anyone else, looks like a fucking perfection against his alabaster skin.

Kage is truly beautiful, but he knows it, and he wants to use it against me. He wants me to want him, and he'll take my desire however he can get it.

"Not to crazy people," I murmur, my eyes tracing over his long black eyelashes in jealousy. Mine always point down, so I have to curl them, but they aren't that long and thick. His skin is like porcelain, perfect and unmarred, which is even more annoying. His hair is glossy and luxurious, giving him that just fucked look, but I don't care.

"Like what you see?" he asks, and I realize he was letting me stare. "I did it all for you."

"What?" I feel my brows furrow as I try to make out the meaning of his words. Like most people, words are thinly veiled lies or sometimes threats. People in our industry wield them like weapons of war, but not Kage. He says exactly what he means. It's unnerving and slightly terrifying.

There is something very scary about a man with a truthful tongue.

"I know you like to match your partners, even though you won't admit it. You also don't like traditional clothing, so I picked this for you. Does it please you, sweetheart?" he asks, his voice whisper quiet, like he's telling me a dirty secret. His dark eyes hold mine, drinking down my every reaction as if using them to learn my secrets and truths. I've never been observed this closely, and I grew up in front of a camera. My poker face is excellent, but in front of Kage, it feels weak.

"It's acceptable."

He grins like I gave him the biggest compliment. His fingers trace over my cheekbone, his eyes following the movement as he leaves a trail of fire in his wake.

"How about we make a deal, Fallon?" For once, he's serious, watching me with thinly veiled hope and excitement.

It's almost contagious.

"Or a bet?" he hedges.

"What for?" I ask, even though I shouldn't. I should draw some ground rules and leave Kage to his fantasies of me, since they will never match up to who and what I truly am. Once people get the real thing, they don't want me.

They all want the idea of me, nothing more.

"Whoever kisses the other first loses." His sly smirk has my eyes narrowing.

"And what does the winner get?" I mock indulgently.

His dark eyes trace over my body as if he has a right to it. When others do it, I feel dirty and used, but when Kage does it, every nerve ending comes to life as if responding to him.

"Whatever they want, sweetheart," he murmurs.

"Whatever?" I scoff, looking away.

His hand grips my chin and pulls me back around, and my heart stops as he nearly presses his face to mine. "Whatever they want. We both know you'll win, and I'll let you. I'll be the loser every single time, and I'll be happy about it. Whatever you want, Fallon, take it because it's yours. If you want the world, I'll give it to you."

The car glides to a stop, and a tap on the roof tells me they are waiting for me to come out, but I'm locked in a staring contest with Kage. His tongue darts out to wet his lips, and I follow the movement. "Deal?"

I don't know why I reply, "Deal."

The smile he aims at me is so full of joy, I almost stutter out a breath. "Good girl, sweetheart. Wait there." He slides out of his door, the sound of it closing loud, and I jerk, my heart thundering as if I just ran a marathon.

What's happening?

Slowing my breathing, I swallow and put my mask on just as the door opens. His hand reaches in, waiting for me as he blocks their view. "Ready?" he asks softly.

"As always." I lay my hand in his and slide from the car, noticing the way his other hand presses against the doorframe above my head so I don't hit it on the metal, and then he takes my arm, shutting the door as he leads me away, ignoring the security whose job he just stole.

The lights of the flashing cameras are so bright, they blind me for a moment, and I cling to Kage's muscular arm as I force a smile and try not to wince. Their screams blend into one, and when I can finally see, I have dots in front of my eyes, but I wave and smile before letting Kage guide me onto the red carpet.

Barriers separate fans and reporters, all of them clambering to get the best picture or overhear gossip. The old theater, the most historic in the city, is lit up brightly with banners and posters for the movie. Other stars walk the carpet ahead of us, the actual stars of the movie, but every single eye seems to turn to us as we make our way down it. We stop every now and again to pose for a photo, and each time, Kage lets go of my arm and steps back, turning his face away from the cameras so they only capture me.

I frown at that, and then he takes my arm again, leading me farther down. This time, he leans in despite the questions and phones being shoved at us. "You look so beautiful. You shine just like a star tonight, sweetheart. Listen to them scream for you, all wanting to be you." His whisper makes me shiver, and then he steps away again as I pose for photos, trying not to let my reaction show.

Every time we stop or turn, he leans in to whisper to me just like that, driving me crazy.

"All I keep imagining is your dress on my floor."

"I wonder if they know just how incredibly lucky they are to be near you and get your photo."

"How could I even compare to your beauty?"

It pisses me off because I hate that my heart flutters at his words, making me smile. When he tries to step away again, I grab his arm and pose for the photo, letting them all get what they really want—Kage and Fallon.

I feel him looking at me, but I don't meet his eyes. I turn my head, making sure to get my best angles like I was taught. His other hand slides around my waist, tugging me closer until I feel his hard chest touch my side, the soft material of his suit brushing against my bare leg.

I can barely breathe. His scent wraps around me, and his warmth thaws me, but I force my usual smile onto my face, and then we move closer as I sign autographs and pose for fan photos.

"Fallon! Fallon!" I smile despite the mics being shoved at me. "Are you here with Kage as a date?"

"I'm just her plus one." He grins, clearly not wanting me to make a remark. “Fallon is the true star of the show tonight. I’m just here to support her.”

It’s not a no, the insolent bastard.

“Kage, just yesterday, you said your dream is to work with Fallon, and now here you are.”

“Was that a question?” He chuckles as I raise an eyebrow at him. He said that?

“Are you two collaborating?” another calls.

His dark, hungry eyes find me. “Hopefully one day, but I’m a patient man. Now, if you’ll excuse me, I need to make sure Fallon gets inside before the movie starts.”

I wave and sign more autographs, relieved though I’ll never admit it that he fielded the questions for me. I feel raw tonight, and despite my cool attitude and confident smile, interviews still freak me out after the one last year stabbed me in the back.

His hand finds my back, guiding me through the throng, and I start to notice the way he moves his body to block fans or greedy reporters reaching for me. Despite them screaming his name, he ignores them, his entire focus on me.

He’s protecting me as if I’m something precious.

I hate that it’s working.

K ♥ F
Golden Love
I'll be with you.
I'll wait for you.
Golden Love
Can't you see
I'm your fool?

SEVEN

KAGE

"You know you'll lose, right?" she murmurs at my side, the dark room only heightening my need to feel Fallon. I'm fighting a losing battle, wanting to drag her onto my lap and fuck her right here for all these snotty fuckers to see.

I don't like to share, though, and when Fallon melts for me, which she will, it won't be in front of anyone else.

"Hmm?" I hum, my thoughts focused entirely on her. Every movement is burning into my brain despite the fact that my eyes are on the film premier with every other person here.

"The bet because I'll never kiss you, so you'll lose." She says it so matter-of-factly, I can't help but smile and turn my eyes down to her. She sits stiffly in her chair, the man on her other side laughing loudly at something in the film.

"Then I'll happily lose," I admit.

Her lips purse until she smiles, shaking her head. "You're a strange man, Kage."

"Yes, but aren't you intrigued?" I murmur, making her grin wider, and I feel like I won a fucking war. That smile is for me, just me, nobody else.

My eyes find her in every room, and my soul cries for hers. There isn't a moment of my existence since I met Fallon when I've had peace —until now, with her at my side, smiling at something I said.

She focuses back on the film, but my eyes are only for her. I drag them over her stunning face, burning every inch of it into my memory.

"Eyes on the film," she orders. "It's a masterpiece."

"No, but you are. I'd much rather spend two hours staring at you. Don't mind me though. Keep watching, sweetheart."

I swear a slight blush stains her cheeks, but she doesn't dignify my comment with a response. Instead, she tries very hard to watch the movie for the next two hours while I watch her. I'm absorbed in every minute facial expression that gives her away. When she wants to laugh but doesn't want anyone to know, her lips twitch. When she's sad, her nose crinkles, and when her eyes widen, she's enraptured.

She's fucking beautiful, so much so it hurts.

When the movie is over, we both clap with everyone else, and she greets and speaks to the director and producer as well as some actors. I stand at her back where I belong, letting her shine, and shine she does, bigger than any star.

That's my girl.

The after-party is surprisingly calm. There are tables spread across the fancy hotel with meals and drinks being served. Crew members and actors mingle, laughing as they tell stories from the film and congratulate each other on another amazing movie.

Fallon joins in for a while before sitting at my side and reclaiming some of her peace. I block any attempts of men coming over with my glare, making it look like we are having some stolen moments. She needs just a minute to regroup. Everyone hangs on her, looks at her, or watches her, and it must be exhausting.

"I don't know how you deal with it," I comment.

"With what?" she asks, her eyes finding mine, and I'm glad to see she doesn't seem tired of me, just everyone else.

"All the fawning. Even other celebrities fan over you," I murmur softly.

"They fawn over you too."

I don't respond. I've noticed the looks, but I don't care. I'm here for her, no one else.

She sighs, gazing over the elegant ballroom. "You get used to it." She smiles, but it's humorless. "I have been thrust into these situations since I was young. My entire childhood was spent in parties like this, sometimes doing my homework in the back." She swallows, her eyes finding me. "I eventually realized it was easier to just give in and play the part they wanted rather than fight them. My father taught me to be the perfect guest and always have a perfect smile and response. It's exhausting, if I'm honest, but it's as easy as putting on clothes for me—a habit, although not necessarily a good one."

"Your father taught you that?" I'm not a fool. I know who her father is. Everyone in the world does. Agille was a legendary artist who died some years ago, leaving her and her mother behind before she died too, or ran away—no one knows. I know everything I can about Fallon, but surprisingly, their relationship is secretive. She was seen at her father's side all the time, but to me, she always looked sad and he never looked interested, but maybe I was wrong.

"I spent my entire life being formed into his perfect protégé, but I never quite compared to him. Even now, they whisper about it. My father was a legend. He was good at being a rock star."

"And at being a father?" I ask.

She glances at me, her eyes dark with something unfathomable. "Like I said, he was good at being a rock star. It was his life, which became mine. Being a good father had nothing to do with it. I was an extension of him, just like his guitar, something else to use, not like they will ever know that. The world worships my father and puts him on a pedestal, but no one knows the real him. Only me."

"Yet you say nothing?" I ask.

"What would speaking about it do? He's dead, they love him, and I will be compared to him until the day I die."

"Fallon—" I reach for her. She looks so alone right now, so lost, that it makes my heart hurt. She inhales sharply, and it's so out of the blue my eyes track hers to find what she's watching.

"Is that—"

"My ex-husband," she answers, her throat working as she watches him. "And his new girlfriend."

"What is he doing here?" I ask.

"She's the producer's daughter. She's trying to make a name for herself," she replies. "She's a pretty young actor, making her way up. She's just someone else for him to cling to. It's the closest he'll ever get to fame and he knows it."

Our eyes go back to him as he works the room, holding her arm proudly, but I see what she sees. He's a leech, butting into conversations and hanging onto his girlfriend's fame. She looks awed by him. She's young, just like Fallon said, barely twenty, with straight blonde hair hanging to her waist. Her round face is turned up to his as she gazes at him with worshipful eyes. No doubt he has love bombed and preyed on her need to feel a connection, yet he never once looks at her.

Poor girl.

"How long has it been since you've seen him?" I ask.

"A year." She glances at me, smiling. "I kicked him out the moment I was home. I didn't see him after. Why would I? He broke my trust and ruined our marriage. There was nothing to see him about. In all honesty, I expected to run into him before now."

"Are you okay?" I question.

"I thought I would feel something, but I feel nothing when I look at them. Doesn't that make me twisted and cruel?"

"No, it makes you, you," I murmur as I lean in. "My Fallon, who doesn't let fools like that have her heart or tear her down. He never deserved it in the first place, and you knew that. That's why you never truly loved him. Deep down, you knew he wasn't worth loving. It was never a relationship, it was a transaction, and you were always paying the higher price. There can never be real love when you aren't equal. He used your name and your money, and part of you hated that about him." She looks at me, her eyes wide. "Tell me I'm wrong. Tell me you didn't use that inequality as a way to keep him at arm's length because it's easier when they owe you something than it is if they don't."

For a moment, she just stares at me, her eyes so wide I could drown in them.

"Who says I'm capable of love?" she counters, unwilling to focus on anything else I said since she knows I'm right.

"I do, and I can't wait to feel it," I murmur.

The entire world disappears, and for a moment, my heart stops as she leans in, glancing at my lips, and my head starts to scream at me.

Fallon is going to kiss me.

She's finally going to kiss me.

"Still not letting you win," she whispers with a cruel grin as she leans back.

I release a shaky breath, my heart racing a million miles an hour as she picks up her drink and casually takes a sip. Meanwhile, I'm left reeling, but I can't swallow the smile that curls my lips. Fallon is playing my game. She's talking to me, and she's here with me.

All my dreams are finally coming true, and before she knows it, she will be mine, and I'll show her just how capable of love she is, and if not . . .

I'll love her enough for both of us.

"I need the bathroom." She stands, and with a dismissive turn, she heads past her ex and his new girlfriend. He turns as if feeling her, his eyes seeking her out, and I know then he came here on purpose.

He might have cheated on Fallon, but he never wanted to be discovered. He wanted to keep the kingdom she built, and he's here to try and get her back, the fool. Downing my drink, I stand, ignoring the women and fans calling to me, and then I follow after her.

Fallon is mine. Maybe it's time I made them all aware of that, including her.

I'm going to lose the bet, and I can't fucking wait.

I pass him, but he's too busy staring after Fallon. "Baby?" the young actress calls, laughing self-consciously as she tries to get his attention. "Don't you agree?"

"Oh, sure," he replies, looking at her and forcing a smile.

Shaking my head, I head down the corridor and to the wooden bathroom door. I know he'll follow her, and I'm going to make him realize she's not his anymore.

I push through the wooden door, finding Fallon drying her hands in front of the marble vanity. For a moment, I just stare, and her eyes raise in the mirror, narrowing on mine.

"Kage?" she says, turning to me.

I cover the four steps in one big jump, and she flinches.

"I lose," I snarl as I grab her perfectly coiled hair and pull her to me, crushing my lips to hers. I swallow her gasp. Her hands beat my chest before they slow and then grip my jacket, and I grin in victory.

I back her up until she hits the sink, my tongue sweeping inside her mouth to taste her. My groan echoes around the room as I hold her tightly. Her taste burns into my brain, as does the softness of her lips and the catch in her breath.

I could kiss her forever, and I know now that I can never let Fallon go.

It has never felt like this . . . never been like this.

I try to get closer, to merge our mouths into one, but she pulls away, panting. My chest is rising rapidly as I stare into her wide eyes. I rub my thumb across her lips, smearing her lipstick even more, liking that out of place perfection that makes her real.

I hear footsteps. "Play along, sweetheart."

I crouch down, pushing her dress up and covering her crotch with my face so it looks indecent just as the door opens. She gasps, and there's a curse.

"Fallon?" he says.

"Little busy."

I can't help but smirk as I place a chaste kiss over her panties and lift my head, licking my lips as her ex gapes at me and then her.

"What the fuck are you doing? She's mine!" her ex blunders, his face turning red as I smirk at him. My eyes go to Fallon, whose eyes are wide. Her smeared lipstick makes it very obvious what we were doing.

"She doesn't feel like yours." I grin at him as I lean in and inhale.

"She doesn't smell like yours." I lick my lips as I grin at him. "She doesn't taste like yours."

"You bastard!" He storms across the room, and I stand to meet him. I don't lift my hand, even though it would be easy to hit him back. I let his fist hit my face.

The corner of my lip splits, and my tongue dips out, lapping at the blood there as I grin at him. "Oh, I'm so scared. Remind me who you are again?"

"I'm her husband," he hisses.

"Ex," she retorts, moving to my side.

"Ex-husband. A nobody, right? The only thing interesting about you was Fallon, and now she's gone and you're a nobody. Let me tell you who I am." I step closer, and he steps back. "My name is Kage, and I'm an international rock star with more bank accounts and houses than you could even imagine. My name is screamed around this world. I am something, and Fallon? Fallon is everything. She is the reason I'm here. She's the reason I am who I am. You are nobody. You are nothing. Insignificant." I back him out of the bathroom as he pales. "Just somebody who was lucky enough to be plucked from the crowd to be at her side. But us? We are celebrities, and we are perfect together, so hit me again. I dare you. Hit me. I don't even need to lift a finger to destroy you."

I wait, and I see the moment he decides. He abandons logic when he looks at her, his jealousy and need to be number one taking hold, and he swings. His fist is caught midair by a hand with black-tipped nails—a familiar hand, one I have to hold. She steps into my view, thrusting him away so he hits the wall, and the look of cold hatred she aims at him makes me rock hard.

Her chin is jutted out as she glares down at him like he's a peasant at her feet. Fuck.

"He might not hit back, but I will. You have no right to claim me. I was never yours. You were just a passing amusement, and you have passed. He's right. You are nothing—a failed painter, a failed husband, just a failure—and if you ever try to insert yourself in my life again, you won't have to worry about him. I will fucking ruin you, and you know I can. You know what I'm capable of." She reaches for him, and he flinches, but she simply straightens his tie. "If you ever hit him again, I will cut off your hand, which might be the only worthwhile thing about you, and I'll display it in my house." She pats his chest. "Understood?"

"Understood," he whispers, staring at her like she's a complete stranger.

This is the Fallon I've always known and fell in love with.

She is the one who saved me all those years ago.

This is where my obsession started.

"Good boy, now run back to your cash cow." She takes my hand, threading her fingers through mine as she turns to me. Her eyes land on my lip, and she leans in, her tongue darting out to lick blood away.

"Let's go." She tugs me after her, and I follow willingly.

My soul cheers in victory, my heart overflows, and my hand is clutched in hers, where I belong.

I'm Fallon's man, and she just made that clear.

"Why'd you kiss me?" she asks. She's been quiet since we got in the car. She didn't even bother to tell people goodbye, just left with my hand in hers. She let it go in the car, and I curl it into a fist to maintain the warmth. If this is the only time she touches my hand, then I will count myself blessed that my goddess even offered me that. "Was it just to make my ex jealous?"

"No." I smirk. "That was just a bonus. I didn't like the way he was looking at you."

"What do you mean?" She furrows her brow adorably, and I smooth the lines with my thumb.

"Like you were still his." I reach for her hand, gripping it in mine despite her trying to pull it away. "I've wanted to kiss you since the moment I met you, but I knew you wouldn't let me unless you gained something. That's fine by me. You showed up your ex, and I got what I wanted, which was you."

"You know, you're kind of terrifying," she says, but her thumb darts out and wipes my bleeding lip. "Why didn't you hit him back?"

"He isn't worth it." I smirk as I lean into her touch, but all too soon, she drops her hand. "I didn't need to sink to his level to ruin him. I could do that for you without even blinking."

"Why me? I don't get it. Why are you doing this for me?" It's clear my girl still doesn't understand.

Her brows draw together in confusion, and my heart skips a beat like it always does around her.

"Because I like you," I answer honestly, knowing she needs me to be direct. "I like you so fucking much."

I want to say I love her, but I know that won't go over well.

"Don't, it won't end well for you," she whispers.

"I don't care. I like you." I move closer, invading her space, and for once, I see her retreat in fear. "I like you a lot, and I don't plan to stop, so do your best. Push me away, hurt me, use me, wreck me, just don't stop. Don't turn your attention away from me. Good or bad, I want it. Direct all that ire and all that fucking anger at me. I'll eat it all up. I'll crawl at your fucking feet just for a chance," I murmur, watching her mouth part.

"Why?" she whispers, genuinely shocked and maybe a little scared.

"Because under that ice-cold exterior is a kind, caring, amazing woman who was hurt too many times. I see her all the time, and I want her. I want to protect her and make her happy. In order to do that, I have to keep pushing. Shove me away all you want, I'm not going anywhere," I promise as I lift our joined hands and kiss hers. "You are stuck with me, Fallon, like it or not."

She stares at me before looking away, but she doesn't take her hand back, and I take that as a win.

All too soon, we arrive at her place, and I reluctantly release her hand to help her out. I take it back as I walk her to her door, and she hesitates in the open doorway. Her eyes narrow on me with determination, and I know the next few moments of my life are going to be the hardest I've ever had.

"Do you want to come in and spend the night—"

"No." I kiss her to soften the blow as she bristles at my interruption. Before she can pull away at the rejection, I grip her face. "Look at me, Fallon." She does, and I grin. "I refuse to be one of your fuck boys you spend one night with and toss aside, and that's what you're trying to do. You want to gain the upper hand and get this out of your system. The truth is, sweetheart, there is no getting me out of your system, so even though I would give anything to spend just one moment in your bed, not tonight. This is different, Fallon. We are different. I'm saying no, but I will spend the entire night with my hand on my dick, imagining what could and will happen when you let me into your bed with the understanding that it isn't for a night, but forever." I kiss her, and before she can protest, I push her inside her house. "Goodnight, sweetheart. Dream of me." I shut the door, and I don't leave until I hear her locks click into place.

Good, lock me out.

If she isn't careful, I'll go back on my word, break down the fucking door, and beg her for the night she offered, even though I know it was a tactic.

I'm not playing for a night. I'm playing for forever.

EIGHT

Fallon

He turned me down.

Me.

I have never been rejected in my life, and I don't like how it feels. Despite his promise, I still feel the aching sting of rejection, and old doubts and darkness creep up as I wander through the big house like a ghost.

It has always been like this, as if I don't truly exist in this life or this world.

It's as if I'm a light that is simply turned on to shine for others, and then when I'm switched off, I am forgotten once more.

Nobody cares what happens in the dark, when my light doesn't shine. I smile and say I'm fine when they ask because they don't want to soil themselves with the darkness that festers in my soul.

I was born this way, or maybe I was made this way. I don't know. All I know is that I have fought these demons every day for as long as I can remember. I don't crawl into bed and never come out, instead I disconnect from the world. I just stop feeling. I'm living, but none of it really matters, and suddenly days or months later, I come back online and realize I have been moving along like a machine. I know what it is, although I didn't for a long time until I worked up the courage to go speak to someone.

It's depression.

Every time I have been hurt or let down, it rears its mocking head, waiting for me.

I was hurt so many times, I thought there was nothing of me left, so I never let anyone in. If I did, they could hurt me or realize there was nothing left for them to hurt.

It didn't stop them from trying though.

All the rocks they threw have honed me into the perfect, glittering diamond sharp enough to cut anyone who comes too close. It keeps me safe but alone.

I drift aimlessly through the house until I find myself in the piano room, the one that faces his house. I see lights shining brightly inside, and for a moment, I ache to be bathed in them and feel as much as he does, but I turn away.

I'm not the diamond he thinks I am.

I'm not gentle or kind, and tonight he saw that, and now he doesn't want me, just like everyone else.

I didn't have the option to be gentle, soft, and loving. I had to split my knuckles to protect myself so they wouldn't come back to hurt me again.

I lie in bed for hours, staring at the ceiling. Sleep eludes me like always, but for once, I don't reach for the pills. I want to feel this darkness. I want it to hurt. Maybe that's fucked up, but to me, it's my constant companion.

It reminds me I'm alive, even when I don't feel like I am.

I never tell anyone that I crave the pain or that I was formed this way by my father.

Kage asked about him today, so maybe that's why I take a trip down memory lane, even though he is the very last person I ever want to think about.

He was Agille, the infamous rock star, known for his music, his bad-boy ways, and his epic parties—parties that were some of the worst horrors of my life, parties that scarred me and made me into the ice queen.

Yes, to everyone else, my father was an icon, but to me, he was my abuser. He was my hell, and I don't say that lightly.

I've never seen healthy love before, and maybe that's why Kage terrifies me so much, because what he has for me isn't healthy either.

It's an obsession. Why can't I stop thinking about it?

My fingers trace over my lips.

He tasted so alive, and for a moment, I was alive as well. I came to life with his kiss, with his hands, and then he took it all away, and now I'm left cold and wanting.

Fuck him.

Fuck them all.

I sit in the interview chair. I look calm and composed, but my heart is thundering. I refused a lot of interviews after the one that exposed my ex, but I refuse to show fear when that's what they want. Plus, Jimmy is a good guy. I don't know about his new co-host, Henry, but I don't back down. I've been putting this off, and I can't anymore. My label made that clear.

I need to stay relevant.

"So, Fallon, we saw your stunning debut at the premiere last night." I grin at the pictures that flash on screen. I look good. "And not just that, but with a surprising date, the one and only Kage." The crowd goes wild, and I swallow, swimming through my muddled feelings. "How did that come about?"

I chuckle. "I needed a plus one."

"And you managed to snag the most eligible bachelor in the entire world." Henry chuckles. "How blessed is your life?"

I smile at his snide remark.

"Are you and Kage close? You seemed like it last night." I glance at the photos of us together on the carpet. There's one of me staring into the camera, smiling, and him looking at me with a loving smile.

There are more from the after-party, but I simply laugh—a forced, practiced sound.

"We are friends," I reply. "Although it's new."

"Kage has stated many times that he would love to work with you on some music. Do you see that happening?" Jimmy asks kindly.

"I'm not sure. Kage is a very talented singer." The crowd goes wild, and I wink. "But you know I like to keep my secrets when it comes to my music."

"Very true. Speaking of, when's the next album, Fallon? It's been a year," Henry asks, and the crowd cheers for that. "All your fans are begging for new music."

"My fans are too kind." I blow them a kiss. "Like I said, I like my secrets, but I have been busy for the last year, and I can't wait to unveil what I have planned. Until then, make sure to check out the Easter eggs online and see if you can work it out." There, I plugged the social content like they wanted. I always hated this side of the business. I was never good at it, but I know it's important.

"Well, we can't wait. You are the master of music." Jimmy grins. "Isn't she?" The crowd shouts their agreement. "Honestly, it's like being transported into a different world. We even showed some of our older generation your songs, and they said it was like being back in the fifties again with your soulful voice and rhythm."

"You are too kind." I giggle, another forced sound.

"You are very talented, but I definitely prefer rock." Henry chuckles, and I force a fake smile at the barb. Jimmy frowns at his co-host but chuckles like he's in on the joke. It's clear he is uncomfortable with the comments Henry is making. I'm betting he won't last long. Everyone knows Jimmy is in charge around here. Without him, there's no show, and he doesn't like his guests feeling uncomfortable. That's why so many come back time and time again, because he's actually a good guy who cares, not just about views but the people he interviews.

Henry chuckles. "Okay, okay, enough about music. We all know you are seen with some of the hottest hunks of the year."

I bite my tongue as images of me with some of the men I've slept with come up on screen—ones I never wanted taken. I don't parade them around. They just like to spin that.

"Some say you are out to have fun after your divorce, so who is the latest conquest? Anyone we know?"

I swallow my anger. "Do you ask everyone who they are sleeping with?" I smile. "Or just women?"

He laughs and leans closer. "Only those with such a wide dating history. I mean, come on, from princes to models. You have us all curious with all those love and breakup songs. Do you like breaking hearts for the music?" I raise a brow. "A joke, of course."

"I don't understand the joke. Can you explain it to me?" I retort, refusing to back down since he won't either. It's clear he wants a reaction, so he will get one.

Men like him hate to see successful women, especially one unwilling to conform to his ideals and let him rule them so he can feel powerful.

He swallows, his Adam's apple bobbing nervously as he chuckles self-consciously. "It's just a joke."

"I know, but I don't understand it. Can you explain why it's funny?" When he just stares, I pout. "No? I guess it can't be that funny then," I mock as his cheeks turn red. "But since you are so curious, let's talk about it. You don't want to know who I'm dating, you want to know who I'm sleeping with, and that's why you asked it like that. You believe you have a right to know my personal life, a right to know who I let in my bed. You act as though whoever I'm sleeping with affects my standing or music. I don't ask who you're sleeping with, and you have never asked any men that question nor made remarks about what they are wearing. We have done many of these interviews now, and you need to do better. A woman isn't defined by the cock she is or isn't using. I'm a complex, intelligent musician, and I deserve to be treated with the same respect you give your male guests." He's pale as I look at the crowd. "I am sorry for the course language, but I didn't expect to be so attacked during an interview simply for being a woman and enjoying my life, since we all know he wouldn't dare speak to a man like that."

"Fallon is completely right." Jimmy glares at Henry. "I don't think the way you are speaking to Fallon is appropriate. She has never been anything but kind to us here."

I glare at Henry as he looks around for some help but finds none. Everyone knows better than to fuck with me.

He's just another man bothered by what's between my legs. It won't change anything. No, maybe not for men, but it will for women. I just showed them we don't have to be complacent, meek, and silent.

"I apologize if I upset you, Fallon—"

"No, apologize properly," I demand, sitting back and crossing my legs. My blue-and-white tweed skirt rises with the movement, and I tap my heel impatiently. I look every inch the elegant musician, with my blouse snug across my chest and my hair perfectly coiffed, and right now, he looks like a horn dog. "That wasn't an apology. That was laying blame on me, as if I have no right to be upset. You aren't accepting responsibility. Words have power. You should know that as a journalist, Henry. I demand a proper apology for your disgusting, misogynistic language."

He swallows. "Fallon, I really am sorry."

"Better," I state and look at Jimmy. "I'm sorry the interview took this turn. I was so excited to come here today and talk about what I had coming up."

"And we are so thankful for you coming, Fallon. I truly do apologize for Henry. It seems we have a difference of opinion on what we want for this show." He gives Henry a look before addressing the audience. "We are going to say goodbye to Fallon and hope that we see her again."

I smile, and as the music begins, I stand and shake Jimmy's hand, his expression warm and worried. "I'm so sorry, Fallon."

"Don't be, it's not your fault," I tell him as I take Henry's outstretched hand. I squeeze it hard. "I hope I never see you again, but remember what I said. I do not ever want to see you speaking to another artist like that. You might think you are important and can get away with it, but I have my own ways of destroying someone." I turn and wave at the fans before I head off stage.

I sit in my car, annoyance coursing through me, and I feel my phone blowing up. My social media is off the charts, and I check to see the comments are all in my favor. Even other celebrities are chiming in since it's trending.

I ignore them, and when my phone rings, I hesitate.

"Hello?" I answer.

"Hi, sweetheart," the dark voice greets.

"Who is this?" I pretend I don't know.

He chuckles. "Save the number, beautiful. Nice interview. You were so fucking sexy when you were tearing him down."

"He deserved it," I snap.

"He deserved much more," he agrees. "Don't worry, men like him always get what they deserve eventually. I just called to say you looked amazing. See you later." He hangs up, and I'm left gaping at my phone, wondering what just happened.

He is a strange man.

K♥F
Golden Love
I'll be with you.
I'll wait for you.
Golden Love
Can't you see
I'm your fool?

NINE

KAGE

I mute the interview I'm rewatching, wondering idly if Fallon made it home yet and saw the present waiting for her. I smirk as I imagine her reaction, but then I grab my phone. "Elijah, put me through to JN Entertainment."

"Um, Kage—"

"Now." My tone borders on cruel, leaving no room for argument, and he sighs.

I wait, drumming my fingers on the table, and ten minutes later, after a panicked secretary answers, I address the CEO. Having a name and fame like mine really does come in handy in moments like these. Before, no doors would have opened, never mind phone calls being answered.

"Kage, it's so good to hear from you—"

"Fire Henry," I order without a greeting.

There's silence and then a cough. Obviously, he wasn't expecting that, nor is he used to anyone giving a man like him demands. It matters little to me what he likes or is used to. In my world, Fallon always comes first.

"Sorry?"

"You should be. Fire Henry and offer Fallon a public apology." My tone is lethal. I'm barely able to restrain my anger, but I try for her. She doesn't need me to fight her battles, but I won't sit back and let her be insulted like that.

"Kage, look—" His voice is slick and slimy, but I refuse to cave.

He underestimated just what I would be willing to do for her.

"No, you look. If you ever want me on any of your shows or gigs, you will do this. If not, I will never mention or work with any of JN again, and I will make it widely known why."

"Is that a threat?" he asks.

"No, it's a promise. Fire him publicly and apologize to Fallon." I hang up and wait.

Nobody disrespects my girl, and although she might have dealt with him, I saw hurt in her eyes, and I refuse to let anyone else hurt her ever again.

My phone rings a moment later. "What did you do? JN is calling me, panicking."

"Ignore them. How's it going on the search?" I ask instead.

"Impossible. What you want me to find is impossible," Elijah mutters.

"I don't care, find it. I'm off to the studio. Speak to you later."

By the time I make it to the studio, the news of Henry being fired has already spread, and there is a public statement from JN condemning his actions and apologizing to Fallon while standing with her.

Helen is waiting for me, ready as usual, knowing I hate to be kept waiting. I smile at her and embrace her in a side hug. "Hi, K." She grins. "Good to see you back in a studio, a nice one too."

"Better than the London one?" I tease.

"So much better." She's right. This one is so much nicer. It has a fridge, sofas, and seats to lounge in. It's cozy and warm, and the booth is huge, with every instrument I could need, not to mention the state-of-the-art recording equipment.

For a boy who started with a microphone and not much else, it can be daunting at times.

"Are you ready to make magic?" she asks as she sits next to a worker who nods at me.

"Always." I grin as I strip off my oversized hoodie, leaving me in a white crop top and loose blue jeans. I keep my beanie on as I head into the studio and turn my phone on loud just in case. It won't matter anyway. Every other person and notifications are silenced except for her.

Putting the headphones on, I lift my fingers in an OK sign as we test them. "Did you get the rhythm I messaged you?"

"We got it. Are you sure?" she asks with a deep frown. It's different than my other upbeat rock, but she knows well enough to trust me, and when I nod, she keys it up. I listen to it, my fingers tapping on the mic along with the beat. The lyrics work through my head, and when she plays it again, I start to sing.

Blue like the ocean.

Cold as ice.

I just want to be your paradise.

Melt me, freeze me, never leave me . . .

"Let's try again." I stop, and we rewind, and this time the chorus works like I want.

Taste like cherries with lips so sweet, I want to fuck them every day of the week—

My phone rings, and my heart leaps in joy. I remove my headphones despite being mid-recording.

Ignoring the producer's confused shouts, I step out of the booth, smiling as I accept her call.

"Hi, sweetheart."

"First the flowers, now this. Stop it," she starts.

"Stop what? Spoiling you?" I tease.

"Kage." Helen sighs. "Every minute in this studio is thousands of dollars."

I pull my card without looking and throw it at them. "Then bill me." I turn away, grinning. "Do you like it?"

She sighs heavily. “The painting is beautiful, but Kage—”

“Just say thank you.” She waits, and I smirk. “Say thank you, Kage.”

“Thank you.” Every word is pulled from her, and I chuckle at how pained she sounds.

“You’re welcome. Dinner tonight?”

“No.” She hangs up, but I’m grinning.

I’m getting to her. I know it.

TEN

Fallon

It's been four days since I saw Kage—not that he hasn't tried.

He's knocked on my door every single day, texted, called, and sent presents, but I've pulled away. He's getting too close, and I've pulled back and protected myself like I always do. It helps that I'm in a different city today. I spent the night doing some promo shoots and magazine covers during the day, so when I reach my hotel for the night, I'm exhausted. I just want to climb into bed and sleep. I want my makeup off and my hair unbound.

I want to be alone, just for a moment.

The hotel already has the paparazzi waiting outside. I let my security form a barrier around me as I head toward the lobby. I take some pictures with fans and sign autographs before I slip inside, breathing a sigh of relief as the doors close and cut off their yells and the flashing cameras. Even though I know they can still see in, they can't enter, which is a relief.

Before my label hired security, when I first started out, they used to chase me into hotels and restaurants. Sometimes, it got a bit scary. I had no privacy, and being cornered by big guys shoving cameras in your face is never fun.

I've been here before, though, and I stay here whenever I'm in the city. It's my hotel of choice, and I can't wait to sink into the huge bed I know is waiting for me.

For some reason, my eyes sweep around the waiting room as my heels click against the marble floor, only to stop on the familiar man waiting in one of the chairs. He lifts his head like he feels me and grins, hopping up.

I freeze as he prowls toward me, his hands shoved into his pockets. He has on a green jacket, the shoulders padded, with matching dark green slacks hugging his thighs. His black hair is styled, his eyes are lined, and his lips are pink and glossy. He looks fucking good, and he knows it. His eyes are only for me despite the bustling lobby.

"Kage, what the fuck?" I exclaim when he reaches me. His gaze moves down my body, heating with desire, as if I were naked and not in a white dress and heels. "Are you stalking me?"

"Absolutely, glad you finally noticed." He grins, kissing my cheek. "It's the only way I can see you. I missed your beautiful face, sweetheart. I couldn't last a moment longer."

"Aren't you supposed to act all cool and distant?" I mutter, raising an eyebrow as he leans back, grinning. He's so fucking adorable that I swallow when his dimples appear.

What is it about dimples that makes a woman weak?

"Nah, fuck that, what's the point? It won't get me what I want. I don't need distant and cool. I just need you."

"Smooth." I can see cameras flashing, and I suddenly remember where we are. Rolling my eyes, I walk past him, and he runs to catch up. At the elevator, I sigh. "Do you have a room here?"

"Nope, I thought I could share with you," he supplies.

Grinding my jaw, I turn and storm to the reception. I wait my turn and smile tightly at the woman there. "He needs a room." I nod my head at Kage, who grins happily, leaning into the desk, just watching me. "Stop it."

"We have no rooms left," the woman tells me.

"None?" I frown. "Not even a regular room? It doesn't have to be a suite."

"Um, let me check." She grabs another woman in a matching skirt and jacket, and when she turns, she eyes me distastefully.

She huffs. "The rooms are full like my employee said."

"Okay, I was just checking—"

"Which you do not need to do," she snaps.

"Excuse me?" I gawk.

"Have a good stay, Ms. Fallon." She looks me up and down, and my eyebrows rise.

What the fuck?

"Watch your tone, now," Kage warns, his puppy face transforming into something cruel and cold as he looks at the woman.

She blinks as she stares at him. "Oh, I'm so sorry, Kage. I didn't realize it was for you—"

"No need, I'll share her room since you're full." He eyes her once more, looking at her name badge. "Sarah, right?"

"Yes, yes, here." She hands over her card. "Let me know if you need anything. Anything at all."

Figures. I turn and stomp away. Moments later, he chases me into the elevator, eyeing the card as we ascend. My heel taps angrily, irritation running through me. "Are you mad she was a bitch or because she was hitting on me?"

"Why would it be the latter?" I snap, and he grins, his eyes on me as he lifts the card and pulls out his phone. My heart constricts, anger flowing through me as he dials.

"I don't care what you do," I snarl as I flee the elevator when the door opens and hurry to my suite. "Find somewhere else to stay."

I try to shut the door behind me, but he wedges his shoe in it and kicks it open. Shutting it behind him, he watches me with a wicked grin. "Yes, management please."

Ignoring him, I tear off my jacket and toss it to the bed, leaving me in the skintight white dress with gold buttons as I head to the bar to pour a drink. When I turn, I jump. He's right behind me, looking me over hungrily before he blinks.

"Sorry, yes, I'm here." He reaches for me, but I dart out of his grasp, making him grin as I sit stiffly on one of the chairs, trying my best to ignore him. I don't care if he calls her. Why would I? Let him.

He's nothing to me.

He's probably tired of the chase, which is fine.

"Yes, how much would it take to buy your hotel tonight?" My head jerks up, my eyes wide. I'm sure I misheard him. "I see, one moment." He hangs up and dials someone else.

"Elijah, purchase the plaza I'm in right now, and let me know when it's done." He hangs up, and then he kneels before me on the carpeted floor. He takes my crystal tumbler and licks the rim before shooting it back.

I just stare, unsure what to do or say.

He wasn't calling her?

Why am I relieved?

His phone rings, and he answers, simply grunting before he calls someone else again. "I'm the owner now. I'll sign the paperwork tomorrow, but before then, I want a"—he lifts the card—"Sarah Fredricks fired right now. I also want word going out to every hotel or staff members you have that she is not to be hired in this city again. Make it happen." He hangs up and rips the card, letting the pieces flutter from his fingers.

He bought the hotel.

He fired her.

He bought the hotel just to fire the woman who was rude to me.

Who the fuck does that?

Kage does.

"Why did you do that? You don't need to defend me." I choose to feel angry, not wanting to admit how hard my heart is racing right now. He keeps barging into my life and doing these kinds of things. It's confusing.

"Haven't you realized yet, sweetheart? There isn't anything I wouldn't do for you," he murmurs as he stands and tips my chin up. "Nobody insults you, ever. If Henry wasn't enough of a warning, then she will be."

"Henry?" My brows furrow as I put the pieces together. "You got him fired."

He smirks. "Hungry? I bet you are after the day you had. I'll order room service. Go get comfy. Although that dress is fucking sexy, it doesn't look comfortable."

"You aren't staying here!" I yell, but he ignores me and picks up the phone, looking over the menu.

"You want pasta or meat?" he asks.

"None. Get out, Kage. I mean it."

"I'll order both." He ignores me, dialing.

I stare at him, and he looks over at me. "Either get comfy or I'll undress you myself." Something in his eyes tells me he would, so like a chicken, I grab some clothes and head into the bathroom, only realizing what I grabbed when I get inside, and I groan.

I tug the oversized shirt down and sigh. I'd be better going out naked.

He is going to get the wrong idea.

I stare at myself in the huge mirror, and I want to sink into the floor, but I refuse. Plus, he'd just come in here and drag me out. Summoning all the courage I have, I step out and catch him pouring drinks. He lifts his head, a soft smile on his lips before it widens.

I'm wearing an oversized gray band shirt with the spiked lettering of his name and songs across it.

"I was given this today. I didn't even realize what I grabbed until I was in the bathroom and it was too late," I mutter self-consciously.

His eyes are blown wide, and he's frozen where he stands. "You look fucking amazing in my merch," he whispers, dragging his eyes over me. "I'm going to make every T-shirt I can and give them to you so you can live in them. I might not even let anyone else buy them."

Rolling my eyes, I walk over and sit on the sofa, pulling my legs under me and tugging the shirt over them as I look around the room nervously. I don't know why I'm suddenly so anxious, but I feel like I've been stripped of my armor. I'm makeup free, my hair is unbound and slightly wavy from the style I had it in, and I'm wearing nothing but a cheap band shirt.

I'm not the untouchable ice queen, and it's clear he loves that. He won't stop smiling as he sits far too close on the couch.

"Keep watching me like that and I'll kick you out," I snap.

"I'll sleep outside the door." He grins, and I glare, feeling annoyed.

Kage unnerves me; he always has. I never know how to act or where I stand with him. He unbalances me, and I hate it.

He sees my tension and sighs sadly.

"Relax, Fallon," he murmurs, rubbing my shoulder where his arm is stretched across the back of the sofa. His head is tilted, and his dark eyes are locked on me. "I just want to be here with you. I'll even sleep on the floor if that makes you comfortable. Just let me stay. I missed you."

"You don't know me well enough to miss me."

"Then let me know you. Ask me anything, and I'll do the same to you."

I look away, but he ignores my silence and surges forward.

"Favorite place you've traveled?"

I look at him, seeing his determination, and I know he won't give up until he has an answer, so I take a deep breath and reply, "Probably Italy."

"I loved Italy. We should go sometime. Your turn." I stare, and he rolls his eyes. "Okay, favorite food?"

"Cheap pizza," I admit.

He laughs. "I love you. Mine's cheap burgers. Okay, what's your dream car? I saw your collection. It was big."

I shrug, glancing away.

"Come on, you must have a dream car," he prompts, practically begging me to carry on this game. He doesn't know what he's asking, but it's a stark reminder of my past and just how different we are.

"If I want something, I just buy it," I say coldly.

"Fuck, that's so sexy." He moves closer. "There isn't something you can't buy?" I hesitate, and he grins, finding my weakness. "There is. Tell me."

"1964 Ferrari 250 LM, in bright red with custom black detailing down the side."

"That's an old car, right? Why do you want it so badly?" he asks casually.

I stare into his dark eyes, a little slice of my anger and soul slipping free, unable to hold it back under his innocent question.

"Because it was my father's car. He loved that car more than anything, including me, and I have never been able to find it." I stand, leaving him with more questions than answers.

I feel his eyes on me, but I studiously ignore him. I've already said too much.

K•F
Golden Love
I'll be with you.
I'll wait for you.
Golden Love
Can't you see
I'm your fool?

ELEVEN

KAGE

The table is filled with food, and I watch my girl delve in with satisfaction. She doesn't hold back, taking down platefuls, and it's the sexiest thing I've ever seen—not that I'd tell her. She'd kick me out, and I'm far too happy where I am right now.

My mind keeps wandering back to her answer. I already knew Fallon had a troubled relationship with her father, but I think it goes deeper than I understand, and I'm curious, but I can't push it.

"Favorite color?" I ask around a bite.

She startles as if forgetting I was here. "Gray."

I nod. "Fits."

She swallows. "Yours?"

I nearly jump for joy at her joining in. "Blue," I reply with a secretive grin, knowing she won't understand—not yet. I wait eagerly, hoping she'll ask more.

"Favorite hobby?" Her voice is quiet, but I swear to God it's a landslide in my heart.

She is trying to get to know me. I feel like a fucking king. I can't praise her, though, because she'll close down.

"I like to cook and learn new recipes," I answer.

She grins at me. "I hate cooking."

"I'll cook for you then." I wink. "What's yours?"

"I used to like pottery. I guess I became too busy for it and haven't touched it in a while, plus my label didn't like that it took time away from my music."

I want to throttle them. This girl deserves to do what makes her happy. She gives so much to her music and to the world, so why can't she have something for herself?

"You should start again if you enjoy it," I murmur as I fill her plate again. "It isn't up to them. You have to do things for yourself or what's the point in living? Your life is more than just creating music or being Fallon."

Her eyes rise to mine. "What if it isn't?"

"Then we'll have to change that," I tell her. Her sadness tells me that she doesn't think she deserves anything outside of being a singer. She deserves to live big, even without music, and I silently promise her that I'll give her that.

I'll make her fall back in love with living, then she'll live so hard they won't be able to catch her ever again.

I send the text before silencing my phone. The couch is too narrow and short, but I'd sleep on glass to be this close to her. I expected her to kick me out, but by the time our game ended and we finished eating, it was really late, and I think she felt bad, so she let me stay.

I can hear tossing in the bed, and it's driving me crazy, imagining her sleek curves in nothing but a T-shirt with my name on it. My cock has been hard since she came out in it, but now that I'm in the dark room, my desire is so hard not to act on. I know she isn't ready. I need to win Fallon's heart before I take her body, otherwise she'll discard me along with all the others.

I fist the blanket she threw at me, wondering if she would hear me if I got myself off. Probably, and then she'd kick my ass. I smile when she huffs.

Rolling from the couch, I head her way and slide into the bed on the other side. She sits up, glaring at me. "What the fuck do you think you're doing?" she hisses.

"If you toss and turn any more, you'll fall off the bed. I thought you were feeling lonely, so I figured this was the only way we could both get a good night's sleep." I prop my arms under my head, grinning as I close my eyes.

"Well, you're wrong. Go," she demands.

"No thanks, I'm comfortable," I reply without looking at her.

I can feel her silently fuming, her eyes burning into the side of my face. "Kage."

"Fallon."

I swear I hear her teeth cracking—she's grinding them that hard. "Move now."

"Shh, I'm trying to sleep," I mumble.

"I can't believe you." She sits there until she finally gives up, realizing I'm not moving. With a growl, she flops back. "Why the hell am I stuck with you?"

"Just lucky I guess." I sigh as I roll over and drape my leg over her. She writhes, trying to kick me off, but I'm much bigger, and she eventually gives up.

"Lucky my ass. You're like an annoying Chihuahua or golden retriever," she hisses.

"Guess that makes you a black cat." I crack my eyes open, looking at the dark shape of her face next to me. "Good, I always liked pussy."

"Oh my fucking god!" She groans as I chuckle.

"Just give in, sweetheart, it's easier," I cajole, and she huffs, but I feel her relax, and only ten minutes later, she is snoring softly. I cheer silently in victory. My girl is sleeping right next to me, her warm body under the covers separating us, and despite the fact that I'm cold, I don't move. I don't want to disturb her, even if I freeze to death.

I'd suffer much worse to be at Fallon's side.

Morning comes all too soon, and as soon as dawn breaks through the curtains, I open my eyes, not wanting to waste a moment of daylight. I watch her while she sleeps. It's the most relaxed I've ever seen her, and she looks so much younger . . . softer, like a fucking angel with the light hitting her.

"It's creepy watching people while they sleep, you know," she grumbles later.

"Sure. Good morning, sweetheart."

One of her eyes opens, and she groans. "You're a morning person. I should have known."

"And you're adorable when you're grumpy." I steal a quick kiss from her lips. "I'll go shower and order us food while you get ready."

"Hmm." She suddenly jerks up. "Wait, get ready for what? I'm flying home tonight."

"Which means I have all day with you, so get dressed because we have plans," I tell her, and when I get to the sliding bathroom door, I leave it open. "Feel free to watch me shower if you want, sweetheart."

"You wish!" she calls, and then says, "Wait, who said I would go anywhere with you? Where are we going?"

I can't help but smile as I climb into the shower, purposely using her shower gel to smell like her all day. When I come out, I wrap myself in a towel and head into the bedroom. She's sitting in bed, holding a mug, but her eyes drop to my body.

"Good morning to me," she whispers, thinking I can't hear her. I don't call her out on it since she'll get embarrassed. Instead, I drop the towel as I head to the phone, and her squeal makes me laugh.

She's fucking adorable.

Who knew Fallon had a shy side?

Fuck, I can't wait to explore it.

"Where are we going?" she asks, her arms crossed as she sits in the seat next to me. It's clear my love doesn't like surprises, but tough shit.

We snuck out of the hotel, managing to avoid paparazzi, and I plan to make the most of the day with her in secret.

Just us, no eyes or fans, on a date because that's what this is, even if she won't admit it.

"You'll see, but first . . ." I let the driver know, and when we pull over, I wink at her. "Wait here a moment, sweetheart." I jump out and hurry into the shop.

It doesn't take me long to get what I need, and when I climb back in the car, her eyes lift from her phone and land on the flowers I thrust at her.

"You didn't think I'd forgotten, did you?" I wink as I shut my door, I fasten my seat belt as she continues to stare at the flowers.

"Why blue?" she asks. "I've always wondered."

"I'll tell you one day, when you're ready," I promise as I take her hand. She tries to wiggle hers free, but I just hold on tighter, and she eventually gives up.

Another win.

"You know, Kage, some might consider you a stalker," she comments idly as we drive through traffic.

"They would be right." I grin proudly, pressing my lips to her ear. "Let them call me that, but we both know, sweetheart, that you like it."

"Not a chance." She pushes me away, turning her face to the window.

"Keep on lying to yourself, sweetheart. I can wait." Lifting her hand, I kiss the back as we pull up to the location. "Let's go."

I get out and walk around to her door, helping her out while she turns and looks at the bustling side street, the market entrance proudly displayed.

"A . . . cheap market?" She frowns at me.

Taking her hand, I lead her onto the street and start walking backwards with a grin. "Yes, ever been to one?"

"No, because I was born into money." Her eyes widen as people bump into her. Tugging her to the side, I put my arm around her shoulders so no one else can touch her.

I lower my mouth, ensuring she can hear me clearly.

"I wasn't, and you know what I remember? It isn't the fine dining and money. It's these moments from when I was younger. I have money now, Fallon, enough to buy the world for you. I could take you to every expensive restaurant, spoil you, and buy you whatever you want, but then I'd be just like every other man you dated—forgettable. You can buy all that too. No, today, sweetheart, I plan on being memorable and taking you on dates you've never been on before because I want you to remember them for the rest of our lives, until we are old and gray together. I want this to be our first proper date."

"Presumptive of you to assume there will be a second date, never mind us getting old together." She narrows her gaze on me.

"Sweetheart, I plan on stealing all your dates until the very end. I don't need to pressure you. I know. I always have. I always know what I want, and I knew from the minute I saw you that you were mine and nobody else would ever come close. Don't worry, I'll wait for you to catch up, and in the meantime, I want all your firsts—first picnic, first sunset, first love—but let's start here, first market . . . unless you're scared."

Her eyes flare with challenge, her shoulders straightening. "Fine, where do we start?" she asks as I lead her inside. "It's like a maze."

"That's part of the fun. You walk and get lost, and you find hidden gems. Come on." Holding her hand in mine, I keep her side to the wall so no one can accidently hit her.

I kind of feel sorry for Fallon because she never had experiences like this. Those are the days I remember most—not because of the money, but because I was learning who I was and who I wanted to be. I was finding happiness, exploring this world without judgment or prying eyes, and spending time with friends, and I don't think Fallon ever had that. She always had to be perfect for the cameras watching her, so today, I'm going to let the little girl inside of her out. I'm going to let her have the childhood she missed.

"There are so many people here," she comments as we wander through the short, man-made halls. The building is large, and some of it is outside, but most stalls are inside, selling all sorts of wares, from clothes, hats, shoes, bags, and food to jewelry and homeware. I walk her through it so she can get a feel, watching people shopping, couples holding hands and flirting, families joking and laughing, and teenagers taking pictures and enjoying themselves. "Nobody seems to care what anyone is buying or doing."

"Isn't that great?" I murmur, leaning down to kiss her head. "Here, you can be anything you want. If you want a five-dollar pen with boobs on it? They have it. If you want a T-shirt with your face drawn on it, they have that too." Her laugh is soft and small but there, and I take every single sound as a victory. "Come on, you've seen, now let's shop."

"Here?" Her eyes widen, but I tug her after me, winding through the stalls until I find one selling cheap jewelry. Now, don't get me wrong, it's beautiful and handmade, but compared to the diamonds and thousands upon thousands, maybe even millions of dollars that my girl wears, it's nothing, but that's the whole point. "Pick something," I tell her.

Her eyes are wide as she scans the rows of rings, necklaces, and bracelets stacked across the small stall. A smiling older lady watches us in case we need help. I hold my breath, hoping she doesn't take this wrong, but Fallon smiles at the lady, her hand flowing over the stacks. "These are beautiful," she murmurs. "Did you really make them?"

"I did. They aren't anything compared to the jewels in your ears though." The older lady laughs.

Fallon grins widely. "The ones that half the world owns? They don't compare at all."

Fuck, right then and there, my heart melts.

"You're too sweet, girl." The woman turns to serve someone else as Fallon leans over the rings, checking them out.

"Oh, I like this one." She picks up a simple silver heart ring with a double band, smiling down at it.

"Ah, that one." The lady holds out her hand. "May I?"

Fallon nods, handing it over, and the lady smiles at us as she breaks it apart. "It can be worn as a single heart or as two bands—one for each person to create a heart."

Fallon blinks, glancing from me to the ring as I grin. "We'll take it."

"Wait." She tries to stop me, but it's too late. I hand over some cash and then carefully hand her one half of the ring. While she watches me, I slide the other one onto my pinkie finger since it's so small. Separate, it looks like a half wave, and I can't help but grin in victory when she slides the other half onto her middle finger.

One day, she'll wear another ring for me, and it won't be on that finger, that's for sure.

"You pick one." She smiles up at me so trustingly that I would pick them all if she'd keep looking at me like that.

TWELVE

KAGE

Fallon relaxes after a while, clearly realizing no one here cares. There are no eyes or cameras, just us. She shops, we laugh, and we wander. She talks to people and gives it her all, and the shy smiles she shoots my way makes it all that much better.

The more we walk, the more it becomes clear her bag is annoying her, hitting her side with every step, so I grab it, and without skipping a beat, I slide the strap over my other arm. She doesn't even protest, which makes me smile.

We are walking around the outside stalls when I spot something and drag her over. "Pottery!" I tell her, pushing her to it and wrapping my arms around her from behind, resting my head on her shoulder. It's as natural as breathing, but she stiffens. I still don't let her go, however, and when the man running the stall starts to talk to her, she relaxes.

Call it delusional, but Fallon is totally falling for my charm.

I listen as my girl talks to the man about his wares and the workshop he runs. Her eyes light up with genuine happiness. It's clear she loves this hobby. I make a note of it and vow I'll make sure she gets to do it as often as she wants.

Anything that makes my girl that happy is a win in my book. I even sneak a leaflet and save his number. If I can learn, then I can help her, and it's something we can do together.

After another hour, we find the food court, and I sit her down with a kiss on her head. "Wait here, sweetheart." She sits nervously on the plastic chair at the small table. It's quiet here since it's early for dinner, and she looks around at the rows of food stalls apprehensively.

"Anything you don't eat?" I ask. I should have inquired before. I know from her interviews that she likes spicy food, but she doesn't like overly sweet food.

"Nope, no allergies," she responds almost automatically, still glancing around. "Um, would you like me to pick—"

"Nope, stay here," I respond and then bounce off to grab my girl her food.

She is my girl after all. She just doesn't know it yet.

FALLON

Kage is . . . something else.

I don't know what I was expecting, but it wasn't this.

I thought he just wanted me for the story, for the thrill, but he's still here. He bought a hotel and fired someone who offended me. He chased off my date. He buys me flowers, remembering how many times he has met me. He dresses to match me without a word. He's crude, obnoxious, demanding, and definitely unhealthy, but there's something about him . . .

I watch him bounce around the stalls. He's comfortable here, in his dark jeans and leather jacket, no designer brand name on display. He's just as happy in this tiny, backstreet market as he was at an awards show.

I don't understand him.

Most men I know wouldn't be caught dead in a place like this, never mind take me on a date here to impress me. It's like . . . he's not trying so hard to impress me, but to leave an impression, like he said, and make sure I enjoy myself, not just to experience this as a way to lead in to fucking me.

He comes back while I'm lost in thought and drops an armful of buzzers on the table. One goes off, then he gets up and runs off, and so it goes. He just gets back when another goes off. He has to snag two more tables and push them against ours as the food piles around us. There is so much, it might as well be a feast. I'm pretty sure he grabbed one of everything, and as I sit, wide-eyed, he smiles, waiting for approval.

Usually, I would be annoyed, but I reach for a random tray of meat with a cheese sauce and take a bite. He leans in, holding his breath, and when I swallow, I nod. "It's good."

He grabs a fork and dives in, trying a bit of everything, and I find myself doing the same. There's some candied fruit I'm not a fan of, but the stew is amazing.

"Here, try this." He holds out a spoon to me, his hand under it so it doesn't drop. I take the bite, leaning back as I chew and swallow. The flavor explodes in my mouth. It's spicy but not too much, and crunchy but soft.

"Wow, that's amazing," I admit.

"Right?" He leans over, wiping his thumb over the corner of my lip. "Sauce," he explains, and with a devilish wink, he licks his thumb clean and continues eating.

No, Kage isn't what I was expecting. On the outside, he looked dark and dangerous, but he's a softie on the inside. He carried my bag without a word of complaint, even though it's bright pink, and he let me talk and shop without urging me on or getting bored. He proudly wears the ring and feeds me more food than I've ever seen.

He's almost . . . cute. If, you know, he wasn't stalking me everywhere, but why does the thought make me smile?

By the time we are done eating, I can barely move. "I'm stuffed."

"Nah, that could be us later." He winks, and I groan at his bad joke. "Which was your favorite?"

I have no doubt he already knows. Kage watches every little thing I do with so much intensity, it should scare me, but it doesn't. "Why don't you tell me?" I prop my chin on my hand as I watch him.

Leaning back, he peers at me with his dark eyes. "You would probably say the goat stew, but I think it was the curry." I roll my eyes, and his grin deepens, flashing some adorable fucking dimples.

"What was mine, sweetheart?" he asks casually, but I hear the trap. He's trying to figure out if I watch him as much as he watches me.

Should I lie to throw him off so he won't get the wrong idea?

"How would I know?" I mutter, taking a sip of the fruit juice he got me.

"Guess then," he murmurs, not letting it go.

"Fine, it was the noodles," I mutter, but he catches it, and the smug grin he aims my way lets me know that. Standing, I start to stack the empty trays together to dump them when he slaps my hands away.

"Sit, sweetheart, no girl of mine lifts a hand around me." He clears it all away and brings me a hand wipe. I try to take it, but he kneels and grabs my hands, cleaning each and every finger with careful attention.

"Ready to keep going?" he murmurs, placing a soft kiss on the back of my hand as he stands.

Nodding mutely, I go to grab my bag, but it's already over his shoulder. He waits, taking my hand as soon as I'm close, ignoring my efforts to free myself. The man has no shame.

"Oh, look, a photobooth!" He drags me over to the white cubicle shoved in a corner and pushes me inside. I fall into the chair, and he steps in next to me. It's so small, we are pressed together as he shuts the curtain and hits some buttons.

"Kage," I warn, but he grins at me.

"Smile, sweetheart. I'm going to frame these."

I glare at him as there's a flash, and I turn to the screen just as he leans down and presses his cheek to mine as the flash goes again. "Kage," I hiss, but he turns my face and kisses me right on the lips. This time, the flash is behind my eyes, and then I lean back, ready to shout, but there's a reluctant smile on my lips as it flashes again.

His smile is gone, but his hand is still on my head, our bodies pressed together. There are no more flashes, just us, and I watch him glance down at my lips. "I kissed you to get you to smile, but I'm thinking if I don't kiss you again, I might just die."

“I never said you could kiss me before,” I murmur, my heart racing for some reason.

Nobody kisses me without permission. Nobody kisses me without it leading to sex. That’s how it is.

“Good, then I don’t need to ask this time.” He leans down, pressing his lips to mine. His tongue sweeps across my mouth as his hand slides down, gripping my face. He presses his thumb into my jaw until I open with a gasp. Instantly, his tongue slides into my mouth, tangling with mine as he holds me prisoner in his brutal kiss, but when he pulls back, he lays a softer one on my lips.

I’m panting, my eyes wide as he sits up. “How about we go to the pier next?”

He kissed me just to kiss me? Not for sex or for anything else, just because he could?

Why didn’t I stop him?

We end up at the fair, but I don’t even remember getting there, still stuck on that kiss. Kage, on the other hand, is almost bouncing up and down. We started at the pier before we stumbled upon this. Now, he’s playing every game and filling a bag with prizes for me. He’s won more stuffed animals than I have ever seen, and I don’t have the heart to stop him.

It’s so fucking cute, even I can admit that.

Nobody has ever cared this much about me before.

It’s terrifying because I know once he sees the real me, he won’t want me anymore.

Nobody does.

As if he can feel my mood darkening, he grabs my hand and pulls me over to the Ferris wheel, wrapping his arms around me as we wait in line. It’s busy this afternoon, since it’s a weekend, so we stand together, and I let him pull me close.

I let myself believe that I could be someone this man loves, even though I never could be.

Kage is all sunshine, and I am nothing but a dark moon.

There is a group of teenagers before us, and their giggles only seem to get louder until I get curious and peek at their phones. My eyebrows rise. It's some paparazzi shots of Kage and me, his arm almost touching me as he faces me in the hotel lobby yesterday.

I shrink back, expecting rude remarks, but their next words stop me. "She's just so beautiful. Seriously, it isn't even fair. They look so good together. I definitely ship them."

"Nah, she's way too good for him."

"They are right," Kage whispers in my ear. "You are way too good for me, sweetheart, but that doesn't mean I'm letting you go."

"He's so hot," another says. "Look how he stares at her, and did you see that interview? I keep rewatching their edits on TikTok."

"Do you think I'm hot, sweetheart?" he flirts in my ear. I elbow him, but he just chuckles, not the least bit bothered.

"Do you think they are actually together, or is it just PR?" one whispers while shuffling forward as the line moves.

"Definitely PR," another adds seriously.

"No, I think it's real. Why else would he show up at her hotel? She hasn't been seen with anyone here, right? He's said how much he respects her."

Jesus, just how many interviews of us have they watched? It's impressive.

"I like them together. She's smiling. Look, when was the last time you saw her smile with anyone? She's always so serious," one remarks with a grin. "I think we should ship them until it's real."

"I agree with that," Kage whispers darkly. "Want to give them something to really talk about, sweetheart?"

I frown at him as the girls are directed to one of the cars and us to the next. Just as they slide in, Kage lets out a whistle. They turn to look as he lifts his hat, and then Kage kisses me on the cheek. The screams they let out are feral, and before they can pull out their phones, I dive into the cart. Kage laughs as he follows me, his hat back down.

I watch as they turn, trying to see us as we start to move, but it's no use.

Shaking my head, I grin. "They are going to follow us around all day now."

"Nah, I'm fast, baby."

I smirk. "Not what a girl wants to hear."

He gapes at me. "Was that a joke?" he exclaims. "I'm breaking you down one thing at a time." He lunges over to my side, draping his arm around my back and leaning into me. "Soon, sweetheart, you'll be in my bed and calling me yours."

I elbow him. "Doubtful."

When I turn to the view, I'm smiling once more.

The asshole.

Kage is right; he's fast. We race from the wheel when they call after us, looking like maniacs as we run from the fair and back out into the city. The excitement makes me laugh, a sound so carefree, I haven't heard it in a long time.

We end up walking for hours. My flight isn't until the middle of the night, so when we find a park overlooking the city, Kage disappears and comes back with blankets and a picnic. I don't even question how he got them. I relax, nibbling on the food as the sun begins to set. The sight is beautiful, but I have this strange feeling inside, like I have been missing so much beauty.

"What are you thinking about?" he asks, leaning back on one elbow. He's staring at me, not the sunset, but I shouldn't expect anything else from Kage.

"How often I spend hours waiting nervously for the night to come, not realizing the beauty it holds," I admit honestly, looking away so I don't have to see his eyes.

"Why are you nervous for the night?"

I glance over at him, meeting his dark, unjudging gaze. "Because my demons hide in the dark."

I look back at the sunset, waiting with bated breath. His hand covers mine on the blanket—no words, just a comforting hand, and I want to cry for the second time today.

"Personally, I like sunsets," he says. "They remind me that time keeps moving and that tomorrow is coming. It's a reminder that life goes on no matter what happens. That's what I used to think as a kid when I shared a room with my mom and siblings, cold and hungry. Those sunsets were a promise that no matter how bad things got, I had tomorrow and another chance to be better."

I meet his eyes once more, something bending inside me. I never thought of Kage's past. "You were hungry and cold a lot?"

He smiles softly. "I was. We grew up poor. Happy, but poor."

"I grew up rich and unhappy. What a pair we make," I murmur.

"Your home wasn't happy?" he asks.

"You would think so. I had everything you could ever want as a child—everything but parents' love. I was a thing to them, something to use. I wasn't a child and was never allowed to be. I hated nights the most because they were so long, and I was so alone. At least during the day, I had to attend school or shoots with them and be around people. When I was alone at night, I was scared."

"Just think, on nights you were staring into the dark, so was I. Both of us were hoping for tomorrow to come, hoping for a better future. Now, here we are together, despite everything, watching the sunset and knowing the dark can't hurt us anymore."

"Can't it?" I ask.

"No, Fallon. It can't. Nothing can hurt you, not with me here," he promises.

Others have made empty promises like that before, but I want to believe him.

THIRTEEN

Fallon

Today was amazing.

I would never tell Kage that though. I left him looking like a lost puppy at his new hotel and headed off for my flight. The jet was waiting on the tarmac, and I know I could have delayed or changed it to spend more time with him, but I refuse to reconfigure my schedule or life for anyone ever again, even Kage.

It's strange though. After spending all day with him, the silence doesn't feel as comforting as it once did. More . . . lonely. He filled that space so well, always talking or moving. I didn't even realize how often he filled the silence until I'm surrounded by it. Once, it would have felt warm, a place for me to relax and shed the facade and just be me, but now I miss the constant chatter.

My lips curve as I recall him blabbering all day about random shit. When I realize what I'm doing, I kill the smile and recline back in my chair as the crew goes about their last flight checks. The steward, Jase, knows to leave me alone by now. They've worked for me for a while. He handed me my drink, smiled, and went to help the captain and copilot. I debate calling out, if only just to speak, but I'm just now realizing I don't speak unless I have to when I'm not with Kage. With him, it's almost natural to speak often, to ask something or tell a story.

What is he doing to me?

Today was amazing and probably one of the best dates I've ever had, which is exactly why he did it. He's determined to break down my walls and get me. I still don't understand why. That isn't me putting myself down. I'm rich, I'm powerful with a family name that inspires loyalty and fear, and I'm beautiful and classy with a good image. Outside, I seem like the whole package. Is that what he wants? Someone to be seen with?

No, he didn't want me to be seen today. He wanted me to be comfortable. Which begs the question, if he doesn't want me for my money, fame, or name, then why does Kage want me?

"Sir, you can't—" Jase begins, his face pale as he tries to block the stairs.

"Ah, don't worry, I'm Fallon's boyfriend."

My eyes widen at the familiar voice, and then Kage is pushing past a shocked and confused Jase, waving at me.

"Kage?" I snap.

"Hey, baby," he calls, stowing his bag. He winks at Jase and strides my way, dropping into the chair opposite me with a groan. "Shit, this plane is nice. I should buy one or maybe two, then we could match." He wiggles his eyebrows as I continue to stare.

"I thought your name too many times, and like a bad omen, you appeared," I mutter to myself.

"You thought about me?" His grin grows.

"Nightmares," I retort.

"It counts." He shrugs as he reaches down, lifts my legs, and lays them over his lap just as Jase appears.

"Ms. Fallon, should I call security?" he asks, looking between us.

"No, he's a stalker, but not even security will get rid of him." I sigh. "Jase, this is Kage."

"Hey, my man." Kage waves. "Nice suit, the blue really suits you."

Jase blinks, looking from me to Kage before recognition seems to bloom. It's subtle, since Jase is so good at his job, but his smile grows, his eyes heating as he looks Kage over. "Thank you. Would you like a drink, sir?"

"Nah, I'm good, just look after my lady." He settles back in his seat. "That's all I want." His eyes lock on me. "I missed you."

"It has been an hour," I reply with an arched brow.

He nods seriously. "An hour too long."

I just stare, unsure how the hell Kage knew where I was flying from and also how he had time to pack, change, and get here. He's in an oversized black hoodie and cargo pants. I suppose nothing about him should surprise me anymore.

"Should I tell the captain we are ready to leave, Ms. Fallon? Or are we expecting more company?" Jase asks kindly.

I sigh. "We are ready to go before any others turn up."

"Thanks for waiting." Kage blows me a kiss.

"I wasn't." I grab my magazine and pretend to read it. I feel him staring at me the entire time, so I eventually fold it down and meet his gaze. "What now?"

"You look so beautiful." He grins. "Continue reading. Don't mind me, I'm just looking at the view."

Rolling my eyes, I lift the magazine to cover my face, but I can't stop the small smile on my lips. I ignore him during takeoff, but once we are in the air and I've finished the magazine, I know I can't keep staring at pictures of the band Sanctuary, no matter how pretty they are, so I drop it and lean back in my chair to find him still watching me.

"I lost the bet, you know." He grins. "I kissed you first."

"I told you, you would," I retort.

He leans closer, and I suck in a breath at his proximity. "So did I, but it was so fucking worth it," he says, his eyes dropping to my lips, so I place a hand on his solid chest and push him away before I do something stupid, like kiss him.

"So . . ." I want to change the subject. "You're stalking me around the world and seem to know everything about me, but I hardly know anything about you."

"What do you want to know, beautiful? Ask and I'll tell you anything," he replies. My eyes narrow. No one is that honest. They cover things up and tell half-truths to impress the other person.

"First time you got hard," I say, pushing him.

"In gym class. It was really embarrassing. Something about the way Sarah Peoples was jogging made it happen. Everyone saw." He grins. "Keep asking, sweetheart. I have nothing to be ashamed of."

"Everyone has something they are ashamed of." I frown. "Something you don't want anyone else to know."

"That's where you're wrong. I want you to know everything about me, even the bad stuff, so ask and I will answer."

I stare into his earnest eyes, confused. "First love?"

"You," he says without a moment of hesitation.

"What? You didn't love your first girlfriend?" I joke to cover the uncomfortable feeling within me.

"No, I didn't. I have never loved anyone the way I love you, not even my parents. I know I should feel bad about that, but they were just there. I was supposed to care about them, and in a way, I did, but it was never love." He says it all without a hint of shame.

"Why did you come back here?" I ask, needing to move on before I look too closely at his answer and the fact that he apparently loves me. He's wrong—he can't—he just thinks he does.

He's in love with the idea of me, not the real me.

"For you." He grins. "I spent the last year building my name and wealth so I could be worthy of you. When I figured it was time, I came back to be closer to you."

Jesus Christ, why is every answer coming back to me?

Why am I so hot and flustered?

Maybe it's the intensity in his eyes, the raw truth I hear in his voice, or the way he's massaging my legs like he isn't the least bit worried about what he's admitting when most would bury those dark things deep down so no one would ever see, never mind admit them to another person.

"Why did you become a singer?" There, that's a safe question.

"I was always good at singing. People told me I should try, so I did to earn some money. I was good at it and started moving up through the ranks, but it solidified my choice when I met you because I knew I needed to be as close to you as possible." I frown at that. He met me a year ago, and he was already an established singer by then. Maybe he's confused.

"Ever slept with a fan?" It's something a lot of singers brag about, sleeping with groupies, but I find it cringey.

"Never," he states so vehemently that I truly believe him. "In fact, I've been celibate for a year."

"A year?" I gape at him. "Are you saying you haven't slept with anyone since meeting me?"

"Why would I?" he asks, tilting his head. "I know what and who I want, so why would I risk that for momentary pleasure when it would pale in comparison to the real thing?"

"But I saw you with women and—" I stop, realizing what I said. I didn't go out of my way to look him up, but like me, he's on every news outlet, and whenever he stepped out with someone, they pounced on it.

The sly grin he gives me lets me know I'm not getting away with that, but he doesn't say anything, thank fuck. "For PR or I was working with them, nothing more than that, and every time, I debated having the pictures pulled, but I wanted your attention. I'm glad it worked."

"I wasn't jealous." I point at him in warning. "I was just saying."

"Sure, sweetheart." He grips my legs possessively. "I was jealous every time I saw you with someone new. My only reassurance was that they were never there more than once, so they meant nothing to you."

"What does that mean?"

"They were just something else for you to use and flaunt, like money or fame." He shrugs. "It was obvious to me. They were a distraction, a buffer."

My heart stops as I stare into his dark eyes. This man sees and knows too much, and it terrifies me.

"Next question?" he asks innocently, completely oblivious to my internal turmoil.

"Favorite color?"

"Blue," he responds, and I know I asked before, but I was checking if he was telling the truth.

"Why are you so obsessed with me?" I ask after a pause.

"You aren't ready for that yet," he answers. "You're looking for an excuse to run, and I'm not giving you one. Besides, beautiful, you can try to run from me, but I'll just find you. You forget, I know everything about you."

"Bullshit, you can't know everything about me," I scoff.

"Favorite color is gray, and you tell everyone your favorite book is *Women Don't Owe You Pretty*, but it's actually *Pride and Prejudice*. You can't drink and eat at the same time. You hate the taste of beer but love cheap pizza. You love roller coasters but hate going underwater. You love shopping and watching movies, but you don't like to go alone. You collect vintage art, and you love pottery. In an interview in 2013, you admitted you liked being spoiled by the person you are dating. Shall I go on?"

My eyes widened while he spoke, and I swear they are bugging out of my head. "How?" I blurt, stuttering over the words.

"You are the only thing in this world that interests me, Fallon, so I spent my time knowing every single thing there is to know about you. Good and bad, I want it all." He leans closer. "But I want all those dark, little secrets I see floating around in your head, the ones you are ashamed to share, and I'll have them." He leans back. "But for now, what else do you want to know about me?"

"I'm done asking," I snap, feeling way too vulnerable and exposed.

"Okay, beautiful, how about you get some sleep?" he suggests as I stand, needing to put some space between us.

Does he really know all that?

Just how long has Kage been stalking me? It sends a shiver through me, and not necessarily a bad one.

"I can never sleep on planes," I tell him. "I just don't get warm or comfortable enough."

"Here." He rips off his hoodie, revealing a tight, short-sleeved shirt underneath as he offers it to me. "To keep you warm and cozy," he explains as I stare.

"I don't wear hoodies," I mutter, glaring at the offending article of clothing.

"Sure you do, when they are mine. It's comfy as hell, here." He drags my arms up, and before I can protest, he slides the hoodie over my head, careful of my makeup and hair, and settles it into place. The material is big and baggy, almost reaching my knees, but it's super soft and warm and smells like him. Realizing I'm sniffing it, I drop the material.

"You don't listen to anything I say," I mutter in annoyance.

"I do, sweetheart, just not when I know you're wrong." He takes my hand, leading me to the door at the back. He opens it and pushes me in and then shuts it behind him. "Now lie down and rest."

"Nobody bosses me around," I warn.

"I'm not bossing, sweetheart. I'm asking." He backs me up to the bed until I fall backward, and then his arms go down around my head. "Either you sleep, sweetheart, or we are going to do something very different in this bed. Your choice."

My eyes meet his. The bedroom is small, and there isn't much except a bed, but as I lie on the silk sheets, I know that if I let Kage fuck me, it will change something. He'll have gotten what he wanted, and he'll get bored, just like everyone else, and part of me doesn't want that. I like his attention, for now at least.

I slide backwards, crawling up the bed and slipping between the sheets. His chuckle follows me, but he doesn't seem disappointed. He does, however, climb in next to me, and before I can move away, he wraps me up in his arms, dragging me closer so I'm pressed against his chest. "Before you tell me off, it won't work, now sleep." He kisses my head softly. "You can go back to keeping your distance and pretending you don't want this tomorrow. Tonight, just give in and let me hold you while you sleep—not for you, but for me."

"Fine, for you, and because I'm tired," I mutter as I relax into his embrace.

"Thank you, sweetheart." I hear the smile in his voice, but I ignore it and close my eyes.

I don't expect to be able to sleep, but I must because I jerk awake sometime later, my nightmares chasing me into consciousness.

"Shh, baby, I'm here. You're okay. It was just a dream." Kage strokes my face, his body wrapped around mine in the dark, and I remember we are on the plane.

Blinking, I bring his face into focus while my mind tries to catch up to what's happening. "It wasn't," I croak, my voice hoarse. Was I screaming again? I'm sweating and my legs are weak, which is typical after one of my night terrors. "It was a memory."

He frowns, watching me. "What kind of memory made you that scared? You were crying in your sleep."

"The worst kind," I whisper. "Ones I've tried to forget."

"People only bury something when they've done something bad," he whispers slowly.

"We bury what we fear," I whisper, my voice soft and shaky.

"And what do you fear, sweetheart? Tell me and I'll take care of it. You'll never be scared again," he murmurs.

"You can't take care of my past, Kage. Nobody can." I relax into his grip but look away, feeling too vulnerable.

"Don't ever be ashamed of your past with me. When you're ready, I will be right here, willing to hear it. I promise." He kisses my forehead and wraps himself around me more solidly. "Want me to distract you?"

"Please," I whisper.

"Hmm, well, I told you we were poor when I was growing up, and we really were. I grew up in Section 8 housing, going to a school that had bars on the windows. My dad worked two jobs, my mom three, and I have two siblings, but we aren't really that close. I think it's because we all knew we wanted to get out of there, and when we had the chance, we did. I check on them now and again, and I made sure my parents don't struggle anymore, but they don't understand this life, and I don't need them to. I'm thankful for everything they did to raise us, but now it's my turn to carve my path."

Turning in his arms, I meet his eyes. "Some—no, most people would be terrified of the real you, Kage."

"I don't care about them. I only care about you. Are you scared of me?" he asks, his hands sliding over my body.

"No," I admit. "Not even a little."

He kisses me softly. "Good girl. I'd rip out my own heart before I would ever hurt you."

Surprisingly enough, I believe him.

K F
Golden Love
I'll be with you.
I'll wait for you.
Golden Love
Can't you see
I'm your fool?

FOURTEEN

KAGE

Despite her original protests, Fallon disembarks her jet wearing my hoodie. I spy the cameras from a distance and smile, knowing they will capture it. After all, they got me coming out of the hotel wearing it. Soon, the whole world will know I'm Fallon's, and I couldn't be happier.

"Don't tell me you need a ride too," she calls as she heads to her car that's idling a few feet away.

"Well, we do live next door to each other." I hurry over and open her door before the driver can. She rolls her eyes but gets in, and I slide in next to her, taking her hand. She doesn't even fight me, and I consider that a win. Things have started to change between us. She's opening up and letting me in. Fallon still has so many secrets and layers, but I can't wait to peel each one back.

Like tonight on the plane, I realized there is something in Fallon's past, something that haunts her, and I won't stop until I free her of that ghost.

Besides, she wanted to get to know me earlier. No matter how she rationalizes it, she wanted to get to know me, and that's a good sign. Honestly, I would wait forever for Fallon, but knowing she's softening toward me makes me feel like a superhero.

"What are you going to do with your new hotel?" she asks as we drive into the city.

"Eh, it's a good investment. In fact, I'm considering buying one in every city around the world so when you travel, you have a safe place to stay."

She turns and gapes at me. "Sometimes I can't tell if you're being serious or not," she responds.

"I'm deadly serious." I frown. Does she think I wouldn't? I'd do much, much more for my girl. "Where do you go often? I'll start there first." When she just stares, I smile. "Don't worry, I'll get a list from your management."

"They won't give it to you," she mumbles.

"Sure, sweetheart," I scoff. My phone buzzes, and I pull it out with one hand, refusing to lose the hold I have on her.

Elijah: I think I found it. Want me to proceed?

Kage: Give them anything they want and have it shipped to my girl's address.

Elijah: Understood. Are you back now? The label is mad you canceled those interviews.

Kage: Then schedule more to make up for it.

"Problem?" Fallon asks.

"Just my manager." I hold out my phone. "You want to see?"

"What? No," she scoffs, pushing my phone away.

"Baby, I have nothing to hide from you. Look through my entire phone if you want. I can tell you what you'll find—way too many pictures of you and me stalking your socials, but not much else. In fact . . ." I load up the settings, and when she turns to me, I scan her face and then grin. "There, now you can unlock it with facial recognition too. What's mine is yours."

"You didn't!" She gapes, so I turn my phone and watch her mouth drop open as it unlocks with her face. "What the fuck, Kage?"

"What's your schedule like this week? I don't want to intrude—"

She laughs. "Really?"

"On any important meetings or anything, but I want to know when I can see you again," I finish, ignoring her joke.

She looks away, and I watch her profile. "I'll let you know," is all she says, and I know that's Fallon's way of trying to push me away.

I let her because it won't last. If she thinks she can get rid of me that easily, then she's more delusional than I am.

Fallon is mine, and she's never getting away from me.

I was right. Fallon is trying to avoid me.

Luckily, I was dressed up today so I don't bother changing. I need to look the part to be at her side. My black leather jacket hangs to my feet, and underneath, I wear cinched black pants with a sheer, loose shirt. I know it looks good on me, and I dressed in hopes of seeing her. I guess I was feeling lucky, and I was right to.

It didn't take long to find the restaurant, and I spent time searching the guy she is going on a date with—a foolish attempt to stop the rumors about us online. I've given her time this week, but I'm over it now. Instead, I focus on the man she is meeting. It seems he's some kind of actor with a famous daddy no doubt buying all his roles. He's a pretty boy but nowhere near the caliber of my girl, and he knows it.

I make sure to park around back, and then I rap on the metal fire door. Eventually, a confused waiter opens it. When he spots me, his eyes widen. Good, he knows who I am, so this will work well. I hand over a wad of cash. "I need your help."

"Sure, sure, uh, can I have an autograph?" he asks, taking the money.

"You can, but help me first." I know my smile is evil, but I don't care.

I follow him inside, and after explaining what I want, I hide behind the bar in the fancy restaurant, watching as he goes to take their order. Their table isn't too far away, and she looks really fucking good tonight, but then again, when doesn't she? When the waiter comes back and starts making the drinks, he nods at one of the glass tumblers as he turns away to grab my girl's drink. Grinning, I pull the crushed pills from my pocket and dump them in the glass, and then I stir it as he loads them onto a tray with a wink and heads back to their table.

I wait with a wicked grin as her date takes the glass without looking at the waiter and downs most of it nervously. I'd be nervous too with such a beauty looking at me, and it was just like I was expecting.

The waiter comes back to my side, and I slide over the autograph I promised. "What did you give him? Do I need an ambulance?"

"No, but maybe a plumber." I smirk, watching them chat and drink.

That's right, drink it all.

There's enough in there to take down an elephant, never mind a rich boy.

I wait impatiently, and not too long later, her date pales, stopping mid-sentence. He suddenly jumps to his feet, stuttering something to a confused looking Fallon before he grabs his ass and stumbles through the restaurant to the hallway at the back. I can't help but grin, and then I push away from the bar and make my way to my girl.

She turns and sees me heading her way, her mouth dropping open. I push my coat back at my hips to show off our matching outfits and let her get a good look at her man.

Her pupils dilate, desire filling her gaze, and when I reach her, I lean down and kiss her lips possessively. "Sorry I'm late, sweetheart. I had to find the restaurant." I head around the table and sit where he was, draping the napkin over my lap as I recline back in my seat.

She stares at me in shock. "Um, that's my date's seat."

"Yes, and he's sitting right here. Have you ordered food yet? I'm starving." I drop my eyes to her body and watch her cheeks heat.

"He'll be back any minute. You better go, Kage," she snaps, shaking off her stupor.

I take the wine glass my new friend brings and sip it as I point at everything he touched. "You can remove his setting. I'll need a new one." When it's gone, I meet her eyes and see her glaring, ice frosting her gaze. "He won't be coming back anytime soon, sweetheart, trust me."

"What did you do?" she snaps.

Fuck, I love it when she gets that look in her eyes. Wrapping my foot around her chair under the table, I drag her closer as she yelps. When she's at my side, I lean in so my coat blocks us, grab her hand, and press it to my hard dick.

"Keep looking at me like that and we are going to be leaving before you get your meal, sweetheart."

She snatches her hand back, looking away from me. "I'm looking at you in anger. How are you hard?" she hisses.

"I love your anger, it's fucking beautiful, but I'm hard anytime you look at me," I admit, whispering in her ear. "If you wanted a date, beautiful, then you should have said so. I do like a challenge, so thank you. I was getting a little bored this week."

"Seriously, Kage, what did you do?" she asks, not backing down, her eyes meeting mine boldly. Her icy gaze makes me shudder with desire. I love my soft, needy girl, but I love my hard, icy girl just as much.

"I gave him something to keep him busy all night. He didn't deserve to be here at your side."

She stands abruptly, ready to storm away, so I grab her hand and pull her down onto my lap, holding her there with one arm while I open the menu with the other, propping my chin on her shoulder.

"Kage," she snaps, elbowing me.

I kiss her shoulder. "Stop making a scene, sweetheart, or I'll bend you over my knee for daring to look this beautiful for another man," I warn as she stiffens. "We both know I will, so behave."

"You wouldn't dare," she murmurs.

"Do you want to bet?" I whisper huskily. I know every eye in the restaurant is on us, including the staff and the cameras pressed against the glass outside, trying to get the scoop. "Keep trying and we'll find out."

There's a moment of silence. "Can I at least sit in my chair?"

"No, I like you where you are. You can't run from me now. I'll be your chair, sweetheart. What do you want, steak? No, pasta?" I murmur, still scanning the menu. I'll give it to the idiot, he picked a good place. The food here is supposed to be excellent. No doubt he wanted to show off, but I bet he had to drop his daddy's name just to get in. I only had to show my face.

"Kage, you are being ridiculous. I'm allowed to date. You don't get to show up and do something to my date then hold me hostage," she begins, wiggling to get free, and I groan.

"Keep moving like that and I'm going to make a mess before we even get to dessert."

"You're fucking insane," she snaps as she stiffens.

My waiter friend chooses that moment to turn up, grinning. "Ready to order?"

"Where is my date?" she asks.

"Oh, uh, the gentleman you came in with is . . . indisposed in the bathroom right now. Mr. Kage said he was your date." The waiter grins. Good boy, I'm going to give him a big tip. "What can I get you to eat? The chef said he would make anything you like."

"Then one of everything, please. My girl can't decide." I snap the menu shut and hand it over. "And please make sure to send some water to that poor man. I bet it's going to be a long, long night."

When the waiter leaves, Fallon turns in my arms, her eyes narrowed. "Did you feed him laxatives?"

"More than even models take." I smirk. "I hope you're hungry."

She continues to stare into my eyes. "How didn't I see it before?" she whispers.

"What, sweetheart?"

"The devil in your gaze," she whispers, and my lips tip up in a grin. "I'm never getting away from you, am I?"

"Glad you noticed. It's only taken a year." I kiss her cheek. "Now, if you behave, you can sit on your seat, but if you try to leave, I'm going to bend you over this table, flip your skirt up, and spank your ass red, and we both know I will." I watch her swallow nervously, even as her eyes flare. My girl likes me taking control when everyone else would back down to her. "Are you going to be a good girl, sweetheart?"

"Yes," she whispers, but I arch my brow, her nostrils flaring as she takes a deep breath. "I'll be a good girl."

Kissing her cheek again, I remove my arm. She stands, brushing her hair back and sinking into her chair, making me grin. She watches me with a new look in her eye, a considering one. It seems she's finally taking me seriously.

Good.

"So how has your week been, sweetheart?"

FIFTEEN

Fallon

He waits patiently, a smile flirting on his lips. He's so close I can smell the cologne that follows him everywhere, and despite everything, he looks good tonight. I can see his stacked muscles and abs every time he moves, and there's something about his hair being half up in a ponytail with strands escaping into his face that really does it for me.

He's all darkness and crazy. I can see the madness and obsession in his eyes, but for the first time since—what was his name?—picked me up, I smile a real smile, and I know I'm fucked.

I tried to stay away all week. I told myself I don't need Kage to be happy and that there are others out there. That's what tonight was about, but nothing compares to seeing myself in his dark gaze, feeling his possessive obsession, or the desire he stirs within me.

"Fine," I respond. "Yours?"

"Long. I missed you, but I did get to see you hurry to your car every day, trying to avoid me." People don't say stuff like that, but Kage does like it's normal conversation. The worst part is, I'm starting to get used to it. I can't even remember a single word the other guy said, but Kage? I hang onto everything he says, never knowing what he will do or say next.

It's exciting and should be the exact opposite of what I want.

I like boring, easy to control men. Kage is nothing like that, but I find myself wanting him more and more.

Maybe I just need to fuck him out of my system, like a new addiction you get tired of after a while. That has to be it. I sit back, deciding to sleep with Kage tonight so I can move on from this strange bond we seem to have, and then I can go back to my boring, predictable life and men I can easily manipulate.

That decision seems to lift a weight off my shoulders, and I relax as I reach for my wine. "What else did you do besides stalk me?"

"Started work on a new album. I'm thinking of calling it *Blue Dahlia*. What do you think?" he asks, sipping his drink as he watches me. As always, he gives me his full attention, never once looking away. Some would find it unnerving, and others would be terrified of Kage and the lengths he is willing to go to so he can be next to me.

"Maybe you should call it *Stalker*," I respond, and he laughs, his head thrown back. I can't help smiling, but I drop it when he looks at me.

"I'll name a song that for you." He winks knowingly as plates start to arrive, and there are so many, they have to drag another table over. I blink in shock. Usually when I'm on a date, I pick at my food—not because I'm ashamed of eating, but because a previous date took a picture and I was torn apart online for how much I eat. I was young then, and it created a bad, unhealthy relationship with food for me for a long time. It's something I'm still working on, but here Kage is, buying me the entire menu, and when I start to reach for food, he looks so fucking proud, I can't help but want to try it all.

What is it about this man that does that to me?

Despite arriving through the front door, my date wanting to show me off, Kage takes me out the back way, knowing I wouldn't want to be seen leaving with another man. It's another drop in the bucket that seems to overflow when it comes to Kage, and when we head home together, I know I'm going to fuck him tonight. I'm going to get this out of my system, then tomorrow, I'll let him go.

I'll go back to my normal self.

When we pull up at my house and he gets out and walks me to my door, I turn to him and press my body against his, rising up on my toes and kissing him. He groans, cupping the back of my head and kissing me back. I deepen it, sliding my hand under his coat and across his chest, swallowing his gasp.

My back hits the door, and he pins me there as he dominates my mouth, his hand hiking up my thigh and lifting it over his hip as I explore his muscles. Desire has me rocking my hips into him, knowing it's going to be so good.

He pulls back, and with dark, lustful eyes, he presses a promising kiss on my lips. "I told you, sweetheart, I won't be another body in your bed—not until I know you'll keep me there forever. You think fucking me tonight means you can walk away, but that isn't happening."

My eyes widen at how easily he read my intentions. I feel annoyed and embarrassed about being turned down a second time.

Second!

By the same guy!

I turn around to unlock the door when he crowds my back, pressing me against the wood. "That being said, I never promised to behave all the way, and I can't leave my girl needy, can I?"

"Let me go," I order, pushing back, but he pins me there effortlessly and pulls my skirt up. No one would dare touch me like this, nor would I let them, but when he presses his palm against my needy cunt over my underwear, I freeze.

"Shh, stop fighting, sweetheart. You've been such a good girl tonight, so let me reward you. Let me take the edge off so when you've decided I'm yours, I can spend all night between your pretty thighs, knowing you've been waiting for me." His voice is dark, menacing, and so silky, I lose myself in it.

"That's a good girl. Keep quiet for me so they don't find us. I'd hate to have to kill someone," he growls as his long fingers slide across my wet cunt. "They call you an ice queen, beautiful, but you are all warm and wet for me. I guess I make you melt." I elbow him as he chuckles, pressing his thumb into my clit.

Desire slams through me so hard, I almost cry out. He stokes that desire, petting me softly while whispering in my ear. "I'm yours, Fallon. If I knew you wouldn't walk away tomorrow, I'd be in your bed, and I'd spend all night worshiping you, but I won't risk this, won't risk us, so you're going to be a good girl and let me finger your cunt until you come, and then next time, I'll get on my knees for you and lick your pussy clean until you promise to be mine forever."

Fuck.

My eyes close, my breathing becoming labored as I tilt my hips back, demanding more.

"Please," I whisper, the only sign of weakness I'll give him, but Kage rewards me for it. Two thick fingers slide into me, rubbing that spot not even I can reach until I cry out, rocking my hips for more. His thumb rubs slow circles around my clit until I drip down his fingers. My heart hammers, and my hands clench against the wood of my front door.

His heat presses against my back as his lips slide across my neck, tasting my pulse. "You feel like heaven, sweetheart. I bet you taste even better. I can't wait to find out, but first, I want to feel you come."

I'm always in control. I'm always—

My eyes cross as he slides a third finger inside me, dragging a moan from my throat as my legs begin to shake, widening of their own accord as he plays my body as easily as he plays his audience.

My head hits the door with a bang as I let him fuck me.

"We can't have you hurting yourself, sweetheart. The only marks you will wear will be the ones I give you."

His hand slides between my face and the wood to protect me from it, but I bite his skin to muffle my moans, and he groans behind me. His touch becomes demanding as he drags pleasure from me.

"Come for me. You know you want to. Let me feel it. Give me something to get through tonight. Soak my fucking fingers so whenever I look at them, I'll think of you." His dirty words spur me on, and before I know it, I'm tumbling over the edge. I come with a muffled groan, my hips jerking as my cunt clenches around his invading fingers. I shudder as I rock my hips, riding the waves of pleasure until it's finally over, and I slump.

"Good girl," he praises, slowly removing his fingers from my greedy channel and straightening my panties and skirt.

Turning me, he kisses my lips softly. "Goodnight, sweetheart. Dream of me. I know I'll dream of you." He steps back, but he doesn't leave. When I turn and slip inside, slamming the door, I finally hear him walk away.

Pressing my back to the door, I stand there, feeling more confused than ever.

SIXTEEN

Fallon

I'm so confused after everything that's been happening. Kage is a wild force of nature, and he's determined to wreck my life, but I keep letting him push his way in then leave. I know why he's doing it, and shit, I even know he's right, but it makes me feel confused and fed up.

Maybe that's why I find myself wandering my house, the usual insomnia and demons chasing me in the dark until I find myself in the living room. I sink onto a couch, looking around at the empty space. For a moment, I imagine it filled with life, with his laughter. Would I still feel so alone? Would I still be so scared all the time?

Would it be enough?

I click the TV remote, letting the leather cushions swallow me until it consumes my body. No one would notice or care if I just let go.

A familiar voice from the TV has me jerking upright as horror and memories assault me.

There, like a ghost conjured from the darkest parts of my soul, is Westie, my father's best friend and bassist. He's older, his hair is grayer, and his eyes and mouth are lined with age. For a moment, I remember how beautiful and oh so fucking dangerous he was.

He was one of the worst parts of my past.

I can't even focus on the words he's saying in the interview. All I can do is stare. I haven't seen him in years, since they all took a step out of the spotlight after my father's death—a decision they didn't make lightly, but one that was the trigger for me to finally step forward. Once more, though, I feel like the scared teenage girl facing down the bigger, more experienced man. When the sound seems to filter through my ringing head, I grab the remote and increase the volume, scarcely breathing or believing what I'm hearing.

"I think it's important to keep the memory of Agille alive, but also to do justice to his story and his rise to fame. That's why this docuseries is so near and dear to our hearts. Everyone has this perception of him as this bad-boy rocker, one of the most talented to ever live, and yes, we want to show that side, but we also want to show the man who was our leader and our friend as well."

"Are you fucking kidding me?" I screech as I leap to my feet.

They are making a docuseries about my father?

It's clear it's for fame, money, and the spotlight it will bring, but I wonder how they will gloss over his life. How will they portray his home life? Will they make me the villain? The weak child? All that pain, all that shit I survived will become nothing but a carefully crafted footnote in their story to the top. Everything I endured will become meaningless.

Anger fills me at the idea. What I went through was real, what I survived was real, but this will make it nothing but a lie. Everything I have fought to forget, to move away from will all be brought back up.

I'll never escape him.

I've tried so hard to surpass him, to give him one last fuck you, but I never will. I will always be remembered alongside my father, and the bitter truth is, nobody will ever speak out against him, not even those who know the truth. They will sit in the interviews and call him a legend, and I'll be forced to endure it silently.

Well, fuck that.

I'm not that little girl anymore. I know more now, and I have a voice.

They don't get to make him the martyr and me the villain in my own life.

They don't get to pull apart my past and make me relive it without giving truth to everything I went through.

I can't breathe as I watch Westie discuss more details about it, something they never even asked my permission for. Don't they need that?

All the pain, anger, and hopelessness I have tried so hard to run from consumes me until I crawl back onto the couch and bury my head there.

How can they do this to me?

Isn't surviving it once enough?

I stare at the screen until it cuts out, and I still stare at the blank, empty space.

They ruined me. They broke me.

I have nothing but rot and darkness within my soul, and one day, it will consume me. Even the doctors feared what lived inside me long before they gave it a name, and it all started with them, with him, and those are the thoughts that chase me into waking nightmares.

The room spins, the bottle of amber liquid sloshing in my hand as I fall into the booth. The party is in full swing, and faces blur before me, including some of the biggest names in the world. I hear laughter and moans, and it all blurs.

My arms shake, and my skin is sweaty. I know I shouldn't be doing this.

I know this isn't right, but no one cares.

No one even noticed me here, trying to hide away with alcohol clutched in my hand. My father is somewhere in the party, celebrating another award win. His band is with him as they fuck and shoot up, leaving me to the circling sharks. Even in my own home, I'm not safe. I tried hiding in my room, but it didn't work. In fact, it only made it worse. There was nowhere to escape to then, no company to help me. No, it's better to be here, surrounded by people, even if that means I have to accept the bottles they hand me.

I should have stayed at Kayla's, but I think her mom is getting suspicious and slightly sick of me.

All I want is to be left alone to do my homework in peace. I have an essay due tomorrow, and I really want to pass to prove to all the snobby kids at that elitist school that I'm as smart as they are and that I didn't get in on my father's name alone.

But no.

When the crowd parts and he comes toward me, I know tonight will be no different than the others.

"There she is, our favorite girl!" Westie shouts, needle marks showing on his arms. He always gets sloppy and overly touchy when he's high. My father either doesn't notice or doesn't care, and I don't know which is worse. "I wondered where you were hiding. Have a drink, princess." He thrusts another bottle at me. "We are celebrating."

"She's too young," someone comments as they pass, but they don't intervene, like it's a joke.

"Nah, our princess is mature for her age, aren't you?" He grins as he slides in next to me, his legs coming up to block my exit on the other side, not that I can get my body to move. "Do you want to feel as good as I do, princess?"

"No, I'm okay." I force the words out, hoping he'll leave me alone tonight.

"Oh, come on, don't be boring. Your dad said you could. Besides, we are celebrating!" He pulls out the baggie and wipes off the table, starting to lay it out.

Most girls my age are worried about boys and the dance that's coming up.

My worry is that one day, they are going to push too much into my system and I won't wake up.

I don't want it, I don't like the feeling of being high, but if I say no, he won't stop there. I try anyway, even as he cuts the line.

"No, Westie, I'm okay. I'm tired, and I have to be up early for school—" I gasp as his hand grips the back of my head. His expression

is mean now, and I swallow out of fear, trying to shrink away from him as he leans in, the stench of alcohol on his breath overwhelming me.

"Didn't we teach you that it's rude to say no, princess? Don't embarrass us or your dad like that." He forces my head toward the table and shoves the rolled-up bill into my hand. When I hit it back, he smashes my head into the table. "Don't make me mad, princess. I'm celebrating."

Tears crowd my eyes as I fight against his hand, but it's no use. Despite him being high, he's stronger than me. They all are, and they always have been. I'm just too skinny, too weak, and too young. The attention was once flattering when I was younger. I was their princess, their girl, their daughter when every girl my age wanted it, but as I grew up, it all changed, and now I hate it.

I would give anything for a normal life, a normal upbringing, with a father who loved and protected me.

I snort the line, hating the feeling and hating his hand as his hold softens in my hair.

"Good princess." His hand slips lower, and revulsion twists my insides. This time, I snort the line on my own, wanting to be numb . . . wanting to forget whatever they are going to do to me tonight.

I jerk awake with a scream. So many memories crowd my head, it hurts. My hands clamp down on my ears as I scream, tears falling down my cheeks.

No, no, no, no.

They aren't here. I'm safe. They aren't here. I'm safe.

I repeat it as I run through all the grounding techniques I know, but it doesn't help. The darkness reaches for me, trying to swallow me whole, and something tells me if it gets me tonight, it will be the end.

Rolling from the couch, I crawl from the dark, empty room, searching for something, anything to cling to. I need something to anchor me in this world so I don't fall into the darkness where my memories haunt me. My head lifts, and out of the window, I spy the lights on in Kage's mansion.

Without conscious thought, I drag myself to my bare feet and stumble out of my front door, my entire focus on the lights. If I can get there, I'll be safe. The darkness won't reach me.

My silk nightdress whips around my bare legs as I clamber through the gap he created in the wall, thankful for it right now. Ignoring my stinging feet, I run and stumble to the front door. My heart pounds as fear nips at my heels.

I crash into the door with desperate, clumsy hands, struggling to grab the doorknob. It opens, and I fly inwards. It's unlocked. I look around with panicked, unseeing eyes before scrambling for the stairs.

"Kage." It's a croak.

Was I screaming in my sleep?

Gripping the banister, I drag myself up the steps on shaky legs, crying the entire time. "Kage," I call louder. "Kage!" It's a sorrowful scream as I reach the top and collapse. "Kage, Kage, Kage, Kage."

"Sweetheart?" There's a bang, and then I'm lifted into solid, safe arms. "Fallon, look at me. What happened?" he asks, holding my head up. He runs his hands over me in panic. "Fallon."

I focus on his eyes as the darkness ebbs away from his light. "Nightmares," I rasp, knowing he won't stop until he knows. "I need you."

He blows out a breath, holding me closer. "I'm here." He kisses my head, warming my skin with that one touch. "I'm here, sweetheart." I close my eyes as he carries me deeper into the house, his arms my safety net. Suddenly, I'm lying on something soft, and I startle, reaching for him in my panic, but he slides in next to me, pulling me into his arms. "I'm here. I'm here. I'm not going anywhere. You're safe. You're safe." He repeats it until I'm breathing again. "That's it, sweetheart, breathe for me." Something warm tucks around me. "You're freezing."

"I'm sorry. I'm so sorry," I whisper. "I couldn't see a way out, and then I saw your lights on and I just . . . I just thought if I could get here, I would be safe. I'm sorry."

"Don't you ever be sorry. I'm glad you came," he replies, holding me tightly.

"It tried to get me."

"What did, sweetheart?"

"The darkness," I whisper.

"Shh, I won't let the darkness get you," he promises.

"It already did," I admit. "It got me, Kage, and I'm so fucking lost."

"I know, but I'm here now. You're safe, and I won't let you wander alone," he promises. "Now just breathe for me and let the light soak back in."

I don't know how he knew I needed that, but I do, and I sink into his warmth. The light of the room burns against my eyelids, chasing away the last of the lingering memories and thoughts. I'm not a fool, I know what happened in my past will never go away, but I hoped one day it would get easier.

I was wrong. It only seems to get harder.

I have been told I need to deal with it, to find the trauma that stalks me and confront it, but I can't. I couldn't ever speak the truth to the array of doctors I saw. I just lied and lied and lied until it became second nature . . . until I even believed the lies.

I'm okay. I'm always okay.

I don't know how long we lie here, him holding me, protecting me, until I force myself to sit up, ashamed and empty once more. I go to slide off the bed, but he captures my hand and sits me on the bottom.

"Let me look at your feet." Before I can protest, he drops to his knees on the floor and lifts my feet, checking them with a sad smile. "Just some small cuts, nothing that can't be fixed, sweetheart. Nothing I can't fix if you let me," he murmurs, and I know he means more than my wounds.

He can't though. Can't he see that? Nobody can.

I watch with sad eyes as he carefully lifts each foot and washes them before applying ointment and then wrapping them in big, warm socks that reach mid-calf.

"Your door was unlocked," I murmur numbly. It's always like this after one of my storms—numbness, nothing, until I don't even feel connected to this world—but when he meets my eyes, electricity fires through me, making me feel again.

"It will always be unlocked just in case you need me. It will never be locked, not to you," he promises as he picks up my hand and kisses it. "You were okay when I left you. Was it just a nightmare?"

I know I have a choice. I could lie once more or I could accept the helping hand. I could let someone in. I'm starting to think I can't do this all alone.

"I saw an interview . . . . They are doing a docuseries on my father and his life." I choke back a bitter laugh, blinking the tears away. "It was all buried with him, and it never truly left me, but I could handle it. Seeing that brought everything to the surface." I meet his gaze and confirm what he probably already suspects. "My father wasn't a good man. I didn't have a good childhood, and now they are going to play it everywhere. It will be a lie, and I just felt like it was making me helpless again, like I was back then, hiding the truth and forcing me to lie like I did for all those years."

He's quiet for a moment, and I'm worried about what he will say and what he will think of me now.

Will he still want me?

"So what do you want, Fallon? What do you want to do? Tell me and I'll help you. I'll do anything. Just say it, sweetheart. We'll regain your power, your voice, just tell me," he begs, anger and determination in his eyes, and it's what gives me the strength to speak again.

"I want the world to know the truth. If the world wants the dirty details, then they can have them, even if it ruins me. For once in my life, I don't want to be a liar. I want to tell the truth, the entire truth. I want to open my wounds and let them feast on them. I want . . . I want to riot. I want to fucking tear them all to pieces. I want them to pay."

He doesn't ask how or why, but he kisses my hand before he leans up, cupping my cheeks. "Then that's what we'll do."

SEVENTEEN

KAGE

It took Fallon over two hours to fall asleep, and even now, she's making these little noises that rip my heart apart.

I thought loving Fallon meant loving all of her, and I thought I knew everything, but I was wrong. She hid it well. She lied so convincingly to everyone, even to herself. I never knew about her past, and now that I know some of it, I want to kill them.

How dare they hurt this angel?

I wish I could go back, wish I could protect her, but I can't. Instead, I hold her and silently vow that no one will ever hurt again. Whatever she chooses now, I will deflect the blows meant for her because I love her.

I need to know what I'm protecting her against though. I know she won't tell me until she's ready, and I don't want her to, but I can't lie here and do nothing. Grabbing my phone, I drape my arms around her and look over her shoulder as I search.

There are pages and pages of articles about her father and the band. It's only when I dive deep that I find some random online musings about old parties where people were caught doing drugs and illegal shit —her father included—at her family home.

Was she part of them?

Was she forced into those parties as a child?

I can't find much else. Whoever was doing cleanup did a very good fucking job of it. Everything about her father are memorials and fan pages singing his praises. Her name is always mentioned as the beloved daughter, so it seems even in that she can't escape him, even though she changed her name.

Sighing, I drop my phone. I want to protect her, but I don't know how.

Fallon is the strongest person I know, so I know she can handle it, but she doesn't need to alone. The fact that she came here tonight . . . Fuck, my heart beats faster, knowing she reached for me in the dark when she was struggling. She feels safe with me. It tells me I'm doing something right, but I need to do more. I need to be more. I don't want her to struggle with her nightmares forever.

Maybe I could force her to move in with me. She doesn't seem to have them when she sleeps in my arms—nah, she would probably murder me. One day, though, I'll convince her to, but until then, I can sneak over every night when she's asleep and hold her. It's worth the risk of her wrath if it keeps her safe, even from her own mind. I might not understand what that's like, but I'll become the best at understanding for her.

When Fallon comes down the next morning, I expect her to look shy, ashamed, or maybe even angry and storm out, but I should have known better. She rises to every challenge. Despite what happened, she looks as perfect as always, wearing nothing but her long, lace nightie with her hair unbound, her face free of makeup. She tilts her chin up, eyeing me with an arched brow as she gracefully slides into the seat next to mine at the head of the table. "Good morning." She looks like she belongs here, like she was made to be here. Fuck, she acts like she's leading a goddamn business meeting with the way she deliberately folds the napkin over her lap and looks around.

It makes me hard as hell, but my desire isn't important right now.

What we discussed last night is.

"We need to make a plan," I tell her as I lean back, "on how we are bringing down this docuseries."

""I'm surprised you haven't already done it." She smirks as she grabs some toast and spreads jam on it.

Chuckling, I watch her, far too happy to have her in my house. "I did try. The company that's making it, however, isn't one I have connections with. They are big, and this will take more than me threatening them."

Nodding, she takes a bite as she watches me. "This could ruin you," she says after swallowing. "I have no qualms about what I'm doing by exposing the truth and bringing them down, but this could ruin your career, Kage."

I rub my thumb along her lip to remove the jam there. Her eyes widen as I suck it clean. "Ruin me. Use me all you want, Fallon. I'm yours. We are doing this together."

"Are you sure?" she asks.

"More sure than I've ever been before. I created this life for you. If you want to wreck it, then do it." I shrug as I pile more food on her plate and watch her eat it. "So where do we begin?"

EIGHTEEN

Fallon

Kage and I look really fucking good. We dressed to cause them stress.

His black hair is messy and hanging in his face, and his eyes are smoky and lined to the point where I'm debating asking him to do my makeup. His ears are filled with earrings, a giant cross hanging from the left lobe. His suit jacket looks like snakeskin, but it's a deep black and buttoned low, exposing his built chest and the ink across it. His hands are covered by sheer gloves, and his pants match his suit jacket. It shouldn't look so slutty, but it does, and I kind of love it.

Following his theme, I chose to wear black as well. The dress is short and long-sleeved, buttoned down the front with a triangle collar and frills down the sides of my chest. I added tall black boots and a wide red belt, with triangles draping over my hips, making them look wider. I add some black shades and dramatic earrings, and when we step out of the car together, I know we make quite the sight.

The Hall Movies building stands tall above us, a skyscraper with glittering windows. This is just the first step in our plan, and we make sure to walk slowly for the paparazzi we called to catch us walking in. It will raise questions and get the public talking just like we want.

Once inside, we head past reception, the lady there scrambling to her feet. "Excuse me!"

I pull down my shades and eye her. "No." We head through the barriers and into the elevator, hitting the floor Kage's assistant told us about. They made the meeting, playing on every channel's need to get into our good books. They might not be willing to pull the docuseries after a call, but they want us to be friends.

Hence, we head right to the CEO's office and walk in.

He gets to his feet, blinking in confusion as we sit in the chairs opposite his desk. "We still have ten minutes," he begins, confusion and apprehension swirling in his eyes.

"Sit." I tilt my head, forcing out the next word. "Please."

He does slowly, his eyes wide as he looks between us. "Your manager didn't mention what you wanted. Is it to discuss the series following your life we pitched a few years ago? I'm very glad to finally meet you, Ms. Fallon, and of course you, Kage."

"No, it isn't." I lean back in my chair, watching him. "Are you a betting man, Mr. Perrier?"

"Um, no, not really?" It ends as a question.

Sitting behind his huge desk, with the city view through his floor-to-ceiling windows, he must feel like a god. He is anything but. He might have money and power, but everyone in this world knows my name, and I wonder how many know his.

"I have seen the docuseries you are due to produce on my father." He blanches. "First, I find it disgusting you didn't even ask my permission."

"I'm sorry, Ms. Fallon, but we don't need your permission—"

"Did it sound like I was finished?" I snap, and he sits back, his face turning red. I'm guessing he's never been spoken to like this before. He would throw us out if we were anyone else. "I want you to put a stop to it. Pull the project."

He blinks, his mouth opening and closing. "We can't do that," he yells. "It has been announced, funding is secured—"

"Kill it," I demand.

"No." His nostrils flare as he leans forward. "I respect who you are,

Ms. Fallon, but not even you have that power. We can't and we will not pull this series. We feel it's important, and the public clearly agrees. I'm sorry you don't want the truth about your father out there—"

"Oh, I want the truth out there." I smile. "But nobody other than me gets to be the one to tell it. It is no one else's story. It isn't that you can't—it's that you won't. You want the money and recognition. When was the last time you had a hit? Your movies are tanking at the box office, and your shows aren't getting renewed. You are failing, and you know it. You need a Hail Mary. I was going to offer you one, depending on your attitude, but I won't now. You want to be the captain of this ship? Then you will sink with it."

Standing, I pull my shades back down. "It's a shame you're not a betting man because personally, I wouldn't bet against me. If you want to be my enemy, then fine, you're my enemy, but be prepared for what that means." I turn and walk away.

Anger courses through me. I wanted to give them the chance to backpedal. I wanted to work with them, not against them, but I guess we have no choice.

I won't back down.

Since they are so obsessed with the truth, then they will get it, and it will drown them like it did me.

K♥F
Golden Love
I'll be with you.
I'll wait for you.
Golden Love
Can't you see
I'm your fool?

NINETEEN

KAGE

I needed something to cheer my girl up after that asshat refused to pull the docuseries, so when I get the text that I've been waiting for, I grin widely. I dropped her off at home at her insistence, but I hurry over now as Elijah waves the delivery truck in. I watch them unload it and inspect it before signing and taking the keys.

"Go away, Kage, I need to think," she calls through the door.

"Fuck thinking. I got you a present. Come see." There's a moment of silence, and then the door creaks open and she peeks out.

"If it's your penis, I don't want it."

"Not this time." Grabbing her hand, I pull her out and stop her before her dream car, placing the keys in her open hand. "Surprise, baby."

She gawks, running her eyes over the red supercar that we searched high and low for. I might have spent a small fortune buying from what I believe to be a drug dealer who really didn't want to sell it. "Is that the 1964 Ferrari 250 LM?"

"Not just any, that is your father's car. We tracked its history to make sure. It's the right one, right?" I worry, glancing from her to the car.

She nods silently.

"Do you want to drive it?" I urge her, pressing my hand against her back. "Go on, it's yours."

"Are you sure?" she asks softly. "This couldn't have been cheap."

"Baby, when are you going to realize I would buy this entire world for you? Or that I can twice over? It's yours, so enjoy it however you want," I tell her, needing to see her smile.

"However I want?" she asks, a strange look in her eyes as she glances at me.

"However you want." I nod.

She tilts her head, eyeing it, and then heads inside. I turn, confused, but she comes out a few moments later with an open bottle of Champagne in her hand. She drinks from the bottle, and then my eyes land on the crowbar in her other hand.

Prowling to me, she thrusts the bottle into my hands. "Hold this."

Blinking, I take the bottle as she swings the crowbar over her shoulder and turns toward the car. My mouth actually drops when she slams the bar into the side of it. It's a slow hit, but then she does it again, harder. She laughs as she walks down the side, dragging the crowbar along its perfect paint, the sound making me wince.

"Um, Fallon?" I'm so confused.

She stops at the back of the car and brings the crowbar down on the window, smashing it in. Glass shatters everywhere before she looks up at me. "He loved this car more than he ever loved me." She brings it down again. "He protected it more than he ever protected me." She rounds the car, and with a scream, she slams the bar into the window, smashing it in before slamming it against the front as she keeps moving. She brings it down again and again, getting into each swing. Her eyes are crazed, and her chest heaves when she turns to me. "You said it was mine."

"It is." I shrug. "Burn it for all I care. It's yours. I'll just be here, watching the show."

Her eyes land back on the car. "He used to shout at me if I even so much as came near this car. Now look at it, Daddy!" she screams. "Look at your perfect fucking car." She brings the bar down with each word before she presses one heeled foot against the hood and gracefully climbs up, standing on top of the car and bringing the crowbar down over and over again.

My eyes widen, but I can't stop myself from laughing when she blows her hair from her face and grins at me. It makes my heart clench. Her makeup is smeared, her clothes are falling off one shoulder, and her hair is a total mess, but she's never looked so beautiful and carefree. If I didn't already love her, I would fall in love all over again.

Taking a sip of the Champagne, I clap and cheer her on.

I watch her wreck what I thought was her dream car, but money means nothing. I'd buy a million of them if it would make her feel better.

Tears fall down her cheeks, though, and I hate how much this is hurting her as much as healing her. She screams as she jumps up and down on the top of the car, and I wait, protecting her from here. She climbs from the car and smashes the lights in before dropping the crowbar, silently crying. I let her, knowing she needs this. I'm just here for when she needs me.

"I fucking hate you," she whispers softly. "I hate you, I hate you, I fucking hate you!" she screams, her chin wobbling. "Why didn't you protect me? Why was this car more important to you than my innocence? Why wasn't I ever enough?"

My heart breaks, and I wish I could drag her father from the grave and kill him all over again for what he put her through. It's there in her tone—the hero worship, rejected love, pain, and agony.

She loved her father, but he didn't love her.

"I hope you're rotting. I really fucking do. I'm going to tell them all your dirty little secrets and let your reputation crumble. I'm going to destroy everything you worked so hard for, everything you sacrificed your life, your marriage, and your kid for. I'm going to destroy it and fucking laugh while I watch it burn," she promises, wiping her tears away.

I watch with fascination and pride as my girl climbs into the smashed car, turns on the engine, and puts it into gear before getting out. She grabs a rock and presses it to the pedal, then she comes and stands next to me, taking her Champagne and sipping it as we watch the car drive into her pool.

I chuckle. "Well, that's one way to cheer you up."

"I feel so much better now," she says, handing me the bottle. I take a drink, both of us watching the car sink in the water. "I suppose you'll leave now," she murmurs, turning her gaze to me, still glassy with tears. "Now that you've seen the worst of me, seen the crazy in me . . . I'm a mess."

I rub my thumb under her eyes, smearing her mascara like war paint. "No offense, baby, but you've always been a fucking mess, and this only makes me love you more." Turning to her, I cup her cheeks as I press my forehead to hers, the sinking car behind us. "I'm not going anywhere, so scream, cry, whatever you want, and I'll be right there through it all. Let them create stories and rumors because the only things that matter are what you and I think and that we have each other."

Our feet dangle in the water above the million-dollar sunken car. Two empty bottles of Champagne sit between us. Night has fallen, and the only lights come from the pool, illuminating the car and the backyard where we sit.

"Do you feel better?" I ask, breaking the silence we've been sitting in, as comfortable as it was. I'm worried about how she's feeling. She's felt and gone through a lot today, and she looks exhausted.

"Yes and no." She's quiet for a moment. "He loved that car more than life. He bought it with his first big paycheck, and it was his prized possession. It was more than a car to him. It was a demonstration of what and who he was. He cared more about it than he ever did me. Hell, he would show it off and protect it from drunk partygoers, but not me. I was a nuisance, something he could utilize. I was a prop, not a daughter." She laughs bitterly, taking another drink. "They all think they want the truth, but they don't. They want the rock star story he presented. Nobody will admit to what he was really like because it means admitting what they were like too. They were no better. I have lived with what happened to me when he was gone and they were quiet, but they are back, needing money and fame and using my past, my trauma, to make it, and I'm fucking angry, so no, I'm not okay. I don't think I will be until I destroy them."

She looks at me. "How fucking dare they? How dare they think they can use and abuse me like they did back then, expecting my silence? Well, I'm not the same helpless little girl I was then, and they don't get to come back and ruin my life again." Tears fall from her eyes, and she wipes them away. "I won't let them. I hated myself for letting it all unfold the way it did—never fighting back, never speaking out. Maybe this is a blessing in disguise. I'll finally get to say my piece, and when I do, I'm going to watch them all burn. I want revenge, and I don't think I'll be okay again until I get it. I'm tired of being the good girl. I want to be messy. I want to fucking scream and misbehave. I want to act on every impulsive dark thought like everyone else does without worrying about my image. I want to be who I am on the inside without a man dictating what I should do. I'm so fucking tired of warring with myself just to be their perfect girl." Her eyes meet mine once more. "So I'm done. She's dead and buried like that car. From now on, this is me."

Cupping her chin, I press my forehead to hers. "And you are fucking perfection like this. Be what you want to be, what you need to be. I'll be behind you the entire way. If you want revenge, then let's take it. Let's watch them burn. I'll hand you the fucking matches."

She smiles, turning back to look at the car as silence fills the air once more, but it looks like a weight has lifted from her shoulders.

Leaning into me, she rests her head on my shoulder, and I can't help but smile as I press mine to hers.

"Tomorrow will be better," I murmur. "And the day after that, and the day after that. I'll make sure you have an incredible life, Fallon. Your enemies are mine, and your problems are mine. We'll do this together."

TWENTY

Fallon

The house is bigger than mine, and it screams old money. We were escorted in by a butler in a three-piece suit and directed to a sitting room with white couches perfectly placed before a coffee table displaying the latest fashion books. To the left of us is the fireplace with a painting, a portrait of the couple, hanging above it.

I'm surprised because when I knew her, she didn't have money. She was working for it.

Kage and I realized we needed evidence because if they won't stop the docuseries, I will expose the truth myself. To do that, I need more than my voice. No one would believe me without it, so I started writing a list of everyone who might be able to help me, and we began a search. She just happened to be the first person we found, though it wasn't easy. Kage called in some favors, which I didn't ask about since I'm thinking it wasn't legal.

"Are you sure this is right?" I murmur as I cross my legs. I'm wearing a short bouclé skirt and matching jacket, and my sunglasses are pushed up to hold my hair back. Kage looks like a demon in his all-black ensemble and dark makeup, but shit, he looks fine.

"I'm sure. She changed her name and tried to erase her past, but it's her," he promises.

I nod, shifting nervously, wondering if she will remember me. I certainly remember her. She was always at those parties my father and his band held. As one of their favorite strippers, she saw more than most and worked with most of the men there for extra services. If anyone can shed light on what happened behind closed doors, it's her.

The doors to the room open. We both stand as she sweeps in, smelling of Chanel and decked out head to toe, even for lounging at home.

She does a double take at Kage before her eyes land on me, and when all the color drains from her face, I know it's her. She's had work done. Her nose is different, as is her chin, and hell, her eyebrows have been lifted, but it's her. She has the same blue eyes and blonde hair, although it's in a bob now, and instead of a string bikini bottom, she wears a white power suit.

"Fallon?" she whispers before swallowing.

"Sit, please," I reply. She looks between us again before heading to the sofa and sitting down gracefully, crossing her legs. No doubt she's been trained in etiquette, but I remember her sprawled out on top of glass tables with lines on her chest. It's strange.

"Why are you here?" she whispers. "How did you find me?" There's panic in her eyes.

"You married a politician?" I ask incredulously.

"We met through my . . . old work and fell in love." My eyebrows rise, and she purses her lips. "Believe it or not, you can't help who you love. He helped me clean up my past, and we've had no issues until now. Please, Fallon, why are you here?"

"You know why I'm here." I scoot forward as she recoils. Standing, I walk around and sit next to her as she looks at me. "You always knew this was coming and have been trying to run from it. I need your help." I lay my hand on hers because she was a victim too. "It's time to tell everyone what happened back then and make them pay."

"Please, Fallon. I can't lose my husband or this life. Don't ask this of me. It would destroy us." She snatches her hand back and stands, pacing away from me as I rise too. "I'm married now, Fallon. That girl back then? She's dead. I was reborn. She's dead, I'm not."

"I can see that," I snap, my anger taking hold now, although it isn't her fault. "I don't get to walk away from my past that easily. It eats me alive every single fucking day. I don't get to kill who I was and be reborn. I have to live with it. Even my name still makes me theirs. Every single day, I look in the mirror and remember everything they did to me, everything they did to us. You might have been paid for it, but we both know you didn't want it. I need you. I need everything you saw and experienced. Please, Sarah, surely you want them to pay for what they did."

"You think I don't want to?" she shouts, pushing her hair back. "You think I don't struggle to sleep, remembering it all? Even when I hold my kids, I wonder if I will have to protect them from men like them. I go to parties with my husband and they are there, eyeing me, and I feel sick and dirty all over. No matter how much I change or how much money I have, I'm still a whore to them." Tears spill from her eyes. "I can't outrun my past, but I'm trying, so don't ask me to do this. Don't ask me to risk my family, my children for this. I lived through it. I won't do it again. I can't." She sobs. "I can't, Fallon, not even for you. I'm sorry if that makes me weak, but I just can't."

Stepping closer, I take her hand. "It's okay. I'm sorry. I was being selfish. I get it. If I could run from this, I would."

"No, you wouldn't." She smiles sadly. "You were always so strong, but look at you now. I might not be able to help you, but there are others who can." She hurries away, scribbling something down and ripping off the paper before handing it to me.

I nod in thanks and step back. "I really am sorry, Sarah, for coming here. I didn't think it through. I don't want to take your life from you. You deserve to be happy and loved. I'm glad you found that. Not everyone has to live in the past, and I hope you know, whore or not, you've always been the woman before me."

"Fallon—"

"Mom?" The door bursts open, and a girl and boy come in and run to her, wrapping their arms around her legs.

"Hi, babies, did you have a good time with Daddy?" she whispers, crouching and looking into their eyes.

"Mom, you're crying. Are you sad?" the girl asks.

"No, baby, I'm okay. I'm just happy to see some old friends." She stands, looking at me.

"Your mom is an amazing woman. Take care of her for me," I tell them as I nod at Kage, and we head toward the door.

"Fallon?" I turn back to see her arms wrapped around her children as she watches us. "Make them pay."

Sarah reminded me that I'm not just doing this for me, but for every woman they hurt back then. I wasn't the only one, after all, and where there is one, there will be many. Men like this have a pattern of abuse, and it didn't stop with me.

The name she gave me isn't one I'm familiar with, but when we pull up at the cemetery, I'm shocked. We head inside, and after searching, we stop at a grave that matches the name on the paper.

LENNIE MILLER.

BELOVED DAUGHTER AND SISTER

1990-2005

She died the year before my father died.

"Excuse me, who are you?" I turn to see an older, frail-looking woman. Her hair is gray, and her skin is slightly tan. She's short and round, but as she watches us with friendly brown eyes, I see a quiet strength in her. "Did you know my daughter?"

"Your daughter?" I turn back to the grave and then look at the woman. "You are Ms. Miller?"

The woman nods, clutching flowers, and I step back as she struggles to her knees. Kage helps her place the flowers and clean the grave, and then he assists her to her feet. "Thank you, my knees aren't what they used to be," she says, and then she glances between us again. "Did you say you knew my Lennie?"

"I don't think so."

She frowns at me in confusion, and I sigh.

"I'm Fallon—"

"Fallon? Agille's daughter?"

I swallow as I nod, and she looks me over.

"Come with me."

We end up at a cute little two-story house after following her urgings. It's just a short walk from the cemetery, and it's immaculate. Ms. Miller hustles around the cute kitchen, where we sit at a round table. She quickly sets out tea and cookies before sitting and looking at me again. "You don't look like him, but you have his—"

"Eyes," I finish. "You knew my father?"

"No, not really." She reaches over and pours me a drink, her hand shaking on the porcelain, and I cover it as she meets my gaze. "I only know him because of my daughter. I have been trying for years to expose the truth about what happened to her."

"Her death?" I ask.

"That and before." She nods, sitting back. She wraps her hands around the teacup and stares into it. "It doesn't matter how many times I tell it, it never gets easier. Most dismiss me as a grief-stricken old lady. They don't care about the truth."

"I do," I assure her. "I was given your daughter's name for a reason. Can you tell me what happened?"

She takes a deep breath, and I swear she ages before our eyes as she starts to speak. "My daughter was a model. She was a teenager, but they scouted her when she was young, and she was so determined because it was what she wanted." She smiles sadly. "She was so headstrong that we could only agree. We traipsed around the world with her, but it happened right in our backyard. Her manager took her to an awards party. He didn't mention an after-party, and we must have fallen asleep waiting for her to come home. She was gang raped." She meets my gaze. "At one of your father's parties. Her manager dropped her off at a hospital. She had her stomach pumped, and they patched her up before she had to find her own way home. We woke up to her crying. She was never the same after that night, and she never got any more jobs. Her manager quickly dropped her. She was forgotten, and no one cared about her or what we had to say. We went to the police, but no one cared." Tears fill her eyes as she pauses. "She eventually killed herself, unable to handle it."

She delivers that news with stoic coldness, but I can see the agony and grief in her eyes, and I know this woman has never and will never get over what happened to her daughter.

We watch her, silent and horrified, and she takes a sip of her tea. Shame fills me. It was my father's sin, but I blame myself.

"My husband blamed himself—we both did. We should have gone with her, should have protected her." She laughs bitterly. "We were fools, and he couldn't handle it. He killed himself just six months later, leaving me alone. I wanted to follow them, to be with them and hopefully find peace, but I couldn't. If I did, then there would be no one to fight for justice. I have been doing it every day since, not that anybody cares. Nobody listens. I'm forgotten just like her. I lost my daughter, my husband, and my life."

I take her hand as she starts to sob, and Kage takes her other one. As she cries, I look around the house. It's frozen in time, no doubt from the year she lost her husband and daughter. I bet nothing has changed. She's like a ghost, and I understand how that feels.

"You aren't forgotten. I'm sorry it took me this long to find you, but you aren't alone. Your daughter wasn't the only one who was hurt in that house, and I'm going to make them pay. I'm going to make everyone listen," I promise as she lifts her tear-stained face.

"We can't do anything. You are one person, and everyone ignores a small wave," she murmurs.

"But enough small waves make a tidal wave they can't ignore," I tell her, holding her hand tighter. "I will make them remember your daughter and what they did to her, to me, to everyone."

She watches me sadly before threading her fingers through me. "I heard rumors, but I didn't know if they were true. I'm so sorry, my child."

"It's not your apology I need to hear. They didn't destroy me then, and they won't now—plus, we aren't alone." I look at Kage. "There will be more of us out there, and I'm going to find them. I'm going to create an army of angry, vengeful women and shove it in their faces until they can't ignore it. Will you help me?"

"With anything you need. Let's bring them down," she replies before wiping her eyes. "Excuse me, let me clean myself up. Drink and eat, I'll be back." We watch her climb to her feet with a new strength in her steps.

Getting to my feet, I leave Kage sipping the tea as I wander into the attached living room, looking over the pictures displayed proudly above the fireplace. My eyes catch on one of a girl, her daughter. It's clearly from a model shoot, and she looks beautiful. Picking it up, I smile at the excitement in her eyes. Her deep brown eyes match her mom's.

The longer I stare into those eyes, though, the more horror fills me. My entire body turns cold as I stare into a face I've seen before. It was just once, but it was enough to stay with me even now.

"Beautiful, isn't she?" comes a voice, and I startle, almost dropping the picture, but I catch it and put it back. Ms. Miller watches me worriedly.

"Stunning." I nod, my voice hoarse as I glance back at the photograph again.

Memories claw at my throat, and I know we have to get out here. I won't dishonor her daughter any more than she already has been, nor will I traumatize this woman any further.

I won't give life to it here in a place of love.

K♥F
Golden Love
I'll be with you.
I'll wait for you.
Golden Love
Can't you see
I'm your fool?

TWENTY-ONE

KAGE

"You're really quiet," I comment.

She has been since we left Ms. Miller's house after exchanging information. Ms. Miller also gave us the name of someone she has been trying to track down, and with a few calls, I managed to find him. It's where we are now, outside of the restaurant he currently runs, waiting for him to appear since Ms. Miller thinks he knows something about the past.

"Fallon?" I reach over and take her hand, finding it cold. I blow on it, warming it as I crank the heat in my car. "Baby, you're scaring me. Talk to me."

"I knew her," she whispers, swinging her head to look at me, and I see tears swimming in her eyes. "I saw her daughter the night that happened. I saw her."

"Sweetheart," I murmur. There is so much agony in her voice, and when she shakes her head and looks away, my heart breaks for her. She's trying so hard not to break.

"Don't be nice to me right now or I'll cry. I don't think I'll stop, and I hate crying in front of people," she warns, her nails digging into her exposed thigh. Frowning, I carefully pull it free, kissing the mark, and instead, I press her nails into my arm.

"Cut me if you need to."

Her eyes meet mine once more, and she swallows. "I recognized her eyes. They haunt me. I should have seen it before, but there were so many, I tried to forget. I did. I forgot that night until now as much as I could, but now it's here." She slams her hand against her chest. "Needing to come out."

"Then let it out," I beg. "Don't suffer in silence. Talk or scream, but don't hurt yourself over it, baby. Let me help, even if it's just to listen, please." I wish I could do more. I wish I could reach inside her and rip those memories free so she could breathe without worrying about them. I would do anything to make this easier for her.

"What if I tell you and you hate me like I hate myself?" she whispers brokenly. The way she watches me wrecks my fragile heart.

"Fallon," I snap, and she looks at me again. "I could never hate you. You could tell me you murdered or stole and I wouldn't care. There is nothing that will stop me from feeling this way about you or being at your side, and one day, you will realize that, but for now, trust me. Please, trust me."

She searches my gaze, her lips wobbling. "I was there the night she was raped. I remember her dancing and having fun at the party, then I lost track of her and the other models they brought. It was an album release party, which always made the band happy, and they pushed drugs on me, but it was different that night. It wasn't just coke or the usual. It was . . . It was to make it easier for them. I was their princess, their favorite little girl, and they *loved* me so much, Kage. I can barely remember that night, but I remember being carried upstairs. One of the doors was open, and when we passed, she was there, lying on the bed with her head turned to the door, tears flowing down her cheeks. I think she was drugged too, and she couldn't move. There were men around her and one on top of her. Our eyes met for the briefest moment. Her brown eyes locked on mine. She knew what was going to happen to both of us and was unable to stop it. I always remembered that look—the hopelessness and understanding. We were two strangers tied together in hell. I hated myself that night for not helping her."

"Fallon, you were drugged." I force the words out, breathing past my fury and horror at what my girl went through. The way she casually spoke about being drugged and taken advantage of makes me think it happened a lot, but she doesn't need my anger right now. It does nothing. She needs me to listen and support her. This is her life, her past, and she has every right to be angry.

"Still, I blame myself," she admits.

"Do you blame her?" I ask, and when she shakes her head, I grip her chin, forcing her to look at me. "Then don't blame yourself. You were young; you were drugged and abused. You didn't need to be her savior, you just needed to survive, and you did. You survived, baby, and I'm so fucking proud of you for that."

"Did I? Because part of me is still back there. The worst thing is, part of me believes I deserve to suffer because without it, I would be happy. I would be free, and I don't deserve to be. How could I after everything?" she whispers. "Maybe I deserve to suffer. Maybe I deserve to be unhappy for the rest of my life, this darkness dogging my steps until it claims me."

"Never. It will never get you," I vow. "Not while I'm here, and I'm not going anywhere. You need to stop blaming yourself, Fallon. You need to stop taking the responsibility of the world on your shoulders. You are a victim. You were a victim. Say it."

She hesitates. "I'm a victim."

"Again," I demand, "until you believe it."

"I'm a victim," she says softly. "I'm a victim," she says stronger. "I'm a victim, and I'm fucking angry!"

"That's my girl." I kiss her softly. "Be angry and hurt, but don't ever give up on me. Don't ever let them win. You didn't survive all that just to let them win now. If you have to, live out of spite until I can make you live out of love."

"Why are you so good to me?" she asks, leaning into my hand, her glossy eyes softening as she watches me. "Even now, even knowing everything, you want to be at my side."

"I want you more than I've ever wanted anything in this world, sweetheart. Perfect or messy, I want it all. I want every inch of you and always will. It isn't even just a want. It's a need. I can't breathe without you. I'm here, and I will always remain here," I promise, kissing her softly. "Can you breathe easier now?"

She nods, taking in slow breaths. "We have to get revenge for her."

"We will," I murmur as something catches my eye. It's a man heading to the restaurant. "That's him. Are you ready for this?"

"As I'll ever be." She pulls down the mirror, wiping under her eyes.

"You look perfect as ever, baby," I tell her as I get out and help her from the car. Hand in hand, we head to the restaurant. The closed sign is on the door, but it's unlocked, so we push inside. The man we followed turns, blinking before putting his bag down.

"We are closed," he tells us.

He's in his mid-forties, with a short gray-and-black beard and matching peppered hair, thick glasses, and a mole on his cheek just like the picture, but he used to have jet-black hair and gold grills when the parties were happening.

"Dion Smith? Or better known as DJ EasyS?"

He stumbles into a chair, staring at us in horror. He changed his life, just like Sarah, but we found him, and it's clear he knows.

I sip my coffee as Dion watches us, his hands playing with a napkin in one of the booths. Fallon sits next to me, watching him carefully. He can't even meet her eyes, no doubt realizing who she is.

"I guess I always knew this day was coming. It's like I've been looking over my shoulder the entire time," he admits, finally looking at Fallon. "I know who you are and why you are here."

"You remember me? You worked a lot of my father's parties. You even look the same," she says.

"I remember you. I remember everything, even if I wish I couldn't." He looks down at the table. "I was lost back then, Fallon. I thought reaching the top was the only important thing, and I didn't care how I did it. I wanted money and the lifestyle, and to achieve it, I looked the other way about a lot of things I shouldn't have. When I got clean and sober, I left and never looked back. I tried to live a better life, but I knew I couldn't atone for what I did. I want to now. I was hoping we would meet again one day and you would give me a chance to be a better man than I was when I was a kid, someone my kids won't look at in shame."

"I appreciate that. Not many would want to speak out on what happened back then. Most have tried to move on, to forget, and don't want to damage their lives. Others pretend not to know." She smiles as she reaches for his hand. "For what it's worth, I don't blame you. Yes, maybe you could have done something to help, but maybe that would have ended badly for you. We all know the violence they were capable of. What matters is that you do something now. You've seen the docuseries announcement?"

"I have." His lips form a scowl. "We all know they are doing it for money, since they could never do anything after your dad's death. They must be desperate."

"And desperation makes them weak." My girl smirks as she sits back. "I'm not that young girl anymore. I have more money and power than any of them, so it's time we showed everyone the truth. If they want fame and recognition, then I'll give it to them. I'll make it so they can't go anywhere without people pointing and knowing."

"Have you thought about what this means for you if this all comes out?" he points out, but I narrow my eyes in warning. He spares me a look, paling slightly. I don't interrupt, however, because my woman can handle her own business. I'm just here for support.

"I don't care." She shrugs. "I refuse to be ashamed of what I survived or embarrassed about people finding out. How can I when others are going through the same thing, still hiding it or living with it? Maybe if I speak out, they can start to heal too . . . and maybe I can as well."

He watches her sadly, but she smiles.

"And I want to make them pay. I want them to beg for me not to destroy them."

"Your father was a scary man, Fallon, but you? I'd fear you more. You're downright terrifying," he says, but he smiles as she leans back.

"I'll help you in any way I can, but you'll need more than me. You'll need as many people as you can get so they can't argue or fight back."

"I know. I need more victims."

"You want more? Go to the top where it all started. Go to the man who facilitated it all and covered it up—the parties, the drugs, the girls . . . Go to their ex-manager."

TWENTY-TWO

Fallon

Dion is right. I should start at the top, not the bottom. My father's old manager would know everything, and if we lean on him enough, he'll crack. After my father died, he lost his golden ticket. Rumor is, he's running new and smaller bands now, trying to find that golden child to take him to the top again. I remember him as a sleazeball who craves money more than anything. It will make him an easy target, but even so, Kage wants to do some research first so we have things to use against him, since he has connections. He also probably already signed for the docuseries.

"You need to eat," Kage orders as he tugs me after him into a restaurant. We've managed to avoid detection all day, but in a place like this, there are bound to be cameras, so I try to pull my hand from his, but he ignores me. "Fallon," he warns, stopping outside of the upscale bistro. "I said I'll help you, and I will, but I also need to take care of you. You can't go up against them weak, which means eating, sleeping, and taking care of yourself. Now, are you going to walk into this restaurant and eat, or am I going to have to carry you, tie you to the chair, and force-feed you."

"You wouldn't dare," I snap.

Smirking, he steps closer as I tilt my head back to meet his gaze. "You really believe I won't?"

As I stare into his dead eyes, I know he would. I know he would do that and so much worse to look after me. I still don't get his obsession with me, his need to love and be around me, but I have to admit it's addictive.

I've never depended on someone before, and there's a reason for it. I don't want to be vulnerable and let them in to hurt me. I didn't have the option to be gentle, soft, and loving. I had to split my knuckles to protect myself, just so they would never come back to hurt me again. If I want something, I buy it. If something is wrong, I fix it. I don't need a man to help me, but Kage? He makes me want to be weak just so he can save me.

"Good girl," he praises, making those words seem filthy as his thumb traces my lips. "If you eat a full meal while I watch, then I'll eat you after."

"Hmm, I am sweet enough to be dessert, but why would I settle for a starter when I could find someone willing to give me the full course when you're not?" I tease, my eyes dropping to his body.

"Sweetheart," he purrs, making me shiver, "I'm a whole fucking feast, and if you try to go for someone else, we both know what will happen. I've made it clear you're mine, so accept it and you can have me. Say it. Say you're mine."

I swallow as he backs me into the wall, uncaring about anyone watching, and honestly, I don't care either. I forget everything but his eyes and mocking lips.

"Say it, Fallon." He tilts his head as if to kiss me. "Say you're mine and I'll fuck you right here. I'll spend all day and night making you come on my dick until you never feel empty again."

I glance at his lips, wanting what he said. I've never wanted someone as badly as I want him. Usually, I have them as soon as I want them, and he knows it. He's teasing me and making me crave him. "You wish," I retort. "I belong to no one, but you, Kage?" I slip my hand down his chest to grab his hard cock, and he hisses. "We both know you're mine, following me around like a needy little puppy begging for a taste."

"A puppy willing to risk everything for you." He pushes into my hand. "I've made it very obvious. I'm yours, Fallon, but I'm glad to see you're finally accepting that. It means you're that much closer to giving in to me."

"You're fucking delusional," I mutter, but I can't help but smile.

"There it is, that smile I hang onto. Do you know how fucking crazy it drives me when you smile? Fuck, sweetheart, you're so goddamn sexy when you're cold and cruel, but when you smile at me, you make me want to drag you down the aisle before you're ready."

"Aisle?" I scoff. "You wish."

"I will marry you one day, Fallon. I'll have my ring on your finger and take your name as mine," he promises darkly. "I'll do whatever it takes to get it. You dream of revenge, while I dream of you."

"I . . ." My words die as a voice interrupts us—a familiar voice.

"Fallon?"

We break apart, and I feel my expression go cold as I stiffen, staring at the familiar redhead. She's older, but she looks exactly the same. She's wearing designer shades that push back her shoulder-length, dyed red hair, and she has the same mocking green eyes and perfect complexion. She's dressed in the latest designer dress and heels with a bag hanging from her shoulder. I wonder how she can afford it. She was a model when she met Yuri, my father's bandmate, but she has long been forgotten.

"It is you." Her smile is cruel as she heads my way. She's by herself, which is strange because from what I remember, she usually has a publicist and cameras in tow, clinging to any form of fame she can. For a moment, fear and shock freeze me in place before I remember who I am. I'm not the same teenager being threatened by her because her fiancé touched me without consent. She blamed me then and probably still does now. He could do no wrong, and she turned a blind eye to what happened at those parties to secure her bag, and it worked. She heads our way, stopping before us.

"You look . . ." She runs her eyes over me. "Older."

Nice barb.

"So do you," I respond with a wicked smirk. "I guess there is only so much plastic surgery can do, right?" I widen my eyes innocently as she glares. I never fought back. I was always too scared to speak and worried what she would do. She has a glint in her eyes—she always did—a spark of someone willing to do anything to get what she wants.

"Yes, well, you'll have to give me the number of your doctor," she responds, glancing at Kage. "Who is this? Your latest fling?"

"I don't have a doctor," I respond with glee. "It's all natural. I guess I have my mother to thank for that." I don't introduce Kage. I won't let her get her claws into him. It wouldn't surprise me if she tried. I'm surprised she hasn't divorced Yuri yet and tried to find someone younger and richer. It's bound to happen though.

"Hmm . . ." She runs her eyes over me. "We were actually going to call you. We heard you tried to stop production on the docuseries." Her frown is filled with fake, syrupy sweet worry. "I know it's hard for you, missing your father, but the world deserves to remember his legacy, don't you think?"

"You mean you deserve the money you'd earn from lying on camera?" I respond, refusing to play the game she wants.

"Fallon, you seem angry."

"I'm so glad you noticed. I thought I was going to have to spell it out for you, since you always were a bit slow."

Her mouth drops open before her lips form a sneer. "We are doing this docuseries to show your father's life."

"I know. You all seem so obsessed with honoring him," I murmur, "so I'll do the same. They want the truth, right? A peek behind the curtains? I'll give them all that. I'll tell them everything that happened."

Her face pales as she stares, no doubt realizing how serious I am.

"You should let your father rest in peace." She frowns, playing the concerned victim.

How fucking dare she?

"No. I don't think I will." I smirk. "I don't get peace, so why should he? Why should you?" I step closer. "You're scared I'm going to ruin you. Let me tell you, Terrie, I *am* going to ruin you. I'm going to take everything you love and I'm going to crush it. You want fame, right? You fucked your way to it and sold your body and soul. I hope it was worth it because you'll regret the type of fame I'm going to give you."

Her slap rocks my head to the side, and I prod my bleeding lip with my tongue as I turn my head. Kage has her hand held midair where she went to slap me again. He's furious.

"Let her go," I tell him, and he hesitates but shoves her hand back.

She thinks she's won. She thinks I won't hit back.

I step closer and slam my hand across her face with every inch of strength I have. I watch her stumble and almost fall on her heels, her shocked face turning back to mine. There is a clear handprint across her cheek, and her eyes water as I reach out and grip her hair, tugging her closer. "How do you like it? Not nice, is it? Don't dish out what you can't take, Terrie." Running my hand through her hair, I straighten it for her. "I'll be seeing you soon. Say hi to your husband for me. I'm sure you'll be on your knees, begging for my help before I'm through, and I can't wait for that day."

I turn to Kage and see him glaring at the woman. "You're right, I'm hungry, so let's eat," I tell him. "We have a lot of work to do when we're done." Taking his hand, I pull him after me, making sure to hit her shoulder as I pass. I dismiss her, giving her my back so she knows she might have scared me once, but not anymore.

Always needing the last word, she speaks, her voice shrill and loud. "You'll regret this, Fallon! We will ruin you! We will fucking destroy you!" she screams after me, drawing a crowd.

"Good luck trying," I call as I open the door and spare her a look. "Many have tried and failed." I blow her a kiss as I walk inside the restaurant, Kage at my side.

K♥F
IST
XY 674243
RIAGE
ssion
Golden Love
I'll be with you.
I'll wait for you.
Golden Love
Can't you see
I'm your fool?

TWENTY-THREE

KAGE

Pressing my thumb into the healing split on Fallon's lip, I meet her eyes. "Are you ready for this?"

"With everything in me." She peers into the LED mirror in the dressing room, then something dark enters her gaze, something unhinged. "Kiss me."

My eyebrows rise as she turns her head to smirk at me.

"Hard, kiss me hard and make my split lip reopen. They struck first. I'm just striking back."

She doesn't have to tell me twice. I back her into the door, slamming my lips onto hers. She groans, her tongue tangling with mine as I deepen the kiss. It turns rough and hard until I taste her blood between our lips, but I don't stop.

Her moans urge me on, and my hand slides down her side, gripping her thigh and hoisting her up until her legs wrap around me. Her dress bunches at her waist so her panty-clad pussy presses against my slacks.

Yes, I matched my outfit with hers again. She's dressed in all black like she's heading to a funeral. It's skintight and short with a wide belt and wider shoulders. Her beautiful hair is brushed back, with curls framing her stunning face, and I grab them now, making a mess of all her hard work. My black silk shirt is undone, exposing most of my chest, and her hand slips in it, stroking my abs. I groan loudly as I pull her dress higher, desperate to feel her soft, perfect skin.

There's a knock at the door behind her, and we break apart, breathing heavily, her lip bleeding like she wanted.

"What?" I snap, my eyes still on her pink lips, wanting to feel them again.

"Um, Fallon? Kage? They are ready for you," Elijah says.

"They can wait until my girl is ready," I reply, gripping her throat as I kiss her again. They can wait; they can all fucking wait. She's all that matters.

"Kage," she murmurs, but when my hand presses against her cunt, she shuts up, kissing me back before she rips away, breathing heavily.

"Not now. If you're good, I'll let you play later."

"Promise?" I ask, dragging my lips across her cheek.

"Yes, but only if you behave," she warns, ordering me around so easily, and I know she's right. I'm like a fucking puppy when it comes to her.

"Fine." I sigh, letting her heels hit the floor.

Reaching up with a grin, she sweeps her thumb across my lips, smearing her blood there like lipstick. "Fasten two more buttons," she orders as she smooths her hair and turns to open the door. "Only I get to see that."

I do so, possessive happiness spreading through me at her admitting even that weakness.

Fallon is mine, she just doesn't know it yet, but the whole world will.

Fallon left early this morning after spending another night in my bed, in my arms, making me more addicted, but she had no nightmares, and it makes me proud. I know she's busy with other things, but I miss her already, so I find myself rewatching yesterday's interview with Elijah before turning to the news. We didn't discuss the docuseries or what we were up to, just gave a quick interview, but the message was clear.

We are coming for you.

"Okay, okay, so we need to talk about the most important thing that happened yesterday. Who saw that interview with Fallon and Kage on *Late Night News*?" a member of the panel asks as I smirk.

"Oh my god, right? It felt illegal to be watching them, like we were interrupting something private. The way they looked at each other . . ." She actually fans her face as if swooning. "I mean, if eyes could speak."

"Kage was so obvious! He was hanging on her every word. He barely looked away from her!"

"I don't blame him. Did you see Fallon? She was stunning yesterday."

That's it, praise my girl.

"I think it's clear there is something between them, and the fact that Kage admitted to liking her so openly? The playboy king? I wonder if he can melt our ice queen."

"I want to know what he said at the end," another says as I sip my coffee.

"There are people online trying to guess and read lips. It's what everyone's talking about. Either way, I think we can all agree the whole world is now obsessed with Fallon and Kage or, as they are calling them, Kallon."

Elijah shuts the TV off and turns to me.

"We were worried about the backlash, and although there are some disgruntled fans angry at you flirting and wanting Fallon, most are supportive. In fact, you have become one of the trending topics online with shipping videos everywhere." I lean in as he turns his iPad and watch some of the videos, my grin only growing.

Good, they are rooting for us. It makes it easier.

"Other than that, you have the studio booked today—"

"Elijah, get me a cat," I interrupt.

"A cat?" He peers at me, blinking at the sudden interruption. "Why?"

"They are indifferent but also chaotic. I like it. It reminds me of my girl. I think she'll like it." I pick up my phone, finding more articles about us. I save them and send her some.

"Kage, earth to Kage," Elijah snaps, and I glance up at him. "Focus on your career, please, at least for one day. You skipped four sponsorship events yesterday. You don't care, do you?"

"No." Standing, I drain my coffee. "Get some of those cat trees and shelves as well. I want it to be happy. Oh, and have that wall dealt with. I want it easy for my girl to come over so she doesn't get wet."

"Why don't I just build a fucking tunnel?" he mutters.

"Great idea, now you're working." I slap his shoulder as I pass.

TWENTY-FOUR

Fallon

"Kage?" I call as I kick off my shoes. It's been a long day. I had a meeting with my label to discuss my plan of action, and then we were running through my new album. I still have some things I want to add, but it's getting there. I don't know why I didn't just go home, but it's become a habit to go to his. I tell myself it's only because we are working together, no other reason.

After yesterday's interview, my phone hasn't stopped blowing up. There were so many questions about my lip, but I refused to answer. Besides, my message wasn't for them, it was for Terrie. Instead, we spoke about music and life, and I showed everyone I'm working against the type of power I have.

There's a sudden meow that shocks me, and my eyes widen as a gray ball of fur shoots my way and winds around my feet. Crouching in confusion, I pet the cat, noticing the collar as I pick it up.

Ice.

Looking around, I notice the ladders and shelves leading up the walls for the cat to climb as well as a cat tree.

"Oh, you met her. That's Ice." Kage grins as he heads my way and hands me a mug. "I'm glad you're back." He leans in and kisses me, and I get distracted for a moment.

"You got a cat?" I eventually ask after much staring.

"We got a cat." He grins. "Our first child together."

I don't even know what to say to that. "Why a cat?"

"It reminded me of you, and when I'm not here to cuddle you to sleep, you still have our baby." He drapes his arm around my shoulders, and with his other, he reaches down and picks up the cat, dropping a kiss on its head. "Let's get your mommy some food. She had a busy day."

What is it about a hot man and a cat that makes me weak?

I let them lead me to the kitchen, where he pushes me into a chair and places Ice on my lap before moving to the fridge. I'm helpless to do anything but cuddle the purring machine as he cooks for me.

After eating, I know I should go home, but I let him lead me up to his bedroom where clothes are already waiting for me. I shower, dress, and slip into bed and his arms with ease, like it's normal. Ice curls up between our legs, purring happily as Kage turns on the TV.

How many nights did I sit alone, listening to my husband snore after I got back late?

How many nights did I wish he would turn over and hold me?

Here is Kage, someone I'm not even dating, and he's doing everything he can to look after me, to make me happy and comfortable, and it's driving me wild. All those worries and desires flee, however, as the news replays an interview. I stop Kage from switching the channel as I sit up, shock filling me.

On the screen, calling from his home, is Yuri, Terrie's husband and my father's bandmate. "I think Fallon's comments were coming from a place of love, but they are from a naïve child. She was young when her father died. She doesn't know much about his life since we protected her from a lot of it. He would be disappointed in her and her response to this docuseries. I don't want to discredit her pain or relationship with her father, since we all know she had a bad year after her husband cheated on her, but I feel like she is taking her anger out on us and his legacy, and that's distressing. I wish her nothing but the best, and I hope she can support us."

Kage turns off the TV, but I stare at the darkened screen in horror and growing anger. "He basically called me an emotional bitch." I laugh, startling Ice. "I knew they would fight back, but I guess I didn't expect it so soon."

"They are just trying to protect themselves. They are scared," he murmurs. "It was a threat."

"I know. He's trying to silence me, just like he did back then." I look at him. "It won't work. I won't let them win."

"I know, sweetheart." Wrapping his arms around me, he slides us down the bed. "Ignore him, ignore them all. The only person who matters is you. They can't touch you. I'll make sure of it."

Nodding, I move closer, breathing in his calming scent. I knew they wouldn't lie down and accept it, but it seems the games are starting early. They will all underestimate me. I might have taken it easy on some of them, but now I won't.

Not anymore.

The game is on.

I fall asleep in Kage's arms, letting him comfort me, all while revenge fills my heart.

K F
Golden Love
I'll be with you.
I'll wait for you.
Golden Love
Can't you see
I'm your fool?

TWENTY-FIVE

KAGE

I'm furious. No, furious isn't even the word.

The deadly fury within me can't be contained in one word.

Sliding from bed, I pick up Ice and put her into Fallon's arms. "Keep her safe while I'm gone, okay? I'll be back soon." I softly kiss both of their heads before I move to the closet and get dressed. Each movement is swift and filled with the anger that chases me from the house to my car. Sliding into my Aston Martin DB 11, I shoot off a text and get a response within minutes.

Firing up the engine, I pull out onto the streets.

I might be a rock star now, but I grew up on the streets, fighting to survive, and nobody, I mean *nobody*, threatens my girl.

The city is busy despite the hour, so it takes me almost an hour to get to the address. I park down the road and kill the engine. Sliding my cap down just in case, I tug my mask up and walk toward the big house at the corner. It screams money, but the closer I get, the more I notice how run-down it is. Hell, the security cameras don't even work, so I shouldn't have worried.

Hopping the wall and fence is easy, and I head to the back sliding doors, breaking off the handle, then I slide them open and head inside. There's no noise or movement, and everything is dark. I step through the wide kitchen and toward the hall. Framed photos hang there, as well as albums and records. I smirk as I take the stairs two at a time. At the top, it breaks off left and right, and I tilt my head, listening. The slight snores to the left make up my mind, and I head that way to wide double doors at the end that are slightly open. After peering inside, I creep over the carpeted floor to the king-sized bed dominating the room. The blinds are open, letting in enough light for me to see the figures under the quilt.

I recognized the orange hair as Terrie, and the man from the TV, Yuri, is snoring at her side, his naked ass out of the blanket. Pulling my knife from my side, I tap his ass. His snoring pauses before resuming, so I head around the bed to try something new. I press the knife to Terrie's throat. Her eyes snap open, confused and half asleep, as she tries to sit up before hissing in pain. Fear fills her gaze when she spies me above her and realizes what's happening.

I don't want to take Fallon's power or revenge away from her, but I won't let anyone threaten her. I won't let this man hurt her again. If I didn't love her so much, I would kill him now for what he did to her, but I know it's important for her to deal with this her way. However, a little threat might make her case stronger and stop him from coming after her so intensely.

Using her hair, I drag Terrie up and keep her on her knees, the blade pressed to her throat as she whimpers.

The sound finally wakes her husband, and he flails as he sits up, rubbing his face. "What is it? I told you to stop taking those sleeping meds." He trails off when he sees me holding the knife to his wife's throat and pales. "We don't have much cash. There are jewels in the box over there, but some are fake. Just take what you want and leave."

"I don't want your money," I reply. "I have enough of my own."

"Then what do you want?" he asks.

"Your death, but that would hurt my girl more. No, she needs you alive for now, but you came after her tonight." I pull down my mask, letting him see my face. "You hurt her. You won't do that again or I will come back here and finish what I started. Leave her alone."

"I can't do that," he whines. "I need the money."

"Here is the difference between you and me. I will kill for what I love, and I would do some very bad things to keep my girl safe, so you're going to back away or I'm going to return and gut your wife while she sleeps, and then I'll hang her intestines around your throat. I won't kill you. I'll leave you here, drenched in her blood, and I'll make it look like you did it."

Terrie screams as I press the blade firmer against her throat, and he swallows. "Okay, okay, we'll leave her alone. Please, just let her go." I feel sorry for him. It's clear he loves his wife, or as much as somebody like him can.

I throw her at him, her blood coating my blade, and I slide it away as I tug my mask back up. "Remember my warning. She isn't alone anymore, and you aren't as powerful as you think. You might have been untouchable back then, but you aren't now. I will carve into your skin until you feel every ounce of the pain you put her through." I leave them crying and holding each other.

This might have been about money for them, but it's about so much more for my girl. It's about reclaiming her power, her body, and her past, and I won't let anyone get in her way. If I have to get my hands dirty for that, I will.

I'll do anything for her.

I would die for her.

I would kill for her.

I would burn with this world for her.

It doesn't take me long to get home, and once there, I head to the kitchen.

Wiping the blade, I slide it back into the knife block and head upstairs, opening my bedroom door softly so I don't wake my girl, but the lights are on and she's awake and waiting.

"Where were you?" she asks, sitting up in my bed. I can't hide the blood on my hands, and I don't try to.

"Warning the people who threatened you," I admit without shame.

"It's what happens to anyone who tries to come after my girl." I stop next to her.

"Are they dead?" she asks calmly, knowing exactly where I went. Maybe my girl knows more about my depth of obsession than I thought.

"No, not yet." I smirk as I lean in, and she shivers, her eyes widening in lust. "Want them to be? Say the word and I'll kill them."

She watches me for a moment. "You would, wouldn't you? If I said so, you'd kill everyone who hurt me."

"Without blinking," I promise, sliding my hand up her neck and across her cheek, smearing the blood there. "Without question."

"You're crazy," she murmurs, but there's hunger in her gaze as she leans into my touch.

"Maybe, but only for you," I murmur, and she flings herself at me, knocking me back to the floor as we tangle in the sheets. Her lips press against mine so hard I taste blood.

Groaning, I kiss her back as she sits across my lap, reaching down and pulling off her cami. Her chest is bare to my hungry gaze as I absorb every inch of her perfect skin and perfect fucking breasts. Her cherry nipples harden for me as she shivers and grabs my hand, sliding my bloody palm across her chest and down into her shorts.

"You're mine, Kage. I'm yours," she murmurs, widening her legs as she presses my fingers to her channel. "Show me."

TWENTY-SIX

Fallon

He freezes under me for a moment, and then his fingers move, sliding inside my wet channel. He watches me hungrily as he strokes me, claiming me.

"Say it again," he orders.

There's blood on his hands and my skin. It should make me sick, but I love it. I love him dirtying my skin. I love how far he is willing to go to protect me. I also love this side of him—this obsessive, crazy side.

Leaning down with a grin, I slide my tongue along the seam of his lips. "I'm yours," I murmur.

His snarl is loud, and before I know it, I'm flipped and my face is pressed into the carpet. It burns my cheek, but I love the pain. I love it even more when he rips my shorts and thong down, his hand coming down on my ass in a slap.

"Again," he demands, his voice as brutal as his hands as he pulls me up. One of his knees nudges my thighs wider as I kneel before him. His bloody hand slides around and up my chest to grip my neck and force my head back so it hits his shoulder. "Say it again. I want you to keep saying it while I bury my cock inside your wet pussy and make you mine. I want you to fucking scream it for the whole world to hear."

he growls. "I've been waiting to fuck you for years, Fallon. I warned you. I let you have an out, but you won't be leaving here now, not until I have my fill."

"Make me," I retort. "If you want me to say it, then make me. You don't scare me, Kage. I can take you. I can take anything you throw at me. I want it. Fuck me. Show me how much you want me. Let me see if you can keep up and satisfy this ice queen."

"I'm going to make you melt," he purrs, tightening his grip on my neck as his other hand slides over my hip and down to my cunt. "You're already dripping for me, my dirty sweetheart. You love it, don't you? You love that I'm willing to kill for you. Their perfect, prim Fallon loves the dirty side of me . . . loves my obsession."

His fingers circle my clit as he speaks, and I gasp, pressing down, begging for more. I'm naked and he's dressed, and something about that makes me weak.

"Don't you, sweetheart?" he whispers in my ear just before his teeth dig into the lobe. "You act all perfect, and they get that side of you, but this good girl wants to be fucked dirty and raw, don't you? You want my cum dripping from every inch of you."

My breathing picks up and my chest heaves as I nod.

"Words, Fallon," he snaps.

"Fuck, yes, fine. I want it dirty. I want it to hurt. I want you, Kage, now fuck me."

"There she is. There's my girl. I love it when you order me around. It makes me hard as hell," he says, pushing my ass back until I feel proof of that.

"I'm tired of waiting," I warn him, moving away, but he drags me back. "Do you have condoms?"

He kisses along my neck. "I'm not wrapping it, sweetheart, not with you."

"I don't fuck unprotected," I snap, moving away. "Not for anyone."

"For me you do," he replies as I push him away. "Name your price."

"You couldn't afford it." I smirk, my eyebrow arching.

Watching me, he pulls out his wallet, takes out a handful of black and gold cards, and presses them against my chest. "The pin is your birthday. Take all the money. I'll sign over the house, my cars, whatever you want. Is that enough, sweetheart?"

I glance from the cards to him. "If I say no?"

"Name your fucking price and I'll meet it, but either way, you aren't leaving here without my raw cock buried in your pretty cunt." He grabs me and throws me onto the bed. My eyes widen as he rips off his shirt and pushes his jeans down, exposing every inch of his glossy, tan skin and muscles, but my eyes catch on his huge, hard dick. It drips for me as he strokes himself. "I've imagined you like this so many times, spread across my bed, watching me, wanting me . . ."

"I'm sure I'm not the only one."

Crawling over me, he smirks as he places a kiss over my racing heart. "Jealous, sweetheart?"

"Never," I grit out, shoving at him, but he doesn't budge.

"Good, there's nothing to be jealous about. I'm yours. I always have been. I haven't been with anyone since I met you, nor do I plan to. Now, I'm sick of talking. I'll pay up later, but for now, you started this, and I'm going to finish it."

He slides down my body, pressing my thighs open as he settles between them, his dark eyes locking me in place as he leans down and blows over my pussy, making me shudder. He brushes his mouth against my folds, inhaling as I arch up, begging wordlessly for more. Rubbing his nose along my clit, he teases me as my heart races. Desire courses through me, heating my blood until I'm wild with it. I need him so badly it hurts.

All this teasing and flirting leaves me vulnerable and needy for him.

I've never needed anyone else like I need Kage. Sex was always a temporary fix for the pain in my soul, but not with him. I'm right here with him. I'm not locked in the past, using pleasure to run from it. I'm just here, feeling it, and he knows it. It's why he waited until I was right here with him, the bastard, so I couldn't blame it on my trauma, because I want him just as badly as he wants me.

"I spent so many nights wondering what you would smell and taste like, it drove me crazy. I touched myself to your Instagram," he admits without a hint of shame as he smirks and then kisses my clit. "And now you're all mine."

"Crazy asshole." I moan as he thrusts two fingers into me, stroking me as he rubs his lips over my clit.

"You were saying?" he murmurs against my wet flesh.

"So good, you're good, please, Kage," I ramble, playing with my breasts and tweaking my nipples as he watches me.

"That's it, sweetheart. Let me see you touch yourself. Let me watch you get yourself off on my mouth." He licks my clit as he adds a third finger, stretching me as I lift my hips and ride his mouth.

His slick fingers pull from my pussy, and he offers them to me. I lean down and suck them with a groan, tasting my cream before he slides them back into me, fucking me with them as he lashes my clit with stern strokes, demanding my pleasure.

My head hits the bed, my hands gripping my breasts as I roll my hips, fucking his face faster as I chase my pleasure. It builds in me, flowing through me so strongly that when I come, I cry out and clench down on him as my legs jerk.

Whimpering, I roll and rock my hips, using him as I ride the waves of pleasure. When I slump, my body limp from the force of my release, I expect him to move away, but he keeps licking me. His fingers spread inside my fluttering channel, going deeper until it nearly hurts.

"Again," he orders.

"I can't," I tell him, but he doesn't care. He keeps licking me and biting my clit while he fucks me with his fingers until I come again, even when I didn't think it was possible. I'm shaky and sweaty as I roll away to escape him, but he follows me, adding a fourth finger inside me.

It hurts so good.

His mouth latches onto my clit, sucking ruthlessly as he forces his fingers deeper. The brutal way he's claiming me hurts, even as it heals something within me.

He pushes me to an edge I didn't even know I had, and then I fall over it.

I scream into the bedding as he continues his assault, making me come again. My hands rip at his comforter as I try to get away, needing a reprieve. He wasn't kidding when he said he wouldn't give up, and he hasn't even fucked me yet.

"Kage," I beg, trying to escape him. He pulls me back to his mouth, his tongue thrusting inside me. I mewl before it slides up and circles my ass, playing with me until I push back.

"You like that, sweetheart. Do you want my cock here too? I'm going to fill every single one of your holes tonight, but I think I'll start with your pretty pussy." He lets me go, and I roll over, scooting back as I stare into his dark, hungry eyes. His chin and lips glisten with my cum as he watches me like a predator. He slides his hands up and around my thighs, gripping hard so I know they will bruise.

I let out a scream as I'm dragged across the bed.

"Where do you think you're going?" he asks as he rolls me, holding his dripping cock in his hand. "I'm not done with you yet. Didn't I tell you, sweetheart, that you won't get to leave here until I've had my fill? That will take all night—well, all our fucking lives, if I'm honest. Now open your pretty thighs and let me look at my paradise."

Before I can speak, he lifts my ass with one hand and impales me on his length.

My scream bounces off the walls at the sudden stretch, pain, and pleasure.

"You can scream, sweetheart, but no one can hear you. No one can save you from me."

Oh God, yes.

My eyes roll back, my back arching as I push down to take him deeper. He lunges over me, his lips meeting mine in a frenzied kiss. Our tongues tangle as my hands slide down his body, my hips lifting to meet his wicked thrusts as he hammers into me. The wet sound of our bodies meeting makes me shiver and gasp into his mouth. He grabs a pillow and shoves it under my back, angling me so his huge cock drags over my G-spot with each stroke. I turn my head, breaking our kiss as I heave in desperate breaths. His lips slide over my cheek and up my neck to my ear.

"You're mine, Fallon, forever. I'm glad you finally realized that. Now come all over your man's cock. I want to feel it. I want to see you come apart with me inside you. I want to bury my cum so deep you will never be free of me."

"Then make me," I retort.

I should have known Kage never speaks without being able to deliver. Despite how many times I've come, he starts to push me toward another release as he straightens, dragging me onto his cock so my ass is almost off the bed, my tits bouncing with each thrust.

Sweat drips down me as he pushes me higher and higher, holding me with one hand as he drives into me, his other hand rubbing my clit until I can't take it anymore.

Screaming, I come around his cock, my cunt gripping him. He fights me as I cry and arch, riding the waves of pleasure. He follows me, hammering into me so hard I whimper, and then he groans, his cock jerking as he spills his release deep inside like he promised.

I slump back as he pulls from my body, leaving me shaking as I suck in air. His hand covers my pussy, stopping his cum from leaving me as he leans down and kisses me softly. When we break apart, I collapse deeper into the bed, unable to hold myself up anymore.

Kage wraps his arms around me, tugging me back as my eyes close with exhausted, sated pleasure.

"Rest, Fallon, you will need it," he promises darkly.

Fire races through my veins, waking me from my good dream, trapping me between wakefulness and sleep. That fire only grows, demanding to be felt and experienced.

Groaning, I bury my head into the pillow under me, sleep mixing with a lazy pleasure until I rock my hips. An orgasm rips through me, and I jerk fully awake to find Kage's head between my thighs. My eyes widen as he crawls up my body and kisses me. "I couldn't resist, baby. Now that you're awake, get on your knees, sweetheart. I had your pussy, now I want that pretty ass."

"Kage—"

"I warned you," he reminds me. "Now get on your knees or I'll make you."

I turn over, but not quickly enough, and he drags me onto my knees and yanks me back to him. His hard dick prods my ass, and before I can whimper a protest, he pushes into me.

My head falls forward, and I bite the pillow, gripping the sheets with my fists. I push back and take him deeper, both of us panting as his hands stroke my back.

"Look at you," he murmurs. "Your perfect fucking ass is split around my cock. You look so fucking good like this, baby. My very own dirty whore with my cum still dripping from your pussy."

Whimpering, I push back, taking him deeper until our bodies lock together.

He's buried to the hilt in my ass, and he lies over my back, his mouth meeting my ear. "Scream for me again, sweetheart. Let the neighbors hear whose girl you are and how good I am to you, letting you rest before giving you what you need again."

Shuddering below him, I turn my face, my eyes catching on the mirror to the left. He's behind me like a dark angel, his obsessive eyes locked on me as he grips my waist and pulls from my ass before spearing back into me. The sight makes me cry out and clench around him as my clit throbs. I can't look away, my eyes locked on him as he fucks my ass.

"Do you like that, sweetheart? Do you like watching your man claim every inch of you? Like watching me fuck you?"

I nod rapidly, moaning as I push back for more.

We look fucking good together.

He fists my hair and lifts my head. "Keep watching," he orders, his voice thick with desire. "Keep watching me fuck you, keep watching while I fill you with my cum again. You'll be seeing this every day for the rest of your life because I will never get enough of you." Each word is punctuated by a hard thrust that has me screaming his name.

I lose myself in him, my eyes locked on our bodies as heat flashes through me so hard, my head feels like it will explode. My ass and pussy clench as pleasure explodes through me, and I fall into it.

I scream his name like he wanted, but he doesn't stop. He keeps fucking me, fighting my body until his eyes meet mine in the mirror. "Mine," he snarls as he buries himself to the hilt and fills me with his cum.

When he releases my hair, I fall forward. "Good girl," he coos, combing his fingers through my messy locks, untangling the knots as he slowly pulls out of me. I whimper, messy and sore, and the bed dips. Moments later, a warm, soft washcloth is pressed against me, wiping my pussy and ass. I part my legs obediently, my face buried in the pillow.

I'm exhausted, and strangely, I feel like I want to cry.

When the bed dips again, I'm pulled into his arms, and he presses a gentle kiss to my head. "You did so well, sweetheart. Go back to sleep. I'll behave for now."

I must sleep for a few more hours when I wake from the bed moving. He has a towel wrapped around his waist, and his hair is wet from the shower. As I roll over and sit up, he drops the towel, his hard cock bouncing free.

He taps my mouth as I peer at him, sleep drifting away as my heart starts to pound in anticipation, knowing what is coming next. My thighs clench together, my sore pussy throbbing despite it all. Early morning light streams in through the windows, hitting his face. "I want this for my breakfast." He smirks. "Open up, beautiful, and let me feed you."

I open my mouth despite my usual reservations, and his hand slides through my hair to grip my neck and tug me closer. I go willingly, placing my hands on his thighs as my tongue darts out and traces his leaking tip. He tastes like mint and male, and I hum, licking him more until his hand tightens on my neck, and his other forces my jaw wider with his thumb. He pushes inside my mouth, and I almost smirk as I push farther down his length despite his resistance.

I keep moving forward until he's all the way in the back of my throat. I hold him there, my eyes on his as he groans, and then I slowly lift my head and slide back down. I bob on his cock as saliva drips down my chin and chest, but I don't care. I make it sloppy and messy, taking him all the way in every time until his hips roll in wild, deep thrusts. His dark eyes burn with love and desire as he watches me, his abs clenching with his movements.

"You're going to kill me, Fallon. I know it, but I'll die a happy man. You were made to be loved, made to be fucked like this by me. Look at you, so goddamn strong and beautiful. No one else gets to see you like this. Just me." His hand tightens as his hips speed up, and I have to hold on. I breathe through my nose as he claims my mouth. I know my throat will be sore later, but I don't care.

He snarls, moving faster, and finally, he bellows. His hips stutter as he pushes down my throat and unloads, forcing it so deep I don't even have to swallow, and when he falls back, dragging his cum along my tongue, I lick and swallow deeply.

"I love you, Fallon." He leans down to kiss me before he releases his hold on me, and I collapse back to the bed. Once again, I fall into an exhausted sleep as he wraps his arms around me.

"Sleep, my love," he whispers, and his words follow me into my dreams.

TWENTY-SEVEN

Fallon

I wake up before Kage. Peering down at his soft, sleeping face, I can't help but smile. I kiss his cheek tenderly, and he sighs, reaching for me. When I move away, his lips tug down in a frown. Grabbing a pillow, I place it where I was and watch as he curls around it. I shake my head as I slip from his bed, silently leave his house, and head home. I did leave a note though, but honestly, I know he'll just stalk me when he wakes. The thought shouldn't make me smile, but it does.

I can't let him though. I refuse to be someone whose life changes because of a man. I am Fallon and will always be. Dressing comfortably in loose pants and a cropped shirt, I shove on a jacket and shades and pick one of my cars at random, and then I drive to the studio, since I'm recording today.

They are ready for me when I arrive, and I head straight to my studio. Everyone knows how I work, and it's like clockwork. That's what happens when you've been in the industry this long. I trust my producer with my music, a friendly girl named Merry. In another life, we might have even been friends, but we both know I keep her at arm's length like I do everyone else. She gets this part of my life—the music and recognition—but she doesn't get the personal side of me—only my friends do. Staring at her now, I wonder why I did that.

"You changed your hair," I murmur.

She blinks, turning to me in shock. "Um, yes. Thanks for noticing."

"It looks good on you," I tell her as she gapes, and I place the coffee on the side. "I didn't know how you liked it, so I got it black."

"Oh, thank you," she replies, sounding confused as she looks at me. "Is everything okay?"

"Fine." I blush and head into the booth to avoid this awkward conversation, but as I sit and put on my headphones, I notice she's smiling down at the coffee so brightly, I feel like an asshole. Was I really such a cold bitch that even getting her a coffee shocks her?

Yes.

What changed? I don't know, but I like seeing her smile, and when she cues the music, I find myself smiling too.

I listen to the song first. It's one we have been working on, but I was struggling with the lyrics. In all honesty, I have been for months. Nothing felt right. It just felt like they were missing something. The second play through, I close my eyes and feel the music. I let everything inside me pour out, everything I've felt and experienced, especially recently. I barely know what I am singing, and when it's over, I'm panting and Merry is blinking. Heading out of the booth, I wait anxiously.

"Was it bad?" I ask.

She doesn't answer, but she hits some buttons and plays it back, and the chorus jumps out at me.

They call me ice queen and him the playboy king.

If only they knew how I make that king fall.

Beg.

How I obliterate everything else until all he sees is me.

All he wants is me.

I meet her knowing gaze as she hits stop. "It's one of the best you have written."

"Merry—"

"Don't." She holds up her hand, grinning at me. "You don't have to tell me, you know that. You can just be you here. I won't ask you anything, but I hope you're happy, Fallon. I really do. It's been a long time since I've seen you this . . . alive. It felt like you were going through the motions for years. I watched it happen, and it made me sad, but there's something different about you right now. You look like you're really here, really living, and I'm happy for you."

"Thank you," I reply softly, and she waves her hand.

"Go back into the booth. Let's make the best album ever."

We spend hours working together, and I let Merry help, trusting her more than I ever have. I let out every raw feeling, and I know she's listening, but honestly, it's kind of like therapy, only better.

Afterwards, I eat the sandwiches she bought, curled up on the sofa as she edits some tracks, the TV on in the background. That's when I see it. Grabbing the remote, I turn up the volume.

Yuri and his wife are standing before reporters. "We have chosen to pull from the docuseries for personal reasons."

"Why?" someone yells.

"Is this because of what Fallon said in the interview?" another calls.

The reporters are looking for the scoop. He looks pale and scared, and he clutches his wife close. Terrie is silent for once, and I gawk. There is no way they would pull from the docuseries, she made that clear, and the threat he left on TV for me drove that home, so then why are they suddenly pulling out?

It doesn't make sense. I watch the entire interview before muting the TV.

There is only one reason he would withdraw. Someone made him, and I know exactly who—the person who came home with blood on his hands.

At least they aren't dead.

Opening my phone for the first time since I arrived at the studio, I see the multiple texts and grin.

Kage: Leaving me in bed, sweetheart? Cold. I'll just lie here, thinking about you.

Kage: I miss you.

Kage: I broke into your house. You aren't there. When are you coming home?

Kage: I tracked your phone. You're working. Fine. Come home after, and let's have a meal together.

Kage: You like noodles, right?

Kage: Ice misses you.

I scroll through the pictures of him and Ice pouting before typing out a message.

Fallon: Stop breaking into my house, stalker.

I snap a pic of me pointing at the TV.

Fallon: Does this have anything to do with you?

My phone vibrates with a call, and I accept with a smile. "It was you."

"You know it." He chuckles. "We have it, sweetheart."

"Have what?" I ask happily.

"We have what we need," he answers.

I lose my smile, understanding what he means. Swallowing hard, I look at the TV once more. "I'll be back soon."

TWENTY-EIGHT

KAGE

While my girl was busy working, I hunted down the man who used to manage Electric Giants and found any source of blackmail I could against him. I know he won't give in easily, hence the need for information. I want to make this as easy for Fallon as I can. Sitting in my car outside of the studio, I check the tracker on Fallon's phone to see where she is—not to rush her, but to make sure I'm ready for when she comes down. The paparazzi are also waiting, the blinding flashes almost burning my eyes as they take pictures of me.

Let them.

When she gets closer, I get out of the car and meet her at the door, my arm out to stop the surging crowd. Ignoring their shouts and questions, I push them away as she moves closer to my side, sparing me a worried look. "It's okay, sweetheart. We can outrun them, come on." Keeping one arm around her, the other outstretched, I push the paparazzi away as I escort her to my car and shut the door, then I hurry around to the driver's side.

I rev the engine and creep forward, warning them that I will hit them to get out. They get the message and finally move from the road so I can pull away. I see some getting into their cars, but before they can chase us down, I slam my foot to the pedal and peel away, weaving through traffic to escape them.

When we finally do, I glance over to see my girl watching me, open-mouthed. "That could have been bad. They get like that sometimes, probably because they saw you as well."

"I'll never let anyone hurt you," I murmur as I reach over and thread our fingers together, laying our hands on my thigh as I look back at the road. "Are you ready for this?"

"As I'll ever be."

The once bustling office is now run-down and out of date, without any security and only a few cleaners working at this time of night. It's easy enough to sneak into the office building and ride the elevator up to the correct level. Once there, we simply open the double doors and head right into his office.

His head jerks up from where it was pressed against the desk—probably sleeping if the confusion and wrinkles in his cheek are anything to go by.

"Who let you in here?" He starts as he sits up, straightening his tie and puffing out his face in an attempt to intimidate us. Blinking, he grabs some glasses and slides them into place. He jerks back, his face pale. "Fallon," he whispers.

"Glad to see you remember me," she remarks as she heads over to the ragged black sofa and sits delicately on the edge, a glass coffee table before her reflecting her beauty as her eyes run over the office. "I remember this being . . . well, more. I guess times are hard." She looks back at him. "Which is why you're doing the docuseries, right?"

"Well, um, Fallon, you see—"

She holds up her hand, and he stops stuttering. "I'm tired, and honestly, being here makes me feel a little sick, so I'll get right to the point." She leans forward, her eyes pinning him into his chair as he gulps. "You are going to pull from the docuseries. You will say you feel it's in bad taste and you want nothing to do with it. After that, you are going to do everything I say. You are going to admit to everything when I tell you to. You will corroborate my stories and others' of the abuse, rampant drug use, and rape within that band. You will be apologetic, you will be sincere, and you will bring the evidence I know you kept." When he goes to deny it, she raises an eyebrow. "You are sleazy, but you aren't a fool. You knew it would come back to bite you on the ass one day, so you kept evidence so they could never turn on you. I want it all." She stands. "I'm going to destroy them, and you are going to help me."

"Why the hell would I do that?" he snaps as he surges to his feet. "That would be implicating myself and ruining my career."

She holds out her hand, and I pass over the folder she looked through before we came up here. Slapping it on his desk, she leans into him. "Because I'm smarter, I'm stronger, and I'm a hell of a lot more powerful. I found this all within a day, so imagine what I could do with two, a week, a month, or a year. You don't want me as your enemy. You can choose to go down with grace or I'll spill all of this and the truth anyway. Either way, you are ruined. You choose how." She steps back, letting him open the folder that details every bank transfer and money laundering he has done in the last two years. It seems he's been a busy boy, profiting from his stars without them knowing, not to mention the shell companies I found, and that was without digging too deeply.

He stares at the paper for a moment before his eyes meet Fallon's. "Why are you doing this, Fallon? Why now?"

"Because I fucking can," she sneers. "Because I want to. Because I'm so fucking tired of all of you playing the victim, and maybe because I'm sick of hearing my father's name on their lips like he is their savior when he was my damnation. You were there. You might not have taken part, but you facilitated raping and drugging as well as abuse of not only me but every woman at those parties. You don't get to get away with that and have a happy life."

"Happy? Look at me." He throws his arms wide.

"It's not enough," she warns him. "Not nearly enough. I want you all to feel every inch of the pain we did. I need it. Now, make your decision. Do I keep digging and ripping your life apart until you can't stand it anymore and have no choice but to come forward, or will you work with me and destroy yourself?"

He looks from her to me, feeling both lost and trapped. He knows he would lose if he stood against her. "I never should have fucking taken that job as their manager."

"But you did, and you did nothing to stop what happened. You made a choice, and you don't get to play the victim now. You have two seconds." She flips up two fingers and slowly lowers one. As she starts to lower the second, he grabs the file and slumps into his seat.

"Fine, fine, whatever you want, I'll do it."

"Good boy." She shoves her shades down. "You can keep that. We have copies. We have to make sure you are behaving. Isn't that what you used to tell me?"

He swallows, staring at her. "I'll do whatever you say."

"Good. Now where's the evidence? I want it. I don't trust you not to destroy it out of spite."

He laughs bitterly. "I'm not that dumb. I might have done stupid shit, Fallon, but I know better than to go against you. You are your father's daughter."

Unwilling to stand by and let him land a blow, I step around and smash his face into the desk as my mouth meets his ear. "If you say one more word, I will start cutting, and I know exactly where I want to begin. Do you understand me? You will be silent unless she speaks to you. You will wait for her every fucking call, and if you so much as look at her wrong, I will carve out your eyeballs."

He shudders under me, nodding rapidly. "Sorry, sorry, it's there." He points at an old cupboard in the back, and I press his face harder against the desk in warning.

"Go get it." Releasing him, I step back and watch with a sneer as he rushes over, not even looking at Fallon. She smiles at me in thanks and to let me know she's okay, but I see the hit landed.

She is nothing like him, no matter what she or anyone else thinks.

She might have collected fame, wealth, and power, but she did it all without hurting others—unlike her father.

We watch him scramble through the cupboard, uncovering a hidden safe. He quickly puts in the code and pulls out a black hard drive, handing it over to Fallon with a scared look.

She holds it up. "If this isn't what I want, I will come back. You might think he was crazy, but I'm much fucking worse. Do not test me."

"The whole family is fucking crazy," he mutters as she turns away. She stops, and I'm about to grab him when she holds up her hand, her eyes landing on him.

"You're right, we are, and I don't think I'm satisfied with just this anymore." His breath shudders out of him as he exhales. "Get on your knees, kiss my feet, and apologize until I believe you."

"What?" he whispers.

"Did I fucking stutter?" She arches a brow, one hand on her hip. "I'm waiting."

He looks at me, and I snort. "Trust me, you don't want to deal with me. I'd make you do more than apologize—I'd make you bleed."

He turns back to Fallon, and she taps her watch.

Heading around the desk, he steps toward her when she tuts. "I didn't say walk. Crawl like the animal you are."

He freezes, closing his eyes for a moment before he sinks to his knees, his shoulders round with humiliation, and then he starts to crawl toward her in his suit. She watches him with a satisfied expression, and when he reaches her shoes, he goes to touch them, and she lifts her foot. "Eh, this is worth more than your entire life. No grubby hands. Apologize now. Beg for my forgiveness."

His head hangs for a moment before his words come. "Fallon, I'm so sorry. I'm really so sorry. Please forgive me. I was a terrible person. I did terrible things. I deserve this and so much more."

"Hmm, I don't believe him. Do you, baby?"

"No," I reply with crossed arms. "Want me to motivate him?"

"No, wait, please! I'm so sorry!" he shouts. "I really am. I'm so fucking sorry." His body shakes as he begins to sob in earnest. The situation he's in must finally be hitting home. I can't help but grin at his pathetic sniveling. Fallon steps back in disgust. "I'm really so sorry.

I wish I could take it all back. I wish I weren't so stupid and desperate. I'm just so sorry. I'll do anything, please. I'll do anything you ask. Please, please don't kill me. I want to live."

Leaning down, she tips his chin up so he looks at her. "Never forget this is where you belong. You are nothing, just a bug under my shoe to crush whenever I feel like it. You live and die when I say so. Now stay here, on your knees, where you belong."

She turns and strides from the office. I follow after her, only stopping to lean down and warn, "Remember what I said," then I follow my girl.

She stores the hard drive in her bag, and we both sit in my car, staring at it.

"What do you think is on it?" I ask.

"Nothing good," she murmurs before sighing and looking at me, a soft smile on her lips. "I'm glad you're here with me, doing this."

Taking her hand, I lean over and kiss her knuckles. "There is nowhere else I'd rather be." I slide my lips up her arm to her ear, where I bite down. "And watching you play with him? Fuck, baby, that was so sexy."

She laughs, smacking me away, and I grin. "You're such a psycho, Kage."

"Don't you forget it, sweetheart." I wink before taking her hand and kissing the back of it, then I press it against my very hard erection. "And just so you know, I'm not lying."

She laughs even harder, her eyes sparkling. I expect her to shove me off again, but she presses her lips to my ear, making me shiver. Her scent wraps around me, the softness of her touch driving me wild. "Then you better drive fast because it got me all hot and bothered watching you defend me."

She leans back, a smile curving her lips, and before she can react, I'm speeding away. Her laughter fills the car the entire time.

God, I fucking love this woman.

The entire world should be terrified because there is nothing I wouldn't do if she asked it.

TWENTY-NINE

Fallon

We are speeding home, his expression hard and determined. He keeps glancing at me, his eyes hungry and obsessive, and I can't help but tease him. I know I shouldn't, since Kage is unpredictable when it comes to me, but he's so much fun to play with.

Leaning over, I press my breasts against his arm as I drag my hand up his thigh so I can squeeze his rock-hard dick. The car swerves as he swears. I sit back and blink innocently as he glares at me. "Fallon."

"Yes, baby?" I purr.

We swerve again, his eyes landing on me. Grinning, I lean farther back in the seat, letting my thighs fall open. I slide my hand up to the waistband and slip my fingers inside.

He looks at the road and then to me. "Don't you fucking dare."

"No? Focus on the road. You're busy, and so am I." I slide my hand lower, and I swear his soul leaves his body with the noise he makes.

He growls my name, and I know I pushed him too far. With jerky movements, he turns the car and speeds faster away from the city rather than into it, and then he pulls over at a dead end. There are no lights except for the ones from his car. When he turns to me, his face is dark, and I swallow in anticipation.

"Kage," I start, but he throws me into the back seat. I land with a gasp, and then he's on me, his lips crashing onto mine. He kisses the fuck out of me, swallowing my noises as I grip his shirt. He finally pulls away, both of us panting.

"Call me baby again," he demands breathlessly.

Smirking, I arch up and lick his lips. "Make me."

The cry that's ripped from my lips as he bites down on my throat is so loud, it echoes around the car. He makes quick work of shoving my clothes out of the way, and then his fingers plunge inside me as he licks the wound.

"Say it," he orders against my skin as he twists his fingers, rubbing my walls until I cry out again, my back arching up. My legs part to give him better access as he bites my neck again. "Fallon."

Sliding my hand up his back, I grip his hair and yank him away from me, breathing heavily as I stare into his dark orbs. "Make me," I demand.

His fingers disappear, and before I can utter a word, he rolls us, the car rocking as I find myself atop him as he stretches out in his back seat. He grips my hips, lifts me, then drops me onto his cock.

My eyes roll into the back of my head, the sudden stretch and intrusion causing a choked sound to escape my lips. It burns, but it soon turns into a fiery pleasure as he rocks me on him. His hands move my hips as I whimper.

"Ride me, let me watch you claim me." He groans. "Just like that. Move those pretty hips and take me deeper. We both know you can."

My head falls forward as I press my hands against his chest and start to work with him. My pussy grows slicker with my want, making it easier to ride his huge cock. Each slide makes my breath catch in my throat as I watch him, and he watches me.

"Good girl," he praises. "Just like that. Look at you. Fuck, Fallon, you drive me crazy. Being buried in your pretty pussy and watching you come apart for me is all I think about, but you know what I crave even more?"

"What?" I ask, sliding my hands up my body to squeeze my breasts, claiming my pleasure.

"That. You using me to get off, taking what you want, and claiming your own pleasure. I fucking love it. I could come just from watching you get off. Come for me, Fallon. Come all over me. Use me for it. I'm yours, every inch of me."

He sits up, turning us so his back is against the seat, our bodies pressed together. The new position drives him deeper, and I clench around him as I cry out.

I kiss him, letting him swallow my sounds of pleasure, and then I start moving for real, using him like he wanted. My desire becomes so thick, I am beyond reason. Everything else flees other than my need to come, and I bounce on him harder, faster, to find what feels good.

Breaking the kiss with a moan, I lean back and slide a hand down my body to grab his on my hip, and then I press his fingers to my clit. "Keep them there," I order. "Keep pressing there while I fuck you."

When he doesn't move, I let go, gripping the seat and moving faster. Each roll of my hips presses my clit into his fingers while he bottoms out inside me. The ecstasy makes me cry out and speed up.

"Look at you," he murmurs, his voice thick with adoration. "My girl, you are magnificent."

His dirty words only spur me on, and when he presses his fingers harder against my clit, I climb toward my release.

My head tips back as my hands hit the other seats, desperate to find purchase as I ride him. When he leans closer and bites my nipple through my shirt, I fly.

I cry out his name as I grind down onto his cock, clenching him as I gasp and writhe. Pleasure rolls through me so strong, it steals my breath.

His groan fills the air, and just like he said, he comes from watching me find my pleasure. My eyes widen as I watch him. He presses deeper into my fluttering channel, burying as far as he can as he fills me with his hot cum.

We shake, our bodies covered in a sheen of sweat, the car still rocking slightly from our movements.

Leaning down, I kiss his lips softly as he groans. "Take me home, baby," I murmur as he jerks inside me, letting me know exactly how much he likes it when I call him that. "I want to play tonight. You'll let me, won't you?"

"Sweetheart, I'd let you carve out my fucking heart, and I'd thank you for it," he replies, kissing me. "But home it is."

THIRTY

Fallon

A lot of people made their names by attending the parties my father held and making connections. Some girls let it destroy them, while others took that pain and used it. They didn't let it consume them. They made the most of it. They were smart and determined, and I respect that.

One of them is Evelyn. She's a model, an actress, and everything in between. She works with the UN and runs charities, and she's a genuinely good person. She was young when I met her, and I only saw her a few times, but she had this way about her. She was a force of fucking nature, and that hasn't changed. We've run into each other a few times over the years, since we run in similar circles, and every time, we just looked at each other, unsure what to say.

I didn't know if she remembered or didn't want to, and I'm sure she felt the same. Both of us were too scared to approach one another, but not anymore. I need her, and I have a feeling she needs this too. She fights for women's rights as a way to get back at those who abused her. She gives women voices, and now I want to give Evelyn's back to her.

There are so many unspoken words in this industry—not just at the parties my father held. It's normal for young, up-and-coming girls to have to pay the "price," as they call it. We know it too well, but none of us speak about it out of fear. Well, fuck that.

I'm taking this back, and I want her by my side, but I understand if she can't. I'm unsure and nervous, but either way, I knock back my drink and head over to her table, leaving Kage at ours. The bar we are in is upscale and filled with rich and famous people, so there are no cameras or prying eyes. She's sitting alone, nursing a cocktail, oblivious to everything and looking as stunning as ever.

She's wearing a sleek black dress that hugs her willowy frame, and her blonde hair is in a tight ponytail, her makeup expertly applied. Diamonds dangle from her ears and on her fingers. She's an intimidating woman to approach, but when I stop at her table, I see the emotions in her gaze before she blinks and looks at me.

"Fallon?" she asks softly.

"Can I sit?"

She nods, watching me with confusion. We have barely spoken in years, so when I slide into the chair opposite her, we both just drink each other in. We are survivors, and we know it.

"Need another?" I nod at her drink, and she looks down at it, a sad smile curving her lips.

She pushes the glass around, and then I realize it's full. "I don't drink anymore," she says. "Too many bad memories. I used to like the way it numbed me so I forgot, but then the nightmares were still there when it wore off, and I was shaky and alone and hurting, so I stopped. I realized I could run all I wanted, but they would still chase me. It's better to confront it." She looks at me. "Humans can't live with an open wound, and the sharks smell the blood in the water."

Isn't that the truth?

"That's why I'm here," I tell her, and she jerks her head up. "I'm ready to stop running, and I'm hoping you are too."

Her eyes drop to her drink for a moment before she pushes it away and delicately folds her hands on the table. "Are you sure?" she asks, still speaking in code.

"I've never been surer. They took my childhood," I reply. "They don't get my life, and the longer I live with this secret, the longer they win. It started as revenge, but as I move forward, I'm realizing it's so much more than that. It's about protecting those who come after us. It's about giving strength back to those who survived and voices to those who did not. It's about the truth, and it's about us. I'm hoping you will stand with me, but I understand if you can't. There are others willing to step forward, so don't feel like you have to, but I had to ask."

She's quiet for a moment, pondering my words

"I was hoping this would happen one day," she says softly. "I knew if I stood up alone, no one would believe me. Everything I worked for would go down the drain, and I would be branded a liar, a troublemaker, so instead I waited and worked, giving back to those without voices or power, hoping it would be us one day—be me." Her eyes meet mine once more. "I'm with you. They stole so much from us, but they can't take our voices, our future, or our truth. Whatever you are doing, I'm in. Let's bring the entire house down."

"It's time for you to take your voice back, not just lend it to others," I murmur. "I'm sorry it took me so long."

"Don't be." She covers my hand, and I see understanding in her gaze. "We all cope in our own ways, and you, Fallon, owe nobody a fucking explanation for how you have dealt with it. I'll stand with you throughout it. I won't let them win. I can't. I made my life mean something, but sometimes, I'm still that scared young girl, wishing this world were different. Let's make it different for the next generation, so nobody goes through it again. Let's change the world together, you and me."

That, right there, is the reason she got where she is. She inspires and protects. She's a goddamn entity unto herself, and I'm glad she's on my side. We share a knowing look of two people who survived the worst of this world. It's an understanding.

"So how do we begin?" she asks.

"I'm collecting evidence at the moment, collecting testimonies and people. We don't have enough to convict, since it's our word against theirs, but we can ruin their names and lives. We can make it so the public will never forgive or forget. When it's time, I'm going to expose it to everyone—blast it everywhere and flood the world with it."

"Make it so they can't turn a blind eye this time." She smiles. "Smart."

Taking her drink, I knock it back. "We'll empty the barrel of the secrets and take away their safety, their comfort, like they did with us." Standing, I smile at her. "I'll be in touch. Thank you, Evelyn."

She smiles at me, her expression so bright it's hard to resist, and then I realize I have been smiling more . . . feeling more. "I mean it. Seeing you succeed has given me a drive to do the same. Knowing you were out there gave me comfort, I guess. I didn't have to be so broken."

"Fallon, for what it's worth, you inspire me every day." I frown, unsure, and she grins. "You're so strong and confident, and you always have been. You have this quiet inner strength that I don't think you even recognize in yourself. That's why so many people try to use it, use you, to tear you down. They see it and it scares them. I think if you wanted to, Fallon, you could do anything. Let's show them that. Let's show them what a woman can do."

The news breaks that night as we are eating dinner. We both watch them report on it. Anger courses through me so viciously that I break my wine glass. Without a word, Kage cleans it up and checks my hand before holding me as the reporter tells us what they know.

"The suspected cause of death of Giles Horn, who you might remember once managed Electric Giants, is suicide—" Grabbing the remote, I mute the TV and sit back heavily.

We saw him only today.

"He didn't kill himself," I snap as I look at Kage. "He didn't. He isn't brave enough to do that. He's weak and stupid, and he wanted to live. He didn't do it, I know he didn't."

They said there was a gun found in his hand, so they'll write it off as suicide, but he didn't do it. I'm pissed as hell.

"We visited him, and he withdrew, then a few hours later, he's found dead?" Kage sighs. "No, this was murder. Someone was silencing him. They are worried about what he knew. He was sleazy but not stupid. They killed him and made it look like suicide, which means they know we are after them. It's more dangerous than I thought." I frown, and he smiles sadly. "A man willing to rape and drug women and children won't want that truth to come to light years later. They will stop at nothing to cover their tracks, especially after getting away with it for so long. It could be any of them. We need to be careful. They won't stop now, not after crossing that line. They can't go back."

"I won't stop," I snap. "I'm not giving up or letting them win. Let them come after me. I'll kill them myself. Hell, I'd look good in a prison jumpsuit."

He grins as he kisses me. "I'm not asking you to give up. I'm just saying we need to be smarter. We underestimated who we are up against, and we can't make that mistake again. We'll win this, sweetheart. I'll make sure of it. You focus on your end, and I'll focus on keeping us safe, okay?"

"He's dead. Without his word . . ." I sigh.

"We have his evidence, and we have enough to keep going. I'll pull some strings, call some people, and make them open an investigation into the death so they can't ignore it. That will only add fuel to the fire. Don't forget I'm here, sweetheart. We are doing this together, and I won't let them lay a hand on you. They may be willing to kill someone to silence them, but I'm willing to kill them for even coming near you," he promises, kissing me once more. "They don't stand a chance. They are scared and hiding in the dark, desperate enough to kill. I'll keep you safe, Fallon. Do you trust me?"

"Yes," I answer without hesitation, shocking myself. For someone who swore to live a life without ever letting anyone close, I trust Kage completely.

"Good." Kissing me once more, he holds my hand while he takes his phone out. My eyes go back to the news, and I wonder who was behind it.

Who would be desperate enough to kill and smart enough to cover it up?

They must have connections, power, and something to lose.

It seems the game just got a lot more interesting.

THIRTY-ONE

Fallon

I refuse to hide and look scared. Instead, I do the opposite. I show my face so they know exactly whom they are dealing with. Kage and I still have lives outside this revenge—we are superstars, after all. He has a show tonight for charity, and he was going to cancel, but I wouldn't let him.

This is just as important, and I refuse to lose our entire lives over the past. They can't have that. I stand in the VIP booth to the side, waiting for him to come on and perform. I've seen him online and in interviews, but never in person, and I'll admit it gives me a little thrill. All the fans are screaming for him, holding signs and chanting his name, but he's all mine.

Pushing my lanyard to the front where it proudly says his name, I lean into the rail and wait. I made sure to look extra good since I knew there would be cameras everywhere and fans looking at me. My dress is black and cut high to display my thigh on one side, the other trailing in a long train. The edges of the neckline are white, as are the buttons down the front, and the shoulders are sheer with white diamonds. My hair is curled back and pinned, with some wavy pieces framing my face, and my makeup was pristine, but Kage kissed the shit out of me before letting me out of his sight.

I'm the only one in the VIP booth, which also makes me grin. He doesn't let anyone else come here, and rumor is, he never has. Hell, when he led me to it earlier despite Elijah's protests, he was so happy.

Elijah moves to my side now, checking on me as ordered by his boss. "You know, he's had your name down at every gig, concert, and meeting for years, just in case you turned up, so you could have peace and watch him." I raise my eyebrow, and he grins. "Just thought you should know, and remember, if you need to go anywhere, let one of your guards know."

The guards are another new thing. There are so many of them, I might as well be the president. I don't know where Kage found them on such short notice, but they are clearly capable. He explained they are the best of the best. Hell, he even bribed some to leave their current jobs and protect me, and they take it very seriously. I'll admit I feel safer, which shouldn't make me happy, but it does. It's also the only reason he agreed to perform without dragging me on stage with him, because he knows I'm safe—not that anyone would try anything in this public of a venue, but he isn't taking any risks.

"Fallon! Fallon!" My name being called brings me from my thoughts, and I smile at the fans who've started to notice me. They surge forward, and my guards hold them back. Laughing, I head down the stairs, ignoring Elijah's protests.

My guards surround me, and I roll my eyes, taking the outstretched papers and signing them. I pose for photos and even get a few friendship bracelets before the lights go down, and I hurry back to my booth to watch my man.

The silence is filled with anticipation as screams split the air, then there's a drum hit. It pounds in time with my heart as I lean over the barrier, just as excited as the fans. The lights flash with each drum beat until a guitar shreds and bright red lights shine down, highlighting Kage. He's leaning back with his eyes closed and a smirk on his lips as he plays, his band in darkness behind him. He's the entire focus. I'm just as hooked as the fans, watching as his fingers dance effortlessly across the cords. His leather jacket is open, exposing the sheer shirt underneath that matches my dress. There's graffiti across the jacket that catches the light, leading down to his tight leather pants, which I had way too much fun feeling up in the car on the way here.

His hair is messy, strands falling into his face, and his eyes are blacked out. When they open, they are so bright they steal my heart all over again. They find me, and when his solo finishes, he blows me a kiss, making me grin.

When the music dies off, he grabs his mic. "How are we feeling tonight?" The crowd screams, and he frowns, placing his hand by his ear. "I can't hear you. I said, how are we feeling tonight?"

The thunderous screams make me laugh, and he grins as he looks over the crowd. "I'm Kage, and I'm just one of the amazing acts performing tonight all in the name of the charity Open Mind, so open your wallets and your hearts and let me steal them." He winks as he wanders across the stage as he speaks. He was born to be a performer.

Leaning down, he reaches for the crowd, and they scream louder as he grins and flirts with them, stealing every single heart, just like he is stealing mine.

"I want to thank you all for coming out tonight to play with me, so how about I get started with a favorite of mine? I wrote it a year ago, after meeting someone who I knew would become my everything. This is 'Golden Love.'"

The crowd, if possible, screams even louder and surges forward, testing the security as the music starts and Kage's crooning voice wraps around us. The lyrics hammer right into my chest. They are so full of emotions, you can't help but feel the music. It's a dark, grungy song, which isn't my usual style, but fuck if it doesn't become my new favorite thing.

I guess I always avoided everything to do with him, but there is no denying that Kage has a voice of a fallen angel, and as he dances around the stage, it's obvious he has the body of one too.

His eyes land on me, trapping me as he sings the chorus.

Golden love,
I'll be with you.
I'll wait for you.
Golden love.

Can't you see I'm your fool?

As he spins around, the drums and guitars growing stronger, he dances to the edge of the stage near me and mouths, "I love you," then dances back, leaving me blushing like a fool.

He really is crazy.

Songs blend from one into another, ranging from dark to soft and loving, yet all have one thing in common—his heart and obsession. When he grins into the mic, I can't help but fall for him all over again.

"Okay, okay, I have just one more song for you. It's a newish one, so shh, let's not tell anyone. I'm not supposed to play this yet. I couldn't resist, though, since the person I wrote it for is here tonight." His eyes land on me. "What do you think, sweetheart, should I let them hear it?"

All eyes turn to me, as does a spotlight, and I purse my lips. He's going to die later, and he knows it if his grin is anything to go by.

When he looks at me, though, it's like I can breathe again. I feel like I can live, can see and hear. He brings me back from black and white into full color, and maybe that's why I fight him so much. I have never felt like I deserved to live in color, in the world he lives in. I don't think I am worthy of his love, but I don't care. I'm greedy and selfish, and I will take it anyway because he makes me feel alive.

I run my gaze over the crowd as they scream for us, and when I meet his eyes again, I nod.

"Looks like I have permission." He steps back into the darkness as the lights go down. "So here it is. It's called 'Riot Act.'"

I frown at the name, something niggling in my head, but when he starts to sing, I forget everyone else. There is a spotlight on him as he croons a soft, lyrical melody into the mic.

Abruptly, it bursts into a rock song, but the lyrics remain the same, flowing like a promised whisper.

She's my queen.

Ice under my skin, melting like our souls.

Keep on pretending, it's you and me.

The world can wait.

I'm yours, you're mine.

This life we lead like a riot act.
My girl.
Where she goes, I follow.
Wrap her in my arms so no tears will swallow.
My girl.

It's a confession.

He's telling me he loves me, that he will protect me and be with me forever.

It's a damn love song.

Running across the stage, he leaps down the stairs and races through the crowd as they shout and reach for him. His security fumbles, rushing after him, and then he climbs the raised bars of the VIP booth and hangs from them as he reaches me, leaning over the rail as he sings.

The music trails off, and in front of everyone, he grabs my head and yanks me into a hard kiss before pulling back with a grin. "I love you."

"You're dead," I whisper, but I can't stop my smile as he laughs.

"Looking forward to it." He steals another kiss before dropping down and heading back to the stage. He lifts his arm as the audience screams and the last note fades, then he pulls his mic down, breathing heavily. "I'm Kage. Thank you. Good night!"

Once his set is over, I head backstage with an escort. I wave at the fans, and once inside the corridor, I find him waiting at his set door. He sweeps me into a dramatic kiss, even as I slap him away.

"You're all sweaty," I complain.

"You will be in a minute," he teases, wiggling his eyebrows.

Laughing, I go to slap him away again when there's a sudden commotion behind us.

"Kage?" a female voice calls, making me pull away slightly. I see a woman lingering down the hall, stopped before my guards. "Kage, hi!"

I frown, but Kage is too busy feeling me up to notice. "Kage," I snap.

"What?" He jerks his head up, follows my gaze, and then looks back at me. "What?"

"Kage, I was hoping to run into you," she calls loudly, and my lips purse.

"Let her through," I order, and she rushes toward us on designer heels, a Prada bag clutched under one arm. It is clear she dressed to impress, wearing a skintight number that leaves nothing to the imagination. She's beautiful, but Kage is oblivious, pulling me closer and resting his chin on my shoulder.

"Possessive thing," he teases, but I ignore him.

"Kage, I was hoping to run into you," she gushes.

"And you are?" he asks coldly.

"It's me, Melissa. We went on a date, but then you left to come here for your music. I'm in the country, and I was so glad to hear you were too." She smiles brightly, ignoring me.

"Right." He just turns to me, kissing my neck.

"Nice to meet you, Melissa." I smirk as she finally runs her eyes down me.

"Same." Her expression darkens before she perks up. "We are twin flames. We hit it off so well, and I know we are going to be great together. So what do you think, Kage? We could go on another date or back to my hotel."

Oh, this bitch.

He ignores her completely, but I push him away, and he leans against the wall, dragging his tongue over his lips as he stares at my ass.

"Kage?" she says, unsure.

"Kage," I demand, drawing his gaze from my ass. "Melissa wants to take you back to her hotel to fuck."

He starts to laugh before sobering at my expression. "Wait, seriously? Are you crazy? I just sang about being in love with this woman. Are you dumb?"

She swallows hard, looking between us.

"Sorry, Melinda—that was your name, right? Anyway, I guess the twin flame thing didn't work." I sigh dramatically. "So sad." I turn away, snapping my fingers at him. "Kage, let's go."

He pushes off the wall to follow, but I should have known better. She doesn't want to lose, and she wants him. I don't blame her because he's incredible, but he's mine.

"Are you serious? He's a fucking rock star, a god, a legend," she hisses.

I turn to face her once more, arching my eyebrow. "And?" I challenge.

Her face flushes in anger, her long nails ripping at the leather of her bag when she doesn't get the reaction she wants. "And you're making him follow you around like a puppy. You can't treat him like that. I think you forget who he is—"

"Moira, was it?" I interrupt, loving the way her face gets darker. "I didn't forget who he is, especially when he was on his knees all morning with his rock star, god, legendary superstar mouth on my pussy." Stepping closer, I tilt my head. "How I treat him is none of your business. He is none of your business." I glance back at Kage to see his hungry eyes locked on me. The bastard likes it when I'm angry and jealous, and I hate that it's working. "Isn't that right, puppy?" I grab his chin, pulling him closer, and his eyes dilate. "You're mine, little puppy, aren't you? Bark for me."

He barks then grins after.

"Good boy." I kiss him before I turn back to her. "Since you didn't ask my name, I'll tell you. It's Fallon, international superstar, hall of fame goddess, and ice queen. If you ever speak to me like that again or come anywhere near him or our relationship, I'll show you what I'm capable of. Now, Mirriam, run along home before I get tired of you."

Taking his hand, I lead him away, my heels stomping angrily as he says, "Relationship, huh?"

"Don't push your luck," I hiss.

K F
Golden Love
I'll be with you.
I'll wait for you.
Golden Love
Can't you see
I'm your fool?

THIRTY-TWO

KAGE

Maybe she's feeling the need to claim me and prove to everyone I'm hers because Fallon grabs me in the car as soon as the door shuts. I'm more than happy to oblige. Tonight, my girl didn't run, not even from my live confession, and when that rando tried to move in on her territory? Fuck, it was so hot watching her lay her claim.

"That's it, sweetheart, show them I'm yours," I murmur, letting her rip off my shirt as I lie back. "I always have been and always will be, now they know it."

I help her pull my pants down, and my eyes widen as she lifts her dress and straddles me. She grabs the headrest to her right as we start to move. Her icy eyes hold me captive as she leans down and bites my nipple. The pain makes me gasp, even as I arch up into her. Her teeth dig in harder, and I grip her hips, rubbing her against my length, her panties the only thing between us.

The pain grows in my chest until she pulls back, both of us looking down at the perfect teeth imprint surrounding my nipple, which is bleeding slightly. "Fuck, sweetheart, that's so hot. Do that everywhere."

I expect her to ignore me, but she slides her lips down my chest, making me shudder below her, and then her teeth dig into my abs, and I hiss. My eyes roll back as I push my body deeper into her mouth, wanting her marks all over me.

Fuck, let them scar. I'd love it.

Lifting her head, she blows over the stinging bite as she meets my gaze. "You're mine, but maybe I need to remind you." Reaching down, she moves her panties to the side, and with an angry twist of her lips, she slams down onto my length.

I can't help but yell. She's so fucking tight and nowhere near wet enough to take me. With a determined glint in her eyes, she forces herself onto me, taking all of my length until we are both shaking, our bodies locked together.

She feels like fucking heaven, and then she starts to move, rolling her hips as she rides me, setting a hard, fast rhythm. I slide my hand up her thigh and over her pussy, rubbing my thumb against her clit. Her eyes blow with desire and her lips part.

"That's it, sweetheart, ride me, use me," I plead, rubbing her clit until she's nice and slick and taking me easier. One of her hands slides down my chest, while the other holds onto the headrest as she rides me.

It's such a fucking sight, I want to take a picture and remember this forever—the possessive glint in her eyes, my blood on her teeth, and her perfect dress pulled up as she fucks me. There is nothing like seeing my ice queen melt.

I might be crazy, but Fallon is pure fire under all that ice, and I love it

"Did you fuck her?" she asks as she speeds up her hips.

"Who?" I frown, lost in the way she's moving. She's all I can think about, so who the hell is she talking about while rocking my world?

"Melissa." I must still look confused because she slaps my hand away, pins it against the seat, and snarls. "The woman from a minute ago."

"Oh." Realization hits me, and I grin. Her eyes narrow in warning, and she clenches around me so tightly, I swear my soul leaves my body. I groan beneath her, pulling her down to take me deeper, but she pushes me away and slows down. "No. Not one of them. I just used her to try to make you jealous. Hell, I didn't even know her name—any of them. I didn't touch them. When they tried to touch my hand or flirt, I pushed them away," I admit without shame, and her eyes flare.

"You made yourself look like a player to make me jealous when I didn't even know you?" she scoffs, rolling her hips. "You fucking weirdo."

"It worked." I try to tug her down, wanting to taste the fire on her lips, but she resists. "I never fucked any of them. Why would I? You were all I wanted and all I thought about. They wouldn't even compare. Hell, I couldn't even get off in my own hand without imagining it was yours."

"You really are obsessed," she remarks, but it seems to pacify her, and she smiles as she speeds up, riding me once more. The driver has to know what we're doing, but I don't care. I wouldn't stop my girl even if the world was ending.

"You're finally starting to get it." I lick my lips as I watch her pretty pink pussy take my cock deep, wishing her panties were gone so I could get a good look.

"Stop talking," she demands, sliding her hand up her body to squeeze her breast through her dress as she clenches around me. Her moan fills the air, making me grit my teeth to stop me from rolling us and driving into her pussy until she screams.

She needs to be in charge right now. She needs this, so I'll give it to her.

I'd let her torture me this way for the rest of our lives.

Her hand hits the roof of the moving car, her blazing eyes locking on me as she fucks the life out of me. I would die a happy man right here, being used for her pleasure.

"Whom do you belong to?" she asks.

"You," I murmur. "I'm yours, Fallon."

Her groan fills the car, her head falling back as her hips speed up, and I know she's close. Her breath hitches, and she cries out, her cunt clamping down on my length so hard I see stars.

I stop moving and let her recover, but when her eyes land on me again, they are filled with a wicked gleam.

Sliding from my hard cock, she tugs her dress down as she eyes me, arching an eyebrow as if to dare me to protest. I nearly fucking come from that look alone. "You annoyed me tonight. You let her get too close to you. You are mine to use, no one else's. This is your punishment. When you have been good, I'll let you come inside me again. Until then, I'll keep using you for my own pleasure. Understood?"

It's another ploy to push me away, but it won't work.

My cock drips with her cream as I put it away, then I sit up and kiss her cheek, grinning. "Completely," I murmur against her skin. "I'm just fucking honored to have your cum on me, sweetheart. That's enough for me. I've told you before and I'll tell you again, use me all you want. If you want me to crawl on my fucking knees or if you want to tie me to your bed, hard and ready to be ridden at all times, then I'll do it. I'll do anything for you."

"Psycho," she mutters, but she's fighting a shy smile.

"You know it, sweetheart. I'm your psycho. Now take me home and ride me all night. Punish me."

Her lips purse, and she glances at me, her icy eyes sliding down my body. "If you hold out all night, I'll let you come when the sun rises."

"Deal."

Doesn't she know I've been holding out for years? One night is nothing.

I've waited my entire life for her.

We stumble into the house, fumbling as she backs me toward her stairs, never once breaking our kiss. We hit a table and something crashes, but I don't care and neither does she. My back hits a wall, and my head hits a painting. I feel it fall and smash to the side, but I don't pull away from her as her hand slides across my chest.

"Ms. Fallon?" a shy, embarrassed voice calls from somewhere behind us. "Um, are you okay? Do you need anything?"

She turns her head, peering at whoever it is, but I don't. I kiss down her neck as my hands hit her ass and hoist her up. She wraps those delicious long legs around me. "No, you can all leave."

"Yes, Ms. Fallon." There's restrained laughter in the tone and then fading footsteps. I don't wait for them to be gone; they can watch for all I care. I slide my hand under her dress and rip her panties off so she can't use them to hide herself from me again.

I debate going upstairs, but I won't make it, so instead, I drop her to the steps, pressing her back with one hand behind her head to stop it from hitting the step and getting hurt as I shove her dress up and drive into her tight cunt.

"Night, Ms. Fallon!" someone squeaks.

"Goodnight," she calls breathlessly, her eyes on me as she lifts one leg and throws it over my shoulder. "Fuck me harder."

Her moans fill her mansion as I fuck her on the stairs like the animal I am.

One hand grips her head, while the other holds her thigh, giving me leverage to drive into her. I bend down and bite her neck as I fill her tight cunt over and over. Her moans spur me on, driving me wild.

"Kage, fuck!" she exclaims, and her back arches as her cunt grips my cock so hard I almost come. I have to fight my own release, causing my chest to heave. It almost hurts as she slumps under me, her eyes closed and lips parted on a breath.

"I'm not done with you yet. I have a promise to keep," I tell her as I lick her lips until her eyes open and meet mine.

I pull from her dripping, clinging cunt, and both of us groan at the sensation as I slide my arms more solidly around her.

She's boneless when I lift her and carry her into the kitchen, where I lay her on the counter. Grabbing one of her fancy cooking knives, I slice off her dress. Her eyes narrow in anger. "That was six thousand dollars."

"Bill me," I snarl, sliding out my wallet and grabbing a stack of cash. I toss it on her chest before adding more. "This is for the others I'm about to ruin."

She smiles, ignoring the money, and leans back, spreading her legs so I can see her juicy cunt begging to be licked and fucked. "Fine, then keep your promise," she replies.

Leaning in, I drag my tongue over her chest and up her neck, tasting her skin until I reach her ear. "I plan to. This cunt is going to be stuffed full of my cock until dawn. Can you handle it?"

"I can handle anything," she responds breathlessly, tilting her head to give me better access. "So stop talking."

Fine. If she doesn't want me to speak, then I'll put my mouth to better use, like licking her cunt.

I'm about to drop to my knees when I see the fruit bowl, and a wicked idea fills my head. Her eyes narrow as I reach for it.

"Kage, what—"

Choosing a peach, I take a bite before leaning down and licking her pussy. "Fuck, it tastes the exact same." I rub the fruit across her cunt, getting it nice and wet before shoving it into my mouth and chewing.

She watches me the entire time, her mouth parted in shock and desire, and when I swallow the fruit, I drag my tongue up her cunt again. "Juicy," I murmur. "So fucking sweet, just like my girl. I want to swallow you like that."

"Then do it," she orders, tossing her leg over my shoulder and pressing her cunt against my face. "I'm tired of hearing your voice. All I want is your tongue, not your words."

Fuck, I love it when she's mean.

Reaching down, I fist the top of my leaking cock to stop myself from coming as I shove my tongue inside her. Her whimper makes my hips smack into the counter, the pain driving me a little crazy as I fuck her with my tongue. I rub my nose against her clit until she grinds against my face, using it to find her pleasure.

She's all I taste, feel, and see, and I fucking love it.

I want more.

I ignore my screaming lungs as her thighs clench around my head, and I lick and suck her ripe cunt until she spills across my tongue with a cry. Her cream slides down my throat as I drink it down, not missing a single fucking drop as her hips jerk. She reaches down, and she can't decide if she wants to push me away or pull me closer, but I'm not going anywhere.

I'll fucking die right here between my rock star's legs with the taste of her pussy on my tongue.

I was made to serve her and bring her pleasure, nothing else.

She finally pushes me away and lies back on the counter, her chest heaving as she throws an arm over her face. "Fuck, I might not survive until dawn."

Smirking, I lift my girl bridal style and head toward the stairs. "You have a two-minute break before I'll be back inside you, sweetheart. You better be ready."

I keep my promise and fuck her all night. She comes so many times, neither of us can count, but if anything, it only makes us more determined to last. My cock aches, my balls hurt, and my body is covered in sweat from how close I keep getting to filling her with my release, only for her to stop and leave me bereft and sore. Part of me even likes the pain and the look she gets in her eyes as she watches me struggle and give into her demands and wants.

The bright early light of dawn spills through the open curtains and over my goddess, who rolls her hips as she rides me. She turns her head and sees it before grinning down at me, her hands splayed on my chest. "You were a good boy. A promise is a promise, you can come."

She doesn't have to tell me twice. Grabbing her hips, I roll us and position her face down, yanking her ass up. I drive into her pretty pussy as she starts to scream, fisting the bedding as she pushes back to take me.

I'm so fucking close from being edged all night, it only takes her pretty cunt clenching around my cock as she orgasms for me to bellow my release. I shove my cock so deep, she whines, and I fill her to the brim with my cum. The pleasure is so intense I nearly black out, rolling my hips until I finally slump onto her, spent, exhausted, and oh so fucking satisfied.

I tug her into my arms and kiss her shoulder and neck. "Punish me any time you want, sweetheart. I'll be ready and waiting."

THIRTY-THREE

Fallon

I'm tired, only having a few hours of sleep, but I don't want to lounge in bed all day. We have things to do. Luckily, the staff isn't in yet, so I drink my tea in the kitchen in peace, smiling at the flowers filling the entire space.

There are so many of them now, they cover every surface. Maybe it's selfish to keep them, but I can't bring myself to part with them when they turn up every day. Leaning forward, I trace a few petals with a soft smile.

"Morning, sweetheart. Did today's delivery come?" He gestures at the fresh bouquet on the table, and I nod.

He kisses me as he walks past. "You must have a whole supplier for them," I tease.

"True. They were hard to find, but it worked out." He heads my way, sitting next to me in his boxers and drinking his coffee—Kage's only vice except for me.

He pulls his phone out and types away on it as I sip my tea.

"What are you doing?" I ask as he stares at his phone. He turns it to me, and I see camera feeds. I frown, realizing they are in his house.

"Checking on Ice and making sure she isn't lonely," he replies without a hint of embarrassment. I hide my smile behind my cup as I watch him. "I had Elijah check on her last night, but I wanted to make sure."

What is it about a hot guy caring about animals that makes women weak?

He lifts his head like he feels me watching, arching one eyebrow, so I force my thoughts in another direction, since my pussy is still sore after last night. Tracing a petal on a flower, I tilt my head. "You never told me about the blue color."

He puts his phone down and lifts my legs onto his lap. One hand massages my calves as he sips his coffee. He always reaches for me, as if he needs to be touching me at all times. I don't think he even realizes he does it, and I'll admit I like it. He anchors me, keeping me in this world when I would easily fall into the darkness that lives within me. His touch is a reminder that he's here and he loves me, that he'll protect me and fight off my nightmares.

"You were wearing that same shade of blue when we first met," he answers, watching me with a soft grin.

Frowning, I look at the flower and then him. "No, I wasn't. I was wearing gold at the awards show."

His smile only grows, reaching his eyes. "That wasn't the first time we met."

My heart skips a beat as I stare into his handsome face. "I'm a bitch, but I would have remembered you."

"Hmm, I was younger then, no one important. I was a nobody. You were a star—untouchable and beautiful," he explains as my frown deepens. "You were young, and I was barely eighteen. I ran into you by accident on a street in London. I was job hunting, needing something to put food on the table, and I accidently bumped into you when I rushed past you, hurrying to an interview. I hit the ground hard. Everyone around me, all your security and fans, started to shout at me and got angry, but you just turned toward me with a smile on your face, then you looked down at me and offered me your hand. It was nothing to you, just a nicety, but that hand was the first to reach for me in the dark. I took it and got to my feet, and you helped straighten my cheap suit. You wished me good luck after I explained I was late for an interview. You even asked what it was for. Hell, I couldn't even remember my own name after looking into your face. I said it didn't matter, and you told me it should matter, that I should only run and chase after something I want—something I'm passionate about, like you with music."

My heart freezes in my chest as he smiles lovingly.

"You were right. I was just wandering until that point, not even thinking about my future because I didn't think I had one. After one run-in with you, I wanted to be better. I wanted to be someone who could be worthy of the look you gave me—worthy of you. You had on this long, blue silk dress. I remember it so clearly. We were kids, Fallon, but you looked like you had it all figured out. You were on top of the world, and I was at the bottom, but you looked at me like I meant something. You wanted me when nobody else did."

"I don't remember," I whisper in shame.

"Fallon." He takes my hand and kisses it. "I didn't expect you to remember me. That meeting might have changed my life, but you have changed a lot of lives. I don't hold it against you. I'm honored just to be with you now and know you're mine. It doesn't matter that you don't remember. It was a passing moment for you, but for me, it changed my life. It gave me you. Honestly, it might be insane, but I've been obsessed with you from that very moment. Even when I forced my way into the music industry, it was for you. I wanted to show you I could and that I was worth it. That soon changed, though, because then I wanted to protect and love you."

My heart clenches at his earnest confession. He's so fucking crazy, but he's so kind to me. Every other hand that has ever been offered to me came with anger and pain, while his is filled with nothing but love and obsession.

He would never hurt or leave me.

He's the first person who hasn't hurt me.

"Without you, I wouldn't be here. I wouldn't have any money, music, or a future. I wouldn't have you. That's why when I tell you my life is yours, I mean it. You made me, Fallon. I built it all for you, so tear it down if you want to. I don't care. It's yours," he promises as he kisses my hand. "To everyone else, I'm a rock star, but to you, I'm yours."

"You're insane," I murmur, but it's more like a love confession than an insult. He did all this for me after meeting me for two minutes? My ex-husband wouldn't even be seen at my side at awards shows after being together for years, and my father wouldn't even protect me although he was my dad, yet this man, this stranger, changed his entire life to be in mine.

How could I not love him?

It might be toxic, but I don't fucking care.

He stares at me with those dark eyes and kisses my hand again. "I can wait. Don't rush to tell me." The bastard grins. "I'm not going anywhere."

Isn't that the truth?

Although everyone else in my life has walked away from me, I know Kage never will.

He'll stay until the very end.

He'll make them all liars.

"I think I'll need a greenhouse soon," I say with a laugh, needing to change the subject before I cry or worse—tell him how I feel. That's something entirely more terrifying.

He grins. "Then I'll build you one," he murmurs as he lifts my bare leg, my robe parting as he presses a kiss to my leg and lowers to his knees.

"What are you doing?" I ask as he yanks my chair closer and runs his nose up my leg.

"Isn't it obvious? I'm having breakfast." He smirks.

"The staff will be here soon." I gasp as he pushes my robe open and rubs his nose over my pussy.

"Then they will see me worshiping my girl." He shrugs, throwing my leg over his arm to give him better access.

I should protest, but I widen my legs, leaning back.

I'm unable to say no to him, especially when I want him just as much.

Sensing I'm sore, he softly brushes his lips across my clit and pussy, teasing me with little kisses that slowly wind me up. The gradual, burning desire has me sighing in ecstasy as I lean into my chair while his fingers tease my hole, shallowly fucking me.

His hands slide up my robe and parts it, revealing my body to his hungry gaze. He slowly glides his lips up along my stomach, his touch possessive and tender.

I watch him reach up to the table and grab one of the flowers he sent me. He turns his head and kisses it before dragging it up my body.

Kage runs the soft petals across my nipples, making me gasp as they tighten and tingle at the touch. I watch silently as he runs the flower down my abdomen to my pussy and gently teases it over my clit.

He drives me mad. The pressure isn't enough, yet my hips tilt anyway, and pleasure rolls through me as his fingers continue their slow assault.

He watches me the entire time, obsession and love in his dark eyes. "So beautiful," he murmurs. "My beautiful ice queen."

"Kage," I whisper.

Pressing the flower harder against my clit, he rubs it faster, and despite being sore and tired, I explode again with a whine.

He pulls the wet flower away and kisses my clit before sliding up my body. Kage brushes the flower across my lips before pressing his lips to mine. "I love you, Fallon. I have since I was eighteen years old. I will love you until I'm eighty, until the day I die. I'll spend every single day loving you, and I'll die with a smile on my face knowing we will meet each other in our next life because our souls were born to be together. We are a forever kind of thing."

As I stare into his eyes, I realize I'm starting to believe him.

THIRTY-FOUR

Fallon

Kage has given me back some confidence I didn't even know I lost. I feel untouchable with him.

I leave him on a phone call with his label, and instead of calling my driver, I grab the keys to one of my favorite cars—a sky blue McLaren Elva—and head toward the studio. The top is down, and I grin as I sing along to the radio. I had an idea for a song this morning after talking with Kage, and I want to get it down before I forget. The midmorning sun heats my exposed shoulders, my Prada tank tucked into some flare jeans. It's a casual outfit for me, but the way Kage's eyes ate me up as I blew him a kiss goodbye made me think I need to wear something like this more often.

My phone starts to ring, interrupting my song, and I hit the accept button.

"Sweetheart, you can't come in looking like that when I can't touch you and then leave." I can hear the pout in his voice. "When are you coming home? Ice misses you."

"Uh-huh, just Ice?" I tease as I switch lanes and accelerate.

"Mainly me," he admits with a chuckle that makes me grin. "Come home and we can play."

"I'm heading to the studio first. We can play later. Get your work done," I order.

"If I'm good, will you let me stay with you tonight?" he asks sweetly.

"I'll consider it." I glance over my shoulder, flipping off a black Mercedes as it cuts me off. I accelerate around it and slide into the lane to get my own back, ignoring the honk. I speed through the next two intersections before stopping at a red light, tapping my fingers impatiently on the wheel. "I want steak later. Take me out," I tell him.

"Are you asking me on a date, Fallon?" He gasps teasingly. "I'm honored."

"I can take someone else," I warn.

"You've got it, sweetheart. It's a date."

I can't help but smile as the light turns green. "And no stealing my panties." I know he probably already has.

His laughter fills my car. "Too late—"

My head turns as something catches my attention. I'm just creeping through the green light, but a huge black truck is coming right at me. It doesn't slow. Instead, it speeds up, and everything around me slows down.

"Sweetheart?" comes Kage's voice as I stare at the truck, knowing I won't be able to avoid it.

It's barreling right toward me.

It's on purpose, I realize.

"Kage!" I exclaim as I press down on the gas pedal, but it's no good. The truck hits the back end of my car. I scream, my hands gripping the wheel as I spin, and then a car in another lane hits my front end. I jerk, pain flashing through me, and then the truck hits me again, ramming me. I try to peer through the darkened windshield, but I can't see anything as the truck forces me off the road and down the embankment.

I start to flip, and everything happens so fast, I can't react.

Suddenly, it's silent.

My heart hammers in my chest, and my body is so cold, I can't even feel it.

Everything is buzzing, but sound slowly comes back to me, my ears still ringing.

"Fallon, answer me right now!" Kage roars.

"Kage," I whisper. "I think . . . I think I'm okay." I look down, and my body appears intact. "A car hit me . . . . I'm okay . . . . I think I'm okay—" My vision spins, and I reach up with a shaking hand, touching my head and pulling it away to see blood covering my fingertips as two hands appear before me.

"Kage, I don't think I'm okay," I croak. "Kage . . . Kage . . ." Everything starts to go dark. "Help me."

"Where are you? Fallon!" His shouts follow me into the darkness, but I can't answer, even though I hear the pure terror in his voice.

I wake up to the sound of sirens and voices, but I must pass out again because the next thing I know, I'm looking at the inside of an ambulance before I'm under again. The next time I wake up, I see an off-white ceiling, the godawful color all hospitals have. Groaning, I turn my head and pain spasms through me, making my eyes slam shut as my vision starts to swim.

A hand grips mine, and when I open my eyes again, I blink to find Kage's worried face above me. "Sweetheart," he murmurs with a shaky smile. "There you are. I was worried."

"What happened?" I ask, my memories hazy.

"You were in an accident. You're in the hospital. I got you the best private room and doctor—"

"More like ordered it. You have every single doctor and the hospital administrator at your beck and call," a laughing voice comments. I turn to see Elijah sitting in a chair on my other side, typing away. He winks at me when he catches me looking. "He wouldn't have anything less."

"Sounds like him," I murmur as I look back at Kage. "The other driver—" Everything comes back, and I gulp. "It was on purpose."

"Shh, just rest," he murmurs, propping me up and sitting on the side of my bed as he runs his eyes over my face.

"I must look like shit, huh?" I joke with a cough. He grabs a cup and lets me sip from it. "Kage, you're worrying me."

"You're lucky to be alive," he murmurs, his voice tight. "Your hand and leg are injured—nothing permanent, which is a goddamn miracle—your nose is broken, your eyes are black, and you have a hairline fracture in your cheekbone and a cracked skull. Those are the most serious. It's a miracle," he says, shaking his head, his hands clenched on his thighs as he looks away. "I'm sorry, Fallon. I'm sorry I wasn't there—"

"Shh, why would you be? It wasn't your fault." I take his hand with a smile. "Besides, I got lucky. Like you said, it could be a lot worse. I guess me getting out of the way even a little saved my life."

"Don't joke right now," he snaps before taking my hand. "I almost lost you, Fallon. Do you know how scared I was? I could hear it happening and couldn't do—" He shuts up, breathing deeply. "You're okay, and I'm here. That's all that matters. Rest now, the doctor will be in soon now that you're awake."

I frown as he glances away. He's pale, too pale, and shaking. I guess it really shook him up. If I'm going to be honest, it scared me too, but I'm trying not to focus on it because I might sink into that fear and never come out.

There's a knock on the door and a head peeks around it. "Mr. Kage, the police wish to speak to Fallon." It's one of my guards, and his eyes are lowered, not even glancing at anyone in the room.

"Let me talk to them." Kage kisses me and heads out, shutting the door.

Elijah scoots closer. "He lost it. I've never seen him like that. He was terrified, Fallon, when he heard the accident. Within a few minutes, the entire police force and hospital suffered his wrath. They are scared shitless. He was like an animal. My usually calm singer was a maniac. He only calmed down when you were settled in this bed. I thought he was going to kill someone. There are forty guards out there, and I suspect whoever hit you will end up in a watery grave."

The door opens, and I glance at Kage as he slips inside. So that's what's wrong. He was worried and probably blames himself.

"I told the police they can fucking wait."

I blink at his statement, but it shouldn't surprise me. I hold my hand out, and he rushes my way, taking it and sinking to his knees next to me as I smile. "Elijah, can you give me a second?"

"Of course." He leaves, and when I hear the door shut, I move over in the bed, making room for him.

"Come on."

"Baby, you need to rest."

I arch my brow, and he crawls onto the bed, holding me. I sink into his arms, ignoring the pain it sends through my wrist and head. This is more important. Besides, I've felt pain before, and I can handle it.

"I was so scared," he whispers.

"I know. I'm sorry," I murmur. "Did they catch the driver?"

"No, they got away, but it will only be a matter of time," he murmurs. "From now on, you won't go anywhere alone."

"I know." I might want to be independent, but I'm not an idiot. Someone tried to kill me today, so I won't fight him on this. "It means we are hitting where we need to."

"Enough," he murmurs. "Not now."

"Now is the perfect time to strike." I look up at his face. "Let them see what's happening and the lengths someone is willing to go to. They want to silence me, but they are going to do the opposite."

"Fallon," he begins, but I lean up to kiss his lips.

"When the doctors let me go of course, but until then, just hold me."

"Forever," he promises, kissing my head, but I know that it's going to take him a while to get over what happened.

I almost died today.

It's my turn to shake in his arms, and he holds me silently the entire time.

K♥F
Golden Love
I'll be with you.
I'll wait for you.
Golden Love
Can't you see
I'm your fool?

THIRTY-FIVE

KAGE

I have ten doctors check Fallon over and say she's okay to be released before I will even think about it. She's annoyed, but I don't care. I nearly—I can't even think about it.

The terror I felt when I heard the crash through the phone, her screams . . . It will haunt me for the rest of my life. She was so happy that morning, so excited and full of life. I never should have let her go alone.

Staring into her beautiful face as she listens to the doctors' warnings, I swallow my pain and fury. She needs me right now. She might appear put together, but I know she's scared. She won't let it out, not here, but she will later, and I'll be there to catch her. She nearly died, but it will be the last time a hair on her head is ever touched.

I will make sure of it.

When I find the person behind the wheel, they will wish they tried to kill me, not her, because I'm going to make them beg for death.

My gaze sweeps over her face, memorizing every single bruise and cut so I can pay them back tenfold. The skin around her eyes is purple and yellow and slightly swollen, and her nose has a strap across it to keep it straight after the break. She has more across her cheek, and the bandage around her head makes me want to hit something. Her hand is in a movable wrap, as is her leg. They are giving her a crutch to help her walk, but they suspect it will be okay in a few weeks at most.

She was very lucky, but she will never have to go through this again.

I can't lose Fallon. I just can't.

I have written hundreds of love songs in my career, and every single one has been for her.

Sometimes, her strength scares me. She might be terrified right now, but she isn't backing down, not even with my warnings or the police's concerns. She's determined to face them down and expose them. I'm with her the entire way, but I'm scared for her and what it will do to her. Someone already tried to kill her to silence her, so what else are they capable of?

It doesn't stop her though. She tugs on a hat, not bothering with any makeup, and then nods at me. "I'm ready."

I take her hand, knowing better than to argue. Outside of the hospital, the area is swarming with cameras. They have been there since the accident was announced. We could avoid them by going out the back, but my girl isn't hiding. She wants them to know. She's going to tell the whole world and make sure they have nowhere to hide.

The lights flash, and the shouts reach us before the door even opens. Once we're outside, the men I hired form a wall, their arms out to prevent the crushing crowd from getting near her. She looks around, wide-eyed, but she stands tall at my side, refusing to cower. That's just who Fallon is.

You hit her, then she hits back harder.

Holding up her hand, she waits for everyone to become quiet, then clears her throat. "I want to thank everyone for their concern and well-wishes. The outpouring of support and love has been crucial in my healing. I am truly thankful for every single person." She sounds so sweet, so kind, while looking bruised and hurt. Yeah, the public will be demanding answers and angry on her behalf. She's really fucking good. "I can't go into too much detail because this is a police matter, but yesterday, at around eleven in the morning, a truck ran a red light and sped up before hitting my vehicle. I was driving alone. It then proceeded to ram me from the road before fleeing the scene. The police are searching for witnesses and the driver, and we are confident we will find them."

"Why did they do it, Fallon?" someone asks.

"The only idea that comes to mind is the fact that I have been very vocal about my unhappiness in regard to the docuseries about my father's life. I have been silently working behind the scenes to bring everyone the real truth about my father and his band's life—one that will be very different from the story they wish to portray. That is all I will say for now, but hate will never win. They can come at me a hundred times, and I will come back stronger. They will not stop the truth from coming out—not this time. Thank you."

Ignoring the flashes and the shouts, my men clear a path to the car. I help her in, and once the door is shut, I open my arms. She collapses into them as I kiss her head.

"You did so well, sweetheart. You can let go now. Let it out, beautiful. It's just me here." She melts into my embrace, beginning to sob. I know she doesn't want to cry in front of them, so I give her the privacy to break down and work through what happened, honored that she lets me be here for this.

She trusts and loves me, even if she hasn't said it.

"I've got you," I promise, letting her cry it out and grieve for everything that happened. My girl is strong, but even the strongest things in the world can break under too much pressure. It doesn't mean she's weak or damaged. It just means she needs to crack before we rebuild.

I offer her my warmth and protection and my lack of judgment.

I love Fallon. I love her strength, determination, and passion, but I love the fact that she turns to me for comfort as well, only letting me see this side of her.

"Why?" she whispers, lifting her head. "Why me?" Her face clouds with anger and heartbreak. "Why is it always me? Why is my life one tragic accident after another and I'm just expected to endure it? What did I ever do to deserve all of this?"

This isn't the woman I love. It's the child who was neglected and hurt.

She's asking the questions she never dared ask, and my heart breaks for her as her eyes meet mine once more, overflowing with tears. I wonder how anyone could ever think she is made of ice. She feels everything so deeply. How can they not see she is begging for someone to save her? To offer her even a shred of decency and humanity, something she's never had?

"Why me?" Her lip trembles, and my heart clenches so hard, I can't breathe.

"I don't know," I whisper. "I really don't. I wish I did. I wish I could change what happened to you, Fallon. I wish I could give you a happy childhood."

Her glassy eyes peer up at me, begging me for something I can't offer. I can't take away her past, but I can atone for it. I can do something they never did.

"You'll never get an apology from them for what they did to you, so let me apologize for them—not because of them, but because of you. You didn't deserve a single thing they did to you. You deserved to be protected and loved, and I'm so sorry they hurt you. I'm sorry they stole your innocence and wonder of this world. I'm sorry they convinced you that everything comes with strings and manipulation. I'm sorry they tainted what love meant to you. I'm so fucking sorry, Fallon."

Her hands grip my shirt as I speak, tugging me closer. "Stop, please stop," she begs, but her eyes tell me to keep going. They tell me to never leave her like everyone else has. They beg me to be the only person who will love her when that is all she's ever wanted.

Cupping her face, I press my forehead to hers, forcing her to look deep into my eyes, into my soul and my heart. "I am not going anywhere, Fallon. Cry and scream all you want. You've been so strong, baby, so fucking strong, but you don't need to be anymore. I'm here, and I'm not going anywhere. I will never hurt you, but I will spend every day apologizing to you for the way this world hurt you."

Pressing a kiss to her forehead, I pull her into my arms and hold her, resting my chin on her head as she shudders and cries harder. “I’m so sorry, Fallon. I would change the world for you if I could, but instead, I will spend every day loving you like you deserve, embracing the scars you carry. I will kiss and love them until they are healed. I’m here. I’m right here. I’ll always be right here. I’d cross oceans and take bullets for you, but most importantly, I will love you when no one else does, not even yourself.”

I vow she will never go through this again.

I wish I could shoulder all her pain, but instead, I hold her through it, giving her every drop of my strength when she feels weak.

THIRTY-SIX

Fallon

It's been a week since the accident, and I've been on bed rest. It's driving me crazy, but Kage won't let me ignore the doctors' orders. The reporters out front have only tripled, and the news stories run every hour. My interview is highlighted despite other things happening in the world.

Good, let them be reminded every day.

Speculation has already started about the truth, and secrets are beginning to be dug up, everyone wanting to know what I meant. The police are still searching for who did this, and Kage hates that, so the guards in the house have doubled. I can barely pee without a man in a suit busting in to check I'm alive.

It's constricting and annoying but also strangely sweet.

I haven't cried since the day I came back from the hospital. Tears are useless anyway. They won't change anything, but Kage watches me like he's waiting for me to crack again. I don't blame him, I was a mess that day, but I pulled myself together—or so I thought.

I answer the phone without looking, a rookie mistake, and a voice I never wanted to hear flows into my ears. "Hello, Fallon."

My heart stills, and when I speak, I'd like to say my voice is strong and confident, but it's small. I'm still a little girl wishing for her mother to love and protect her.

"Mother." I pause, swallowing my pain. It's all on the surface, since I'm never able to escape it, especially recently. "You never call."

I haven't seen or spoken to my mother since my father's funeral. She got drunk and caused a scene after the reading of the will and disappeared into thin air once more, barely sparing her teenage daughter a look. Maybe she was scared of what she would see.

She took off when I was young, leaving me alone with him. She said she was done with his lifestyle—the drugs, the alcohol, and the women. She never wanted a child, but she had me and despised me for it since the moment I was born. She hated the way my father doted on me and loved me when he didn't love her. If only she knew the truth, that his love crossed lines. I would have done anything for him to love me less and her more.

I would have run away with her if she asked, even if she hated me for the rest of my life, but she didn't care about me enough to even say goodbye back then. To her, I was a reminder of what she endured in the name of love and fame. She wanted a fresh start—one that didn't include me.

"Yes, well, I saw about your accident." She waits, but I don't speak. My heart flies for a moment until she talks again. "You shouldn't have reacted to it like that." Whatever was left of my childish heart hoping my mother would suddenly care plummets and crashes.

I go ice cold all over, refusing to let her hurt me once more.

I can't keep giving her that power. She never loved me, so why am I always hoping she will?

"Well?" she prompts when I don't speak. "I have seen you speaking about your father. Let it be, Fallon. Don't bring up the past—"

"They brought it up first," I snap, refusing to be cowed. I won't let her chastise me like I'm a naughty child. She gave up the right to have a say in my life a long time ago.

She's just a stranger with a familiar face.

"Fallon—"

"No, you do not get to call and tell me what to do. We both know you are scared—scared of what I'll say, scared it will ruin whatever perfect life you have built without me. I'm betting a mother abandoning her child wouldn't read well, would it? If you don't like the truth, Mother, then you shouldn't have abandoned your child to that monster," I snarl, refusing to sugarcoat it like I normally would. All those years of pain lace my tone, making me bitter and angry.

"Enough!" she yells. There she is, the true version of my mother. She could never disguise her hatred for me. "Apologize to me right now."

My laugh is bitter and slightly manic. "You want me to apologize? To you?" I laugh even harder, until tears fill my eyes, before I swallow it back, gasping through it. "You want me to say sorry? To you? If I was ever going to apologize to someone, it wouldn't be you. It would be me. I'm crueler to myself more than anyone else. I rip myself apart to fit into little boxes. I starve myself. I medicate myself. I drink and numb myself. I don't even meet my own eyes in the mirror out of fear of what I'll see and feel. I have never said anything nice about myself. I hear your voice and I foolishly hope for the love you should have freely given. I hurt myself over and over trying to earn it. If there was ever an apology owed, it's to me, not you—never you. You abandoned me. You didn't care then, so don't start now. This is my life, and you have nothing to do with it. You made that perfectly clear." Breathing heavily, I tilt my chin up as if she can see me. "I will never apologize for what I'll do next. If you don't like the truth, Mother, then you shouldn't have been such a terrible person."

She didn't say goodbye back then, so she doesn't get one now. I hang up without another word.

I'm panting, but my shoulders are loose and my heart is less heavy, less burdened. I've carried that pain, that fury, in my heart for so long, hating her while she didn't even care, and I kept telling myself I'm not good enough to be loved.

I was wrong.

Kage taught me that. As if my thoughts summon him, arms slip around my waist and a chin rests on my shoulder.

"How much did you hear?" I ask.

"Everything," he admits, kissing on my shoulder. "How do you feel?"

"Better," I answer without shame. Kage would never judge me.

He has become my guide, my protector, my lover, and my home.

I should care that he manipulated it this way, but I don't because I'm beginning to understand he was right. I need him, and he needs me. We were meant to be. It doesn't matter how it started.

"And?" he prompts, interrupting my thoughts.

"And?" I repeat, my brows drawing together in a frown, not understanding.

"Are you going to apologize to yourself?" he asks.

"Oh." I blow out a breath, unsure what to say. I always feel raw and exposed with him. He has this ability to see too deeply and understand too much. It's unnerving as well as endearing. Anyone else might just let it slide and tell me it's okay.

Not Kage.

Taking my silence for denial, he takes matters into his own hands.

Turning me, he forces me to meet my gaze in the mirror in my dressing room, where I was when I took the call. My eyes meet his in the reflection before returning to my icy ones.

"Apologize, right now, to you—to the child, the teenager, and the woman. Apologize for not loving her enough. This body keeps you alive. It saved you. This mouth and throat sing songs that transport people. These eyes . . . they saved me. Apologize, Fallon."

"I—" I swallow as I stare into my eyes. He waits, not letting me escape. "I'm sorry for not loving you enough. I'm sorry for believing everything they said. I'm sorry for hating the shape of you, the color of you, the size of you when you kept me alive and housed my heart and soul. I'm sorry for loving everyone else more than you when you are all I have."

"Good girl." His hand slides softly across my hair. "You did so well." His mouth meets my ear. "Now show it how sorry you are. I'll help." He lowers to his knees behind me, and my eyes widen. He slides his hands up my skirt until my panties are exposed.

I gasp, trying to turn, but his hands keep me in place, my eyes on our reflection as his lips move across my ass, leaving soft, devastating kisses. "Look at how beautiful you are."

I have no choice but to run my eyes over my body, trying to see what he sees. I'm beautiful, enough people have told me, but as his voice whispers against skin, I start to believe it. I start to understand that I can use it for my pleasure.

I can love it for me, not what it can bring me.

His hands glide up my inner thighs, parting them so his mouth can brush over my panty-clad pussy, making me whimper. "This world would fall if they heard you like that. You should be worshiped like a goddess. You are untouchable. You are beautiful. You are kind and soft, hard and crazy. You are talented and beautiful. You are everything. Don't you see?"

"Kage," I whisper as he tugs off my panties. I help him, lifting my sore leg, and he lays a kiss there as he exposes not just my body, but my soul. He looks at my fears, worries, and insecurities, and he kisses them, calling them beautiful even when I couldn't.

"You are so worth loving. Don't you see how you captivate this world and everyone in it? How you captivate me? One meeting and I knew you were someone important, someone I wanted to spend the rest of my life trying to live up to. Your soul might be filled with scars, but light gets in and melts the ice, and I will be your light. I will be your poet, your warrior, your king, and your clown. I will be whatever you need because I love you. I love you enough for both of us."

All I can do is stare into his eyes, seeing what he sees. His voice drowns out the one inside me that constantly tells me I'm not enough and never will be because for the first time, I realize I am.

I deserve to be loved.

I deserve to be happy.

He smiles against my inner thigh and places a kiss there before turning his head and pressing one to my clit. His hands part my ass to give him more room as his tongue darts out to taste me.

It's time to stop breaking my own heart, so instead, I hand it over to him, knowing he will keep it safe for me. He will meticulously seal those cracks left by others and my own hands. Kage will love me even when I can't love myself.

"If you ever forget, just look into my eyes and see how much I love you . . . see you the way I do. I will love you when you forget to. I will remind you when you're lost," he promises, meeting my eyes. "I will be right here with you every time, until you love yourself the way I love you."

He shows me without words. His tongue traces across my folds as I watch myself in the mirror. My cheeks heat with a blush that spreads down my chest, lighting up my skin like a ruby is trapped inside. I watch my ocean eyes darken and melt, and I watch the way my lips part. My skin heats under his touch as his tongue slips inside me and fucks me. I moan, rocking into his touch. My hands slide across my body, reclaiming it and memorizing the way my soft skin feels under my caress.

I enhance my own desire, using his mouth to get where I want. Right now, it's not about him, but me. His tongue presses against my clit as pleasure washes through me. My eyes want to close, but I force them to stay open and watch the beauty of my desire.

When I reach the precipice, I allow myself to fall over the edge and into his waiting arms.

I come in his mouth as he hums, licking up my desire until I'm shaking and leaning heavily into his hold to stay upright. He places a soft kiss on my sensitive clit and moves back.

"Look at how much power you hold inside your body. Look at your magnificence."

Panting, I look down as he moves to kneel at my side, gazing up at me.

"Let them hate you, Fallon, let them be jealous, but don't you ever do it again. Look them in the eye so they know you are more than they could ever imagine. Smile and remind yourself of this moment, of me on my knees, looking up at my goddess."

Reaching down, I slide my hand into his dark hair and watch the way his eyes close in bliss. How could I ever hate myself when he loves me? When my body, heart, and soul make this man weak? I might have days where I still fight the darkness, but I know he'll be right here with me.

Lowering to my knees, I tug his mouth to mine and kiss him, telling him everything I can't speak.

He's my stage, and I sing my song with my lips.

K♥F
Golden Love
I'll Be with you.
I'll wait for you.
Golden Love
Can't you see
I'm your fool?

THIRTY-SEVEN

KAGE

My girl is healing day by day, both inside and out. It's been quiet after her interview, which is good because she needs rest. She deserves it, and I'm right here at her side. Elijah is stressed since I have canceled so much, but I don't care. She's more important, and he's starting to realize that.

He knows if he pushed me, I would choose her and walk away from everything else.

I'm trying to protect her from as much as I can, but I will never keep her in the dark, so when I get the news, I turn on the TV as we lounge in bed. Her eyes open, and I drop my phone. "You're going to want to see this."

Her expression morphs from peaceful to worried. I hate that, but I will never lie to her or keep her from any of this. It's her life and her battles. I am simply her general.

She sits up at the headline, pain radiating from her body as I turn up the volume, wrapping my arms around her. "Evelyn Mitchel, Renwood model, philanthropist, activist, and nation's sweetheart, was found dead this morning in her mansion. Police said it was a home invasion, and they are conducting the investigation—"

She turns to me. "It's my fault. She's dead, and it's my fault."

"No." I cup her face. "It's not."

"It is!" She tears herself away from me, looking back at the TV. "She stayed quiet all this time and they left her alone. The moment I approached her and she agreed to speak out, I signed her death certificate." She looks back at me. "They killed her, Kage. They killed her to stop her from speaking, like she was nothing on their road to silence."

"I know," I murmur as I turn off the TV. She's hurting enough as it is. She doesn't need to see anymore. Evelyn was clearly someone special to Fallon. I saw it the other day when they met up. Fallon cared about the model, and now she's blaming herself like Fallon always does. "It isn't your fault. She made her choice, she told you that, and they made theirs. You are not responsible for others' actions. They are the monsters, Fallon. Don't let them make you feel like one or, worse, scare you. That's what they want—to scare you into silence."

She nods, looking back at the blank TV. "I can't believe she's dead. She seemed bigger than life. Untouchable."

"Nobody is untouchable, Fallon. Don't forget that. They have only added fuel to the fire. They've officially crossed into murder now. This isn't a game anymore, which makes what you're doing even more important. They are willing to kill to silence it. You should keep going, Fallon, but only if you want. If not, that's fine. I'll run with you. I'll keep you safe for the rest of your life. Tell me what you want, Fallon, and I'll make it happen," I say, reaching for her. She melts into my arms, holding me close as she processes her muddled emotions and thoughts.

"I want . . . I want her death to mean something—all of their deaths. I want to be the person she thought I was and be strong enough to face the truth no matter the cost. I want them to pay for everything. More than anything, I want her to finally be free, even in death," she admits, her eyes hardening. "I want them to have nowhere to hide. I need to, Kage. This all has to mean something. I can't let their deaths go like this. The world has to know, and they have to pay."

"Then let's do that," I reply. "Let's make them pay. I will never ask you to stop, but I will keep you safe. You won't go anywhere alone, and you'll sleep with me. I won't lose you. Do you understand me? I care about your wants, but if it means losing you, then I would steal you away in a moment and hide you from the world."

"I know." She smiles, even though I expected her to be angry. "We need another witness. Evelyn . . ." She swallows, pain in her eyes. "She was going to talk. We need someone to replace her."

"You have someone in mind?" I ask curiously, knowing she probably needs to keep moving forward or she'll break again.

"I remember her manager. He was a bit of an ass back then, but maybe he knows someone else, someone who was sent with her," she muses. "It's as good a shot as any, right?"

"Then that's where we'll start. I'll tell your guards."

"You mean my army," she scoffs.

Grinning, I kiss her softly. "I told you, I'm your general, now let's go to war."

THIRTY-EIGHT

Fallon

We manage to get away from my house with only a few paparazzi cars following us, and then we lose them in the city thanks to Kage's new driver. Elijah sighed when he called and we told him we were going out, but it seems he's given up on trying to control Kage.

Only I can do that.

I can't let Evelyn's death be in vain. I need to keep pushing before it's too late. We are running out of time. I can feel it. There is only one place I could think to go to get information on anyone who might have been with Evelyn back then—her old management.

She left them when she turned twenty and my father died, but they are still operating. It makes me sick to think of what they are allowing to happen to the young women and men in their care, but I can't fight the whole world—not yet anyway.

We booked a last-minute appointment, saying we wanted to discuss my modeling options. The fucker was so desperate for money, he didn't even stop to question why I would go to him. It tells me everything I need to know though.

Money is his motivation.

He might make me physically sick, but we need him, for now at least. It's what keeps me silent as we wait in his office. The city is spread out beyond the windows behind his desk. Modeling catalogs sit on his coffee table, and there are prints across the walls. It all screams money, fame, and power. It's perfect and intimidating, just like he wants.

Men like him thrive on being the strongest in the room, but he won't be in this room, which is exactly why I get up, smooth down my deep-brown, asymmetrical dress, and push back my wavy hair. I take a seat in his deep leather chair and turn to look out at the view while I wait.

Less than two minutes later, the door opens. Keeping me waiting is another tactic. He's trying to make me feel unimportant and tell me he's in demand. I've played these games, and I know them well. They won't work on me.

"Ms. Fallon, I apologize for keeping you waiting . . ." His voice trails off when I don't turn to see him. "Um, Ms. Fallon?"

I turn in his chair, my eyebrow arched as he hesitates before his own desk. Good, keep him off balance. "Sit." I wave at the chair perfectly placed on the other side. It's lower and smaller than his. Kage waits, and so do I, neither of us filling the silence.

Pursing his thin lips, he sinks slowly into the chair. He's handsome, I guess, but sitting next to Kage, he pales in comparison. He's older, in his late forties, but his hair is brown and styled, and he wears a power suit, no doubt designer. He has a Rolex on his left wrist and a diamond ring on his other hand. Despite this, I know he's desperate to sign talent. It's been a while since he lost his footing in the industry as newer, hungrier agents rise to the top. His standing is hanging in the balance, and he's bleeding money.

He's desperate, and he thinks I'm his meal ticket.

He's wrong. I'm his damnation.

"Evelyn is dead."

He flinches, his eyes widening before he schools his expression, his lips turning down in a practiced sad frown.

Before he can tell me how sad he is, I carry on. "She was working with me on something, and now I need your help to find someone else."

"Ms. Fallon, we are here to discuss your career, but if this is for a show, I can happily find you another model who's better, younger—"

I hold my hand up. "Don't ever disrespect Evelyn in this office, understood?" When he nods, I sit back. "It isn't for a show, per se. I want names of people who, along with Evelyn, were told to work my father's parties."

His face pales. "I don't know—"

"Spare me the bullshit and lies. I'm low on patience today, and I really want to fucking hit you. Don't give me a reason to. I'm trying my best to hold back, but if you keep lying to me or give me the runaround, I'll grow tired of these games and just take my anger out on you, understand?"

"Fallon . . ." He swallows. "What do you want?"

"I just told you. Are you dumb?" I sigh in annoyance. "The list, I know you have one or you remember. You're one of the best for a reason."

"What do you want with them?"

"That's not your issue at all. Give me the list and I'll leave. I'll even pay you for it. However, if you refuse, I'm going to take my frustration out on you." I nod at Kage, and he pulls out the bag, flashing the stacks of bills inside. I might not want to, but I need what he has, and he can take the money. In the end, it will only make him more complicit when the truth comes out.

He will destroy himself. He just doesn't know it.

He snorts, sitting back. "I won't compromise my morals for money. Giving you those names would be doing just that."

"No?" Arching a brow, I stand and walk around the desk. He watches me nervously as I reach into the bag and take out two stacks. When he's silent, I add another. "How about now?" His face turns beet red as he glances from me to the money, so I add another stack, then another, smiling in disgust. "I can keep going all day. Let me ask you, what do you think will run out first? Your morals or my money? I'm betting on your morals, since we both know you sold your soul a long time ago."

"Fallon," he snaps, standing, but his eyes go back to the money. "Why are you doing this?"

"You're a smart man, you know, now take the money or I will go about this a different way. Either way, I'll win and get what I want. Take the money and make it easy for yourself," I warn.

His eyes close for a moment, and when they open, he looks dejected as he nods. Grabbing a piece of paper, he writes down names and hands it over. I scan them before placing it inside my bra and hand him the stacks of cash.

"See? Wasn't that easy? Everyone can be bought with enough money, and I have enough to do just that. Don't forget that in the future. I can play with you all like toys and not even eat into my pocket change. We both know this game is won by power and cash, and I have both. I'm sure I'll be seeing you soon." I gently slap his face as I pass. "Spend the money well. We both know you'll need to stop what's coming your way."

As I head toward the door, my eyes catch on a magazine on the table. Evelyn is on the cover, and my heart hurts until I'm practically running, feeling like I'm betraying her even though it's a necessary evil to work with this man for now. I'll make sure he gets what he deserves in the end.

I have to for her.

"You're just like her, so confident and stubborn. That's why she ended up dead, and you will too," he spits, feeling brave since my back is turned.

I freeze. I could keep walking, but fuck that.

Turning, I stomp toward him on my heels.

I grab one of the catalogs as thick as a book as I go, and I rush him. He stumbles back into his desk, money falling around him as I smash it across his face. He screams as he flips from the impact, hitting his desk. Grabbing his hair, I press his face to the cover of it where Evelyn sits. "Don't forget her name. Don't forget our names. I'll be back for you." Releasing him, I blow my hair from my face and smile at Kage.

"Shall we?" I hold out my hand, and he lays his in mine and lets me lead him from the office.

"Feel better?" he asks once we're in the elevator.

"I really do." I grin up at him as I pull out the list. "Now, we need to get these people to work with us."

"And then?" he murmurs.

"Then it's time. We can't wait anymore. It's time for the truth."

So far, we have tracked down two of the names. They are still working in the industry, but the others have disappeared and either changed their names or they never revealed their real ones to begin with. Kage is working on that as we speak, knowing we are running out of time. Every moment we waste is another minute where whoever killed Evelyn and tried to kill me could come back at us. Once this is in the open, they will have no shields to hide behind.

The first name, Yolanda, agreed after a tearful talk, although she seemed nervous, but I think that's normal. The second name, however, concerns me. Poe is at the top of his game, so he already faces enough criticism. Would he be willing to help us?

I don't remember seeing him at the parties, but it doesn't surprise me that they did the same shit to men they did to us women. Nothing was off-limits.

We are lucky he agreed to meet at a shoot since he's so busy. I leave Kage outside, next to the lounge and snack area for the crew, while Poe's manager lets me into his dressing room. He's sitting on a sofa, his head tilted back and eyes closed. He looks exhausted and no less stunning. I've seen him in so much, but I never suspected this would be the conversation we would have. His short blond hair is spiked, the tips pink, and his makeup is artfully done, with glitter across his face. He's beautiful, which is exactly why he's one of the best, and he also knows how to work the camera.

Like he feels my gaze, he lifts his head and smiles. "Fallon."

I've never met him, but I instantly feel at ease. I sit in the chair opposite his sofa, and he watches me. "I get it." I blink at his statement, and he carries on. "Sorry, just thinking out loud. I finally get why everyone is so obsessed with you. The cameras don't do you justice."

"Nor you," I admit, and he laughs as he sits up. He sighs and rubs his face before tilting his head and watching me again.

"I'm assuming this isn't a social call?" The shrewd look in his eyes surprises me, but it shouldn't.

"No," I admit softly.

"Your father?" he asks. "I saw that you are going to expose him and everyone else. It doesn't take a genius to figure out what you mean."

"Yes, I heard you were at the parties."

"Some." He nods, his features tightening. "Enough before I managed to get my ass out of there, but not without a cost." His lips tilt up in a bitter smile.

It's one we all have.

"I need you, Poe. I need your help. Evelyn was going to speak out." His eyes widen, and I nod. "I think they killed her for it."

He laughs again. "And now you want me to? Even though it could get me killed?"

"So what? You're just going to live with it and pretend you don't know? That it didn't happen to you? Ignoring it doesn't make it go away. They could kill you either way if they know you were there. They made it clear they are willing to silence anyone," I argue.

"Yet you aren't scared?" he asks.

"I'm terrified, but I won't let it stop me. I can't." Pursing my lips, I meet his gaze. "I'm haunted by what happened to me, but it's more than me now. It's Evelyn. It's all of the people who were there. We have to stop this, and the only way to do that is to expose everything. I know what I'm asking, and I know it could ruin your career, but I'm asking anyway."

He considers me for a moment. "I was so angry about everything for years. I let it consume me, and I took so many drugs to forget. I'm clean now, and I'm embracing my healing, which I'm told means forgiveness. Part of me thinks I should just forgive them and move on, forget about it," he murmurs, looking at me. "Don't you?"

"No. Fuck that," I spit. "You don't owe them forgiveness. You don't owe people who hurt you sympathy. You don't always have to be the better person and bury your feelings, letting them build until you explode. You are allowed to feel. You are allowed to feel angry and betrayed. You are allowed to . . . *be.* Doing that doesn't mean you're not healing. It means you are strong enough to face what happened, but I won't force you. I'll even try to cover your name up if you wish, so nobody knows."

"Why?" he murmurs.

"Because I'm determined to protect everyone when no one protected us back then," I reply. "I won't back down, but this isn't everyone's fight. Yours is wherever you choose to be, and that's okay."

"You know what they will say about me if this comes out," he whispers. "I made it up. I slept my way to the top. The rumors about my sexuality will eclipse everything."

"Yes," I answer, not sugarcoating it.

"It could ruin me. Everything I worked for, everything I endured to get here . . ." He sits back. "But I owe it to Evelyn, I owe it to you, and I owe it to the boy who only ever wanted to be in front of the camera—the one they killed. I'll help you, Fallon." He smiles. "Hell, let them try to kill me. I did that enough to myself through the years each time I stuck a needle in my arm."

"Poe, are you sure?" I might have driven him here, but I will give him a way out if he wants it. I won't be like my father.

"You're right. I can't escape my past. I'm allowed to be angry. Evelyn would have wanted this. If she was willing to talk, then we should too. We owe it to ourselves. Tell me everything I need to know. I'm with you."

I tell him everything, and when I'm done, he's smiling. His expression is cruel and filled with vengeance.

It's time for the victims to reclaim their power.

It's time for the victims to become the survivors.

K•F
Golden Love
I'll be with you.
I'll wait for you.
Golden Love
Can't you see
I'm your fool?

THIRTY-NINE

KAGE

I don't like to admit it, but I'm scared for my girl. Whoever is behind the attack on her and Evelyn's and the manager's murders surely have their eyes on her. They were warnings to make her stop, since they knew killing Fallon wouldn't go unnoticed and they wanted to scare her off, but they should have known better.

Threats just make my girl dig her heels in. She's not scared of dying. She's scared of being weak.

It's one of the reasons I love her, but I'm scared for her. She's intent on bringing this world down, and I'll help her, so while she focuses on that, I focus on her safety.

She becomes annoyed by the constant guards, but I don't care. I also won't let her out of my sight. Where she goes, I go. It means I cancel nearly all my upcoming arrangements and leave my team flustered, but whatever.

Fallon always comes first.

We spend two days going down the list she has. All but one agrees to help, and we both know when it comes down to it, they still might pull out, so the more the better.

"What now?" I ask, sitting next to her in the living room. She is looking at the papers spread before her, my laptop open as we review the evidence, making sure we have everything in order before we make our move.

"Now, it's time," she murmurs and grins over at me. "Elijah knows what to do. Tell him it's time."

Picking up my phone, I drop him a text, leaving the finer details to him. We need to keep it as quiet as possible, but once we have the date and time confirmed, we can relay it to everyone we collected.

Fallon sits back. "It's ready. It's finally about to be over."

My phone rings, and I answer. "Okay, so for the dates—" Elijah starts to ramble, his perfectionist side coming out. I roll my eyes at Fallon as she laughs, and when the doorbell rings, she gets up to get it.

"Elijah." I sigh as he carries on. "Elijah." I keep repeating his name louder and louder until he finally stops. "I trust you. You know what we need, so you don't have to run it all by me."

"You . . . You trust me?" he murmurs.

"Of course. You've been with me for years. I'll let you handle it—" A scream splits the air.

Fallon.

I drop my phone and run faster than I ever have, my heart pounding in fear. I find her in the hallway, surrounded by shattered glass and flowers, but that's not all. Something glitters between the petals, and when my eyes swing to her, she turns and holds her hands up to show me one of them is cut and bleeding. It races down her arm and hits the floor like rain as she blinks at me.

"I thought they were from you. They have razor blades in the petals. I cut myself." Her voice is calm, but she's pale.

"Find out who sent them!" I bark at the guards who rush in. Uncaring about my bare feet, I walk over to her, glass cutting into my soles, but I don't stop until I'm at her side. Ignoring my pain, I scoop her into my arms and head straight to the kitchen. I place her on the counter and step between her legs, grabbing a hand and lifting it so I can inspect the cuts.

"Sir," one of the guards interrupts. I don't spare him a look as I turn her hand.

"They are shallow, just bleeding a lot," I tell her softly.

"Sir, I have the first-aid kit. I'm a medic in training. Do you want me to help?" he asks.

I debate it, but the idea of another man's hands on her, especially right now when I'm on edge, has me shaking my head. "I can handle it. Get that mess cleaned up and check the cameras. I want answers."

The box is placed next to us, and he retreats without a word.

"I thought they were from you," she repeats, sounding odd. She seems detached, which worries me. Fallon has a tendency to retreat into herself, to overthink and push everything away when life becomes too much. I don't want that to happen, so I keep a firm hold on her hand, open the box, and lay out what I need as I speak to her.

"I'd never send you roses, sweetheart. Dahlias for us, okay?" She nods, and I turn to her hand. "This is going to hurt, beautiful."

"Just do it." She nods jerkily, both of us ignoring the blood dripping steadily across us from our position.

She doesn't cry, not even as I disinfect the wounds, but I know it has to hurt.

"You're doing so well, sweetheart," I coo as I clean them up and try to stop the bleeding, but they just keep going, so I grab some bandages and make quick work of binding her fingers. She won't be playing the piano anytime soon, but they will heal. It could have been a lot worse, and she's okay, but that doesn't stop the terror trapped in my chest that started from her scream.

It's a sound that will haunt me. I almost lost her once. I can't let it happen again.

I lick the blood from her hand and arm as she watches. "I'll make them bleed for this," I promise against her skin, watching the goose bumps rise on her arm. I lean in and kiss her so she can taste her blood and my promise.

They will pay for making her bleed.

Cupping her face, I pull away, watching her blink. "Are you okay?"

She nods, looking down at herself. "I need to change. This dress is ruined, isn't it?"

"I'll buy you ten more," I tell her. Hell, I'll buy her every dress in the fucking world if it will get her to smile right now, but she just nods and steps past me. I watch her with a frown as the feeling of something wrong fills me. She's been like this before, distant, like she's not quite there.

I know Fallon struggles with her emotions. I've seen it firsthand, and as I follow her into the hall, I worry they are getting the best of her once more. She's been so strong recently despite everything, so maybe it's all finally caught up to her.

I watch her head upstairs, and then I turn, my eyes narrowed.

"We found this, sir." The guard hands over a folded bit of card, blood staining the front like a watercolor promise.

Flipping it open, I read the hastily scrawled threat, my anger only growing.

Stop now or else these flowers won't be the only thing cutting into your skin.

I hand it back over. "See if you can get fingerprints. I want answers, and I don't want anything like this to happen again. Every delivery is stopped and does not come in unless I approve it. I don't want anyone at this door. This is her sanctuary, her safety. Do you understand?"

"Yes, sir."

My eyes go back to the stairs where my princess just disappeared.

FORTY

Fallon

I don't bother showering, since I don't have the energy. It was zapped out of me. Maybe it's shock, but deep down, I know it's not. It's that swirling darkness that lives inside me rearing its ugly head, telling me I'm not good enough, that I should give up and I can't win.

Instead, I simply slip into my bed naked, my eyes locked on the dust motes floating and dancing in the space before the window, free, floating, and unburdened. It's the way I wish I could be, but everything feels heavy and wrong.

I glance down at my hand. Even that doesn't hurt as much as it should. It didn't pierce the fog. I was doing so well. I hate that it came back now. I hate even more that Kage saw me this way, but those thoughts are dragged under the tidal wave claiming my soul.

Maybe this world would be a better place without me. Maybe Evelyn wouldn't have died. Maybe others wouldn't be struggling with their own pasts if I hadn't brought them up. I'm just a selfish bitch who deserves this.

I don't know what depression feels like for everyone else, but for me, it always felt like this—a weight pressing me down, stealing my energy and my drive, darkening my heart until I can't tell right from wrong.

I fight against it silently. I don't scream or throw things. I just lie here, in the same position on my side, watching the sun move through the sky.

The bed dips behind me, and arms slide around me, tugging me back against a warm chest. I don't have the energy to move, nor do I want him to see me. He'll know.

He'll take one look at me and know like everyone else does.

I am just loud on the outside and empty on the inside.

Dead.

He turns me anyway, rolling me in his arms as he looks down at me, scanning my face and seeing everything I don't want him to. I expect disgust, maybe anger, or even pity, but his expression softens as he stares at me. None of these emotions are there, just worry, which, for some reason, is so much worse.

"Tell me what you need, Fallon," he murmurs, peering down at me without judgment, just wanting to help. "Tell me how to make this easier for you. Do you want me here? Is it better if I'm gone? Do I need to snap you out of it? Tell me, sweetheart. Tell me how to help you."

Working my throat, I try to speak, but when my voice comes, it's rough. "Make it stop."

"How?" he asks, searching my eyes.

"Make it hurt," I tell him, ashamed, but I'm desperate to be rid of these feelings, and that overrides my shame. "Make me feel anything other than this cold dread. I don't need you to make me feel happy, I don't even think it's possible, but I need you to remind me that I'm alive, so make it hurt. Pain is my companion, my constant. It's what has kept me alive this long, so bring me back to life."

He doesn't ask me if I'm sure or tell me no. Instead, he leans down and digs his teeth into my lower lip. I gasp, the sharp pain stabbing through me.

"You want me to make it hurt, beautiful? You want me to remind you that you're alive?"

I nod, wide-eyed, staring up into his dark eyes heated with hunger as he rubs my bleeding lip with his thumb.

"Then keep your eyes on me. I'll be your raft."

He yanks the covers back, tossing them from the bed as he kneels above me. Grabbing the back of his shirt, he pulls it over his head, exposing his stunning chest. A spark of desire ignites inside me as I stare at him, and he unbuckles his jeans before lowering so he's above me, licking down my chin to my neck where he bites. I reach for his shoulders, my nails curling into his skin to keep him close.

He kisses the sting away before sliding farther down my chest, leaving stinging bites until his teeth clamp down on my nipple, making me cry out as my back arches. He bites harder, and I clench my thighs together in need, the pain making my clit throb as desire washes through me. I can feel my own wetness from his rough treatment, his fingers denting my skin and leaving bruises as he releases my nipple, letting blood return, and the feeling makes me clench with need before he gives my other nipple the same treatment. He's making it hurt just like I asked, but with love in his eyes.

It's different from what they did to me.

He's doing this because I asked, because he loves me.

They did it because they enjoyed it. Maybe I should feel bad because I crave this kind of punishment, but I don't care—not with his dark eyes on me.

He leans back, looking me over as I pant below him. "Look at you, so fucking beautiful . . . so fucking mine." Leaning down, he sweeps his tongue down my stomach, making me shiver. "Those feelings inside you can't have you, Fallon. You belong to me. Do you hear me?" When I don't respond, he turns his head and bites my thigh so hard I actually scream. "I said, do you hear me?"

"Yes. Yours."

"Good girl." He kneels above me, dragging his tongue over his lips. "I can't hold back. You wanted it to hurt, sweetheart. Remember that."

I yelp as he grips my hips and yanks me down the bed and between his legs, my head hitting the mattress as he lifts my hips and slams into me. The pain from his invasion makes me whimper, even as my heart pounds, coming back to life.

Desire and hunger fill me, replacing my dread.

His hands pin mine to the bed, pressing them into the mattress, the pain from my cuts making me cry out and clench around his cock as he drives into me. His hard, quick thrusts have me moving up the bed with each one. He doesn't relent or slow down, just hammers into me.

He fucks me so brutally, it borders on being too much, yet it's all I can feel.

He's all I can see.

Those voices disappear, and the exhaustion is replaced as he brings me back to life.

I cry out his name as he fucks me, his lips twisting in a snarl, but then he pulls from my body, making me whimper.

Flipping me, he presses my face into the bed. I fight against him, but he keeps me pinned as he hammers into me, and I love it. I love how roughly he fucks me.

He doesn't fuck me like I'm the ice princess or a superstar, but like I'm me. Fallon.

The woman he wants.

I let the pain run through me, mixing with pleasure inside me until I'm a bomb ready to detonate. When his fingers pinch my clit, I do just that.

I explode with a scream, taking him down with me as he bellows my name.

Gasping for breath, I slump beneath him, my blood burning and skin so hot, I sweat as he wraps me in his arms, keeping me afloat just like the raft he promised he'd be.

I wish I could say one good fuck fixes my mental health, but it doesn't, and I know it won't be long before I have another episode. This one leaves me feeling weak, exhausted, and downright embarrassed, but Kage doesn't care.

He picks me up from the bed and helps me into a bath he must have run before coming to me. He doesn't speak as he gently picks up every one of my limbs and washes them before sliding me lower and washing my hair. His long fingers unknot it, massaging into the long strands until my eyes close in bliss.

I lie in his arms, just letting him wash it all away and take care of me.

He dries me and helps me into a floor-length sleep gown, and then he sits me down before the mirror. I have the strangest feeling that I could weep. I don't because I don't want him to worry, but I watch him through the mirror as he carefully dries and brushes every inch of my long hair. He takes his time, brushing it until it falls in silky waves. He meets my gaze in the mirror and smiles softly before grabbing some hair ties, then he starts to braid it.

"I watched some videos when I realized how long your hair was. I wanted to be able to help you with it," he explains, his eyes narrowed and focused, as if he's doing something very important. For him, he is.

There is no one more important to him than me.

How could I ever hate myself or think I don't belong in this world when someone like him loves me?

As I meet my eyes in the mirror, I mouth an apology to myself for everything I have put this body and soul through, for doubting it and trying to detach from it, and the tears finally fall. He says nothing. Kage lets me cry, and when he finishes my hair, he kisses the top of my head.

"Good as new," he says, and something about that makes me cry harder.

He holds me through it, and when I'm done, he carries me to the bed and tucks me in, sitting against the headboard. "Wait here." He hurries away, and I watch him go, wondering how I got so lucky to meet someone like him.

I don't know how long he's gone, but he comes back with a tray and places it over my lap. There's a bowl of broth, some bread, fruit, chocolate, and water, and when I reach for the spoon, he pushes my hand away. Dipping the spoon in the soup, he lifts it to his mouth and blows before cupping his hand under it to catch any drips, then he brings it to my mouth.

Moving my head closer, I open my mouth and eat carefully. He feeds me the entire broth like this before wiping my mouth with his hand and then feeding me the rest. He watches me eat every bite and drink every drop of water. "Good girl," he praises when I'm done, kissing my head before taking the tray away. When he comes back, he pulls me into his arms and just holds me.

I close my eyes and let him remind me he's here. I'm not alone, and he will always be here, something I never would have believed before. Nobody stays, but he does.

Kage stays.

There's a buzz, and we both look over to his phone on the nightstand.

Grabbing it, he reads the text before he looks down at me, his eyes glinting dangerously. "Three days, that's when it's happening. Are you ready?"

"More than I've ever been," I admit.

Three days.

I have three days until the entire world knows my secrets and I'm not their perfect idol anymore.

I'll just be a damaged, angry woman, and I can't fucking wait.

FORTY-ONE

Fallon

Three days pass quickly with all the planning we have to do. Elijah handles a lot, but I want to be helpful, and surprisingly, he lets me. We grow close in those three days, and as we go over the plan one last time in the car on the way there, he's quiet.

"I'm sorry, Fallon." My eyes widen. I'm unsure what he's getting at as he closes his iPad and focuses on me. "I'm so sorry for what you went through. For what it's worth, I think you're doing the right thing, and I'll be there for you—for both of you. I'll be with you the entire time. We're a team."

"Thank you, Elijah," I reply sincerely. He's smart, and he figured out what we have been up to, plus we needed his help planning, but knowing he will stand with me and not just because of Kage?

I have him on my side, just like I have all of the people we gathered. This knowledge fills me with the strength I need to get through what will happen and the fallout. A little chaos never hurt anyone, though, and I did say I wanted to start a riot.

Hair and makeup take over two hours, but when everything is done, I look like usual perfect Fallon. That's what they want. I refuse to show them an inch of weakness. My hair is perfectly styled, half of it held back off my face, my eyeliner is sharp, and my lips are ruby red. I look like the villain, and I love it.

Standing, I thank the team and then unzip the bag holding today's dress.

Kage and Elijah are busy checking everything over, and I know this building is filled with more celebrities than they know what to do with, but right now, I'm alone, and I let myself feel that because after this, it will never be quiet again.

Reaching out, I run my hand over the silken fabric.

It's white—ironic, I know—but I want to play on their emotions, making me look like the innocent one. It's a mind game, but I'm not above that, not to get what I want.

Pulling it from the hanger, I slip it on. It's cinched under my breasts and flares out around my hips, the hem longer in the back. There are also dahlias sewn across the material—Kage's touch, to remind me who I am and who is with me the entire time.

Turning back to the mirror, I take a deep breath as I inspect myself one more time.

I give myself a smile. "It's time." It's a promise to me, both the woman I see and the little girl hiding within me.

The one they hurt.

There's a knock on the door, and it opens to show Elijah wearing a soft smile on his face. "Are you ready?"

"I'm ready." Turning from the mirror, I take his hand and let him lead me to our destination. Kage waits for me in the wings, and he takes my hand from Elijah, running his eyes over me.

"Perfection," he murmurs, but then he reaches out and tugs on some strands of my hair, framing my face. "And a little wild, just like my girl."

I can't help but smile, and Elijah appears at our side with a producer. "Okay, we're ready when you are, Fallon. This will be going out live as requested. Everyone else is ready for their cues, and your . . . um . . . other guests are waiting outside the audience hall."

I nod, peeking through the curtain to see the packed audience. I invited every rich and famous person in the rock world, including those who were there back then. I don't know if they came, but it doesn't matter.

They will see it everywhere. Cameras are trained on the sofa waiting for me on stage. The feed will go straight to TV, along with the phones ready to live stream. It can't be silenced this time. It can't be stopped.

This isn't just my voice. It's an army, one they won't win against.

Looking back at Kage, I squeeze his hand. "Stay with me?"

"Until the end," he promises, stealing a kiss. "My beautiful, strong girl, you've got this. Show them they fucked with the wrong woman. Show them exactly what you're capable of. Make them all pay."

Stealing some of his strength, I turn back to the stage and school my features. All traces of smiles are gone, and the ice queen is back.

Today, they will know why.

I step out onto the stage with Kage, my eyes on the person I chose to interview me. She stabbed me in the back just last year by exposing my cheating husband. She's the exact type of person I need—cruel, vicious, and willing to ask hard questions to get the truth. She's also trustworthy and well-known.

I was surprised when she agreed, but it seems she doesn't hate me. She was simply doing her job, and I can work with that.

I head over to the sofa, and the crowd cheers, clapping at my appearance even if they are confused. Some probably know what's coming and are here out of fear. I don't spare any of them a look as I sit on the sofa closest to the interviewer's chair. Kage sits beside me, holding my hand. There is nothing else on the stage other than us and the screens above us that will blast the evidence we have.

I wait for the crowd to die down, and then I sweep my gaze over them, but most of the lights are blinding, so I turn back to Louise.

"Fallon, it's nice to see you again." I can tell she actually means it. "Kage, it's nice to meet you." She turns to the camera. "I'm sure everyone is waiting anxiously for what this special live broadcast is about. It's been kept secret until now, and as you can see, we have a very selective, celebrity filled audience." The cameras pan out to the faces of people, who actually wave and smile.

Fools.

When they turn back to us, she smiles. "Honestly, I'm mostly in the dark as well. So, Fallon, why are we all here today? It isn't for a wedding, is it?"

I laugh with the crowd, even as Kage leans in. "She wishes. When I marry her, I will let the whole world watch so they can see she's mine forever."

The host laughs. "Kage, your mic is on."

"Oops." He winks at me to let me know he did it on purpose, and I have to fight my smile.

"No, not a wedding, but something just as important," I add, glancing at one of the cameras. "I'm here today to expose some truths. I know everyone has a lot of questions, and I have been vocal, as has Kage, about the fact that we're unhappy with the docuseries soon to air about my father's life. Then, at the hospital, we informed everyone that someone tried to silence us. Now, we are here to set the record straight. Today, we won't hide anything, and I must warn viewers that this isn't a pretty, fluffy story. You wanted the truth, so you will get it, but don't tell me I didn't warn you."

Louise laughs nervously. "You make it sound like someone died, Fallon."

"They did," I reply without shame. "Many people actually." Mrs. Miller's daughter's image floods the screens. "This is Lennie Miller. She was a young model, and she killed herself. Her mother has been fighting for justice for many years, and today, she will get it. She isn't the only one who died in this war. My presence here today puts me in danger. Just a few days ago, a bouquet of roses and razors was sent to me with a warning. Someone tried to kill me in a car accident, and there have been many more instances. They don't want what I have to say to get out. They want to keep it hidden."

"And what truth is that, Fallon? What is someone willing to kill for?" she asks with a deep frown, wanting to know herself.

"The truth of my childhood and who my father and his band were. They weren't the celebrity idols everyone makes them out to be, nor were they good people. In fact, they were the opposite. They were filled with venom and made into monsters by this industry and those around them who facilitated their drug and alcohol use, as well as other needs that haunt me, even to this day."

"Fallon, what do you mean by that?" she asks.

Taking a deep breath, I clutch Kage's hand tighter, glancing at him for a moment for his strength before looking back at her. "My father and his bandmates abused me throughout my entire childhood." There are some gasps from the crowd, but I don't slow down. "My father and his band threw lavish parties that his entire circle and management not only knew about, but encouraged. They plied models, singers, and underage girls and boys with drugs and alcohol to try to get them addicted, and then they would pass them around like toys and share them between the band and their entourage to celebrate a win or commemorate a loss. If you tried to speak out, you were either paid or threatened. Everyone at those parties was complicit with the rampant sexual abuse and predatory behavior, and most of them are sitting in the crowd today."

There are more gasps and some protests. I ignore them, focusing on the interviewer who has turned pale, her eyes wide with horror.

"Many of the label's managers, models' managers, and assistants knew, and they took part and got paid for it. I have spent years battling with depression and PTSD from what these parties did to me. They have shaped my entire adult life. I was ashamed by what happened and horrified by my own memories." I take a deep breath. Something about speaking this aloud is almost . . . freeing.

I have depression, and I have struggled with it for a really long time—long before I even gave a name to those thoughts inside my head—but I'm not ashamed anymore because I know I'm not alone, and if I can make one more person feel that way, feel seen and understood, then I will speak until my voice gives out. I have depression, and it doesn't make me different, unlovable, or unable to achieve success or a life. It just makes me who I am.

"It took me a long time to realize I have nothing to be ashamed of. I was a child, a kid who should have been protected. Instead, I was hurt by the people I should have been able to trust most. When I heard the docuseries was being made, I knew I could no longer remain silent. Doing so made me part of the problem, not the solution. I couldn't sit back and allow more lies about my father and his friends to spread while the survivors remained gagged and silenced."

"It's a lie!" someone screams.

I don't falter. "I'm not the only one. I've been busy these last few weeks, meeting with people like me—survivors of these horrendous parties—and they are here today to share their stories and prove what happened back then. These are rapists and abusers. They are terrible people, and you hail them as heroes, but it will stop. I won't let others be hurt by their memory."

I look at the wings and nod, and one by one, everyone I spoke to enters the stage. I introduce them as they stand behind me, and then I look into the camera. "Some were victims, and some are witnesses who have lived with the regret of not speaking out sooner. Each has the same horrific stories to tell, and it has gone on too long. This world we live in is broken and ruined. The rich are allowed to get away with whatever they want, and it has claimed lives and stolen innocence. Men have been allowed to get away with this for too long, and today, I say enough is enough. I stand with these survivors, and I will shout the truth from the rooftops. I won't let this world forget or turn a blind eye, not anymore, but don't just believe me." I turn and nod, sitting back with Kage, and we listen to stories just like mine.

They share horrific tales of abuse that have my eyes filling with tears, the pure agony and grief in their words connecting with my heart. It's raw and unadulterated, and no one could ever doubt this is real, but I know they will, so when Poe looks at me and nods before stepping back, I turn to the cameras.

"If these stories aren't enough proof, then maybe this is." We all turn to the screens. "Some took videos—for fun or blackmail, I am not sure. I refuse to show you footage of anyone here, but I will show you the ones I'm in. I don't care if it disgusts you or makes you feel pity for me. All I need is your anger. Watch these and tell me this is all a lie."

Kage holds me tighter as the first video loads. When I first saw it, I was sick, but I know it's important. I was around fourteen at the time, still in my school uniform as I tried to do schoolwork while a party went on around me. It's a CCTV shot, and as we watch, my father's bandmate, Westie, doses me with drugs and then pulls me on top of him for everyone to see. We cut it there and load more, of other parties and other angles.

When I look around the room, I see even the cameramen crying, and one even throws up.

"These are just some of the videos we have. There are explicit ones that show the faces of those responsible for sexual assault and pictures taken of victims and their abusers. I won't show them, but they will be used as evidence. I have spent my entire life afraid of this getting out, but I'm not afraid anymore because living in that fear gives our abusers power, and I won't do that for another fucking second." I turn to Louise.

"Fallon." She stares at me, tears streaming down her face. "I—"

"It's okay," I tell her, knowing she's lost for words. "My own mother knew about this and did nothing, neither did anyone else. It was allowed to happen, and it's still allowed to happen. The truth is out now, and it will snowball. The internet is currently being flooded with files we collected, including money trails, pictures, and testimonies. They can't be taken back or hidden, regardless of anyone's reach or power. We are free. We aren't just victims, we are survivors, and today, we tell our stories. I'm tired of being cast as your villain just because I'm angry and a woman. You can move on without forgiveness, and that's what I plan to do—move on and not hide. I won't give them an inch of power over my future. They have my past, and that's all. What we need is change, in our name and theories." Evelyn's and Lennie's faces show on the screen.

"And consequences for those who are sitting in the crowd, knowing they either let this happen or took part, or those watching at home who are scared their faces will show. Even my father, who is applauded even in death, should be forgotten. All the information I've gathered, along with my witnesses and lists, will be handed over to police after this broadcast is finished," I inform them, eyeing the crowd. "I came here to tell my truth, the one you were all demanding through that docuseries, but also to keep the people I love safe." I glance at Kage. "To keep the other survivors like me safe, so what happened to Evelyn won't happen to us."

"You are suggesting they killed Evelyn Mitchel?" Louise whispers. "Who?"

"Yes, to silence her like they tried to silence me." I take a deep breath. "I'm aware this is a lot to take in—"

A noise has us all turning. It's Westie, and he's on his feet in the crowd. I didn't know if he would come, but he did, and there he stands, full of righteous fury. His face is flooded with panic, as he knows his reputation and life is ruined. "You are destroying our lives, you bitch!" The crowd gasps as he rushes past the cameramen, pulling a knife from his coat, and my eyes widen in horror as screams fill the air.

Cameras topple over as people rush forward.

Time seems to slow, and I realize my mistake.

I thought I was safe now, but I was wrong.

His eyes are narrowed and enraged, and I see my death in his gaze. He's taking me down with him.

I was once his little princess, his dirty little secret, and it seems he's willing to kill to get his revenge. I have no doubt he was behind everything. He might have had help, but he's the one here, barreling toward me.

I don't look away. I can't. If I'm going to die today, I will look my murderer in the eye. I will let him see my fury and my legacy that he can't stop, even if he kills me. What I forgot about, though, is Kage.

He grabs me and turns us, covering me with his body just as Westie leaps at us. I stare up into his dark eyes as he jerks, wincing. The crowd screams, and I hear people running, including our guards, as Kage jerks twice more.

"Die, you fucking bitch!" Westie screams. "You stupid fucking whore. You deserve—let me at her!" I peek over Kage's shoulder to see him being dragged away. "She fucking deserved it! She fucking asked for it. She wanted us. They all did! We were rock stars!"

"Kage," I whisper, looking up into his eyes, my hands going to his cheeks as he swallows.

"Are you okay, sweetheart?" he croaks.

"I'm fine." I slide my hands down his back, and I feel something wet. For a moment, my brain can't figure out what it is, and I lift my hand to see them covered in blood.

It's his. My eyes widen as I scream and struggle out of his arms. He groans and falls back, hitting the floor. I drop to my knees as blood pools around me and soaks into the hem of my dress. I slide my hands over him, seeing blood seeping through his shirt.

"You've been stabbed," I blurt. "You've been stabbed!" I lift my head. "He's been stabbed! Help me! Someone, anyone, help!" I scream.

"Sweetheart." Kage reaches for my hand, covering it. "Shh, it's okay."

"Help me!" Help me!" I beg, but the studio is in chaos.

"Oh god," I hear someone whisper, but I look down at Kage. He's pale and blinking a lot. That's not good, right? Shit, what do you do when someone's been stabbed? I try to remember, but my brain won't work. "You're going to be okay," I promise him. "Get help!" I roar.

"Help is coming, Fallon!" Elijah replies. I can feel people around us, but I only focus on Kage as he reaches up and cups my face. I lean into it as tears spill from my eyes.

"I'm sorry. I'm so sorry," I blabber.

"Shh, it's okay. You're okay. That's all that matters." His voice is softer than it should be. "I'm so sorry, baby. I can't keep my promise to be with you forever, but I'm glad I got to love you, even for a little while."

"No. No." I shake my head, pressing my hand to his chest to try to stop the bleeding, but it soaks into my dress, turning it red. "Help is coming. You'll be fine. You hear me?"

"Baby, it's okay," he soothes.

"No, don't you dare die. I forbid it, you hear me? You can't die. I order you not to," I snap, pressing harder as he groans.

His skin is pale and too clammy, and the puddle around us is too big. He's losing too much blood. Did Westie hit something vital?

"Please, Kage," I beg, a sob bursting from my chest as I stare into his eyes. He's giving up. "You can't make me love you and then leave me. You don't get to do that. You don't get to make me happy, make me want to live again, and do this. You don't get to. Do you hear me? I'm ordering you. I'm ordering you to stay with me." I make my voice firm despite my trembling lips and tears.

His smile is bright despite it. "You're so beautiful when you're mad. I think that's one order I won't be able to keep, sweetheart. I'm sorry."

"Please, I can't do this without you." I lift him into my arms, pressing my forehead to his as I kiss him, tasting blood on his lips. "I can't."

"Yes, you can." He groans in pain. "You always could. You never needed me, but I'm so damn thankful you had me. You're a fighter, so fight, and I'll be waiting for you in the next life, okay? We are eternal, remember? We'll see each other again, I promise."

"No. No. You don't get to say goodbye," I snap, looking around at the terrified and crying people around me. "Help me!"

"Where is the medic?" Elijah screams.

"Fallon. Fallon . . ." I look back down at Kage as his lips tremble, one tear slipping from his lower lashes. "I love you, sweetheart. I always did and always will."

"No, don't say that. You aren't saying goodbye. I'll go get help." I try to pull away, but he reaches up.

"Don't," he rasps, his hand shaking against my face. "Just let me look at you. Let my last vision be of you. Please, that's all I ask."

Shaking my head, I sob harder. "I can't lose you. Just stay with me, okay? They are coming." His eyes start to flutter shut as he coughs, and I hold him tighter. "Just hold on a bit longer, okay?"

"Okay, sweetheart." His words are slurred, and I hate it.

"I'm here. I'm right here."

"Can you sing for me?" he croaks.

Sobbing, I force a random song out, and he smiles even as his eyes flutter shut again. Hugging his head to my chest, I keep singing, and when the song is finished, I trail off. "Kage?" I whisper in fear. He doesn't respond, and I can't stop the sobs shaking my body. "Please, just hold on," I beg him. "I'll sing you any song you want. I'll do anything you want, just don't go."

There's no answer.

"Please," I cry, rocking him in my arms. "Please, help me." I can't even see past the tears blurring my vision as I hold him in my arms.

He's silent and unmoving.

"Please, please, please," I whisper over and over. "Please don't take him from me." Pulling away, I cup his jaw and stare down into the face I have memorized over and over again, the one I took for granted. "I love you," I tell him for the first time. "Do you hear me? I love you, so wake up right now. You wake up right now. I love you."

A laugh makes my head spin, and through blurred eyes, I see Westie lying on the floor feet away, his arms and legs tied while a guard pins him. "How does it feel," he spits, "to lose again?"

My eyes drop to Kage, and I begin singing again, holding him while we wait for help—help that comes too late.

FORTY-TWO

Fallon

Elijah is trying to talk to me, but I can't hear him.

I stare down at my hands, which are red, and blink as I glance at my dress. The entire hem and front are covered in Kage's dried blood. I know I have it elsewhere as well. I should wash, but I can't seem to bring myself to.

That's all I have left of him.

That and the ring on my finger, our shared ring, now stained with his blood from protecting me.

The bright white of the waiting room at the hospital hurts my eyes. I don't even know how I got here. It's all a blur. Once the paramedics surrounded him, everything went so fast. We were flown to this hospital, and I've been kept out of the room . . . .

He didn't hear.

I don't know why, but the thought that he will never hear that I love him for the first time makes me want to scream.

"Fallon," Elijah snaps, and I lift my head to see him. His eyes are red, and he's still crying, but he's more composed than I am. "I need you to tell me what to do. I'm yours now. I signed a contract with Kage that I would work for him and you . . . so now you. What do you want me to do? Please, tell me what to do."

"I'm not your boss. He's your boss," I whisper as I look back at my hands. "It's dry. The dress will be ruined," I murmur. I don't care, not really, but it's all I can think to say.

"Fallon, what do we do?" They are all looking at me, but the truth is, I don't know. "I was told Westie is in custody. He'll be . . . He won't get away with it, and with the evidence you handed over for abuse, he's going to go away for a long time," Elijah tells me.

"Not long enough," I retort, the numbness morphing into anger. "Why should he get to live? Why?" I shake my head, a dark idea coming to mind. "Everyone else uses their money and power to get away with everything, and so will I."

"What do you mean?" Elijah asks as I thrust to my feet.

"Find out where he is being held," I demand. "Now." Elijah hurries away. I don't even know where my phone is or what the news is showing, but I don't care.

I head over to the closed double doors he's behind. "I'll make them pay," I tell him as I place my bloody hand on the door. "I'll make them all pay for what they did to you." Turning away, I head down the hall, my heels clacking as I walk. Elijah is at the end, just hanging up the phone.

"I know where he is."

"Take me to him," I order.

"Fallon, this is a bad idea," Elijah hisses, but I ignore him and the police chief. We bribed him, and when that didn't work, we threatened him.

I used my power and money to get what I want. It should make me feel sick, but it doesn't. I'm just playing the game they created.

Ignoring them, I open the door that leads to the interrogation room. It's empty except for Westie, and when I glance at the camera, the light goes off. I'm free to do whatever I want, just like them.

He lifts his head from the metal table, his eyes widening when he sees me. He looks weak and defeated for once. Gone is the man who haunts my nightmares, and in his place is the monster that hides within—the one who raped and abused girls and boys for fun.

His delusion is almost as big as his audacity, but then again, he is a man.

"So he's dead then?" He laughs. "Shame, I was aiming for you. He was really talented when he wasn't distracted by your pussy, but I get it. It's a good pussy—" His head snaps to the side from the force of my hit. His chained hands struggle against the table, where they are cuffed, stopping him from standing.

He spits at me, and I let it hit my face. He swallows as he watches me, no doubt realizing his mistake. "Fallon, look—"

I pull the knife from behind my back, my head tilted as his eyes widen, and he starts to panic, yanking on his cuffs. "I'm sorry, okay? I'm sorry!" When I step closer, he starts to scream. "Shit, help! Someone help!"

"They won't be coming to help you. No one will," I tell him casually as I stroll around him to his other side and press the blade to his chin so he looks at me. "You taught me that. If you use enough pressure and money, you can get whatever you want." He swallows, trying not to move as I press the blade in deeper. "You took the only thing in this world I love away from me. I'm going to do the same for you."

"All of this for revenge?" he snarls.

"No," I murmur as I slide it down his neck. "All of this for love."

Lifting the knife, I aim it at his chest, just like he did Kage's. His scream fills the air for a moment, and I shake it off. I remember the way Kage's blood felt as it pumped from his body.

"Help!" he roars as I go to stab down but change my mind at the last second and slam the knife into the metal table as he screams. "You crazy fucking bitch! You all deserved it! Even that model bitch. She was going to tell. I thought if I took them all away, you'd stop!"

"You killed her," I comment idly.

"Not by my hands," he says. "I hired someone. You know how good our money is. Fallon, stop this now. It's over." The panic in his eyes makes me happy. I can almost taste his fear.

"I was going to kill you, but I won't. I'm not like you. That's what he showed me, and you don't get the mercy of death. You'll live and rot in jail, with everyone knowing what you did. Enjoy prison."

That's where he's heading. I'm sure the police will connect him to Evelyn Mitchel's and Giles Horn's murders. With that and the attack on Kage, he's going away for a long time.

The thought should make me happy, but it doesn't.

I hesitate at the door, my need for vengeance unfulfilled, so I turn back, and he starts to struggle again. Grabbing the knife from the table, I grip his chin as I yank his head up. "Hold still, I don't think I'm a very good artist," I warn as I press the tip of the blade into his forehead.

He screams and struggles as blood runs down his face, making it worse, but I hold him as still as I can, focusing on what I'm carving, and when it's done, I step back, eyeing my work with a numb smile.

"Better, now enjoy prison." I toss the knife and head out, seeing Elijah's wide eyes.

"Is he dead?" he asks.

"No, but he'll wish he were. When he's sentenced, find some people inside and pay them to make his life miserable, but don't kill him. I want him alive and scared every day."

"Jesus, Fallon, you're kind of terrifying," he says as he falls into step at my side.

"Really? I'm not done yet."

We sit in the car as I stare out the window. "You want what?" Elijah asks.

"Take her house. Take everything Westie's wife owns. I want her reputation destroyed. I don't even want anyone to let her stay on their couch. Ruin her," I tell him truthfully. "I don't care how, just do it. I want her to suffer every single day."

"Fallon—"

"Do it," I order as I look back at him. "As for the others, put pressure on the police. I want them to be made aware that they can't fuck this up. Release every single name of every person at those parties. Destroy them all. I want them to suffer like I'm suffering. I want them to feel every drop of the pain I have right now. Do you hear me? I want this entire fucking industry to bleed like he did. I want them to not be able to look at me without being scared. If you can't do it, I will find someone who can. Do you understand me?"

"Yes," he murmurs. "I'll do it for Kage. I have some contacts."

I look away. "Good, make the calls."

While he does that, my eyes catch on the ring on my finger, the other half still on Kage's at the hospital. They should be together.

They are a pair, so they shouldn't be separated.

"It's done," Elijah says sometime later. "The news is already exposing people. Everyone is on your side. The outcry has started. There are walkouts at nearly all major labels. Hell, there is a goddamn riot outside the studio that was hosting the docuseries. You did it, Fallon. You and Kage did it."

It means nothing without him. He should be here to see it. I'm finding victory isn't the same without my partner.

When I don't answer, he lapses into silence, no doubt feeling my fragile mental state. I feel it too, though I am not sure which way it will go. Either I will crawl into a hole and never come out or I will kill everyone.

Either is possible. It should scare me, but it doesn't.

Kage was my reins. He was the one who connected me to this world. He was the one who kept it safe from me, and now he's gone.

Everyone always called me the ice queen, but I don't feel very royal right now. Queens and princesses are supposed to have happily ever afters, right?

So why don't I?

Why must I endure a life filled with tragedy and pain? Do I get a taste of happiness just for it all to be taken away again? What kind of fucked-up world is this where people who hurt others get to live long, blissful lives, yet I'm stuck suffering alone?

It's fucking bullshit.

"What now?" Elijah asks tiredly.

"Now I'm done. Take me home to him."

"Fallon."

I ignore him, my eyes drifting to the window.

Kage is my home and always will be. I want to go home.

I want to go to sleep and never wake up.

I want to be at his side.

FORTY-THREE

Fallon

I dream of him. His warm hand cups my cheek, and he has a bright smile on his face. I don't ever want to wake up. I lean into his hand, soaking in his warmth and his familiar smile, even though he smells odd, like antiseptic.

"Fallon." His voice sounds wrong, distant, and he starts to fade.

"No, don't go," I beg, trying to hold onto him, but he fades into mist, and my head jerks up from where it was resting on the hospital bed. I was asleep?

It was a dream. This is still a dream. He's looking at me, his hand reaching for me as his lips tilt up. "Fallon."

I blink at his pale yet smiling face. "It's just a dream. It's not real," I tell him. "You're . . ."

"Apparently not dead," he jokes.

"Impossible," I whisper brokenly. "It's a dream. They told me there was no hope, that you wouldn't wake up and you were as good as dead."

"Baby, you should know better than to give up on me." His hand finally touches me, cool but alive. I jerk back, falling from my chair. I made Elijah bring me back here despite the doctors' warnings. They said he lost too much blood, and after the surgeries, they didn't think he would wake up, but they tried anyway.

There was hope, just a spark, but I squashed it. He was dead. He was lifeless. I checked myself. I screamed and cried and begged, and he didn't wake up.

"No, this is a dream, just a mean fucking dream," I whisper, tears falling once more. At this point, though, I don't know how I'm still able to cry. "But still, I'll take it. I'll live in this dream with you if I have to."

"Then come here." He holds out his hand. He's lying on his hospital bed, machines beeping at his side. Shouldn't he have the thingy in his nose and mouth? I suppose since it's a dream, he took it out so he could talk. I shuffle closer.

"A mean dream," I murmur, "but I don't care. I love you, Kage. I need you to know that. I love you, and I'll stay right here with you." I grasp his hand, clinging to him even if this isn't real.

"Does this feel like a dream?" He squeezes my hand and tugs me closer. "Don't I feel real? How about now?" He pulls me down and kisses me softly. "Do I taste like a dream?" he murmurs against my lips. "I'm alive, baby. Now what's this about you loving me?"

"It's you. It's really you," I whisper, my eyes widening. "You're awake!"

He laughs, but I try to stumble away.

"Doctors!" I yell.

"They came in while you were sleeping, apparently just as shocked as you were. I have a long road of recovery ahead of me, but I'm stubborn and alive. How could I leave you when you asked me to stay?" He pulls me back to his side. "Just come here and hold me, that's all I need. Just stay right here forever."

"I promise." I lean in, looking into his eyes. "Are you really okay?"

"I'm okay, sweetheart," he vows, kissing me again. "Now, about this love—"

"Don't push it," I tease before I sober. "I love you. I should have said it sooner."

His face softens, and despite the pain he must be in, he pulls me closer. "I knew you loved me, Fallon, even if you could never say the words. It was in your eyes when you looked at me, in your kiss, your touch, your words, and your actions. You might have been unable to say it, but you showed me a thousand ways, and I would have died a happy man knowing that."

Shaking my head, I wipe at my tears as I lean my head into him. "I thought I lost you forever," I whisper before sitting up, narrowing my eyes on him. "Don't do that shit again, okay?"

His smile is so bright, it might as well have the sun trapped inside. "I won't promise not to protect you because I'll always choose saving you over myself, but I promise to try to stay alive."

"For as long as I am," I order. "You don't get to die before me, okay? I don't want to live in a world without you." It's something I realized when I stared at his silent body. Kage rearranged my world and put himself in the center, and now I don't want to live without him—not that I can't, but I don't want to.

"The moon doesn't exist without the sun," I remind him.

His eyes smolder as he watches me, and he tugs me closer until I'm practically lying on him despite the fact he nearly died hours ago. I try to move away, but he holds me in place. "And the sun can't exist without the moon. There isn't a world in this universe where I would want to live without you, Fallon. Don't you see that? The choice was easy for me. I only exist for you, and you exist to show the world strength and beauty and passion. I would die a thousand deaths to keep you safe. I won't apologize for that, but I am sorry it hurt you. I'm sorry you were scared."

"I wonder if your fans know you're such a sentimental bastard," I choke out, and we both grin. "Just don't leave me."

"Never," he promises as I carefully lay my head on his side. "Now get some sleep, you look exhausted."

I intend to stay awake and look after him, but he's right. I'm exhausted. It must finally win out because before I even know it, I'm slipping back into a deep sleep.

Only this time, I want to wake up.

K♥F
Golden Love
I'll be with you.
I'll wait for you.
Golden Love
Can't you see
I'm your fool?

FORTY-FOUR

KAGE

I watch the slow, even rise and fall of her chest as she sleeps. She's a complete mess, still covered in blood, yet I can't look away. I saw the agony of losing me in her eyes, and if I doubted how Fallon felt before, I never will now.

For the woman who said she would never love, she truly loves deeply. I was happy to spend my life loving her with nothing in return, but knowing she loves me back is a heady feeling, and I don't need the rapid beeping of the machine to tell me my heart is racing at the thought.

The door to my room opens a crack, Elijah's head popping through. When he sees me awake, he rushes inside, practically flinging himself at me. "They told me you were awake. I didn't—"

"Shh." I point at Fallon. I might like Elijah, might even call him a friend, but if he wakes my woman, I will end him.

He nods in understanding, bringing another chair closer and running his eyes over me. "The doctor said you were awake, said it was a miracle. You want to know what I told them?" I tilt my head, watching him even as I brush my hand over Fallon's head to keep her asleep. "Nothing is impossible when it comes to Kage, not if it has to do with his girl." His eyes go to Fallon. "I knew you'd never leave her alone, not even in death, you crazy bastard."

I can't help but smirk, following his eyes to her. "True. What happened while I was out?"

"Uh . . ." He looks uncomfortable for a moment, and when I raise an eyebrow, he sighs. "I told her I worked for her now, just in case you . . ."

"Died," I supply.

"Yup, that. She was pissed, and then she did like a *Carrie* revenge thing and had me bribe some cops." He explains everything that happened in detail since I passed out. I can't help my smile, and when he's done, I look at Fallon once more.

"I fucking love this woman."

"You better. Trust me, you don't want to be her enemy." He goes quiet for a moment. "Are you really okay?"

"I will be. Getting stabbed hurts like a bitch though," I admit.

"Yeah, I bet." He laughs. "The public is eating it up—not just your heroic save, but everything. It's insane out there. They had to call in help to keep control of the riots taking place outside the studio. The news stations are rerunning it over and over too, so there is no getting away from it now. Fallon was right, she needed the public, and they are supporting her like she thought. She'll get justice; they all will. They can't do anything but. Hell, I don't think the music industry will ever be the same again."

"Good, it shouldn't be. My girl is changing the world, and I'm so fucking proud of her," I admit. "Keep an eye out for any threats against her or the others. She wouldn't like it if someone got hurt because of her plan."

"Already on it." He smiles at me. "Trust me, remember? Just rest, you deserve it." He stands, putting the chair back into place before grabbing a blanket from the corner and carefully laying it over Fallon.

He offers me another soft smile, and I know I made the right choice with Elijah. He'll look after her like he does me. He'll protect her and lead her like he does me. It's not about money or fame for him—it never was—it's about the journey, and I'm glad he is here for ours.

"Oh, Kage? You should know she refused to leave you, even for a moment. I know you've been in love with Fallon for years, but it seems like she loves you too. What a great match, huh? You're both fucking insane."

"Rude," Fallon grumbles. "Your voice is so loud, Elijah."

His eyes widen, and he glances from me to her before he ducks out of the room, rushing away. "I'll kill him later," I say since I'm trapped in bed. "Go back to sleep, baby."

"I am." She sighs sleepily, and within moments, her breathing deepens again.

I know I should rest, but I just watch her. I thought I'd never see her again. I was always determined to live my life with her to the fullest, but now, I'll never waste a second.

I fight the exhaustion until it finally pulls me under.

My last image is the love of my life.

I spend a week in the hospital. The doctors mean well, but they are annoying, and Fallon has taken it upon herself to ensure I receive not only the best care, but that I also follow their orders, which means no sleeping with her in my arms or fucking her senseless despite my insistence. She's firm, keeping me in check, and I'll admit I'm brooding—or sulking, as she calls it.

I want our home, our bed, and my girl under me, but from the determined glint in her eyes, I know that won't happen yet.

"Doctor, repeat that again," I order him.

He sighs, no doubt regretting his choice to become a doctor because of me. "You are safe to go home."

"And repeat the second bit," Fallon demands, glaring at me, refusing to back down.

"As long as you get plenty of rest. Your body needs to heal," he grumbles. "Like I have said thirteen times. It hasn't changed. We'll process the release papers right now, and you will be given all the medication you need. We'll also provide checkups in person to ensure you're healing."

"See? I'm free." I smirk.

"To rest," she points out.

"Semantics." I wink. "Doc, how long before I can have sex?"

I swear the old doctor's face couldn't turn more purple, and for a moment, he looks at the ceiling as if praying for help.

"Strenuous activity is not advisable for the near future. We'll sign off on it once you are completely healthy."

"What if it isn't strenuous? What if she's on top and I do nothing?" I ask seriously.

He coughs, glancing at Fallon, who simply rolls her eyes. "Um, I would say no."

My frown is dark, and he swallows hard.

"I'll go process those papers now." As he hurries to the door, I swear I hear him mutter, "I should have become a dentist."

I look at Fallon, pouting. "At least take me home."

"Fine, but to rest," she snaps as she stands.

"Will you be my nurse?" I run my eyes down her body. "In a little outfit?"

"I'll be your fucking jailer," she warns as she leans in, brushing her lips across mine. "And I won't touch you until every single fucking doctor in this hospital has signed off on you being okay."

"Don't challenge me, Fallon. We both know I'll win." I'll get a fucking contract for all of them if I need to. Nobody keeps me from touching my girl, not even her.

Smirking, she leans back. "I'll pack your things. Let's go home."

FORTY-FIVE

Fallon

It doesn't surprise me that the press is congregated around my house when we arrive. Elijah has been fielding more requests for a statement or interviews than any other assistant ever has. We ignore them as we drive through. They slap the car, shouting questions, but Kage's guards force a path through them, and the gate shuts behind us. They will probably scale the wall to get a picture, so when I get out, I tug down my sunglasses and help Kage out. I take his hand and let him lean on me, but it looks like we are just walking together. He would hate to appear weak in front of them.

It doesn't matter that the cameras captured everything—my sobbing confessions and songs to him, his declaration of love for me as he was dying—I won't give them more. This part of our life is ours, not theirs.

By the time we make it inside, he's breathing heavily and wobbling. "Can you make it upstairs?"

"Me? I'm fine." He looks at the stairs, jaw clenching, and I turn to one of the guards. "Bring a bed frame from a spare room into the living room."

"I'm fine—"

I ignore him and lead him toward the living room. "Then do it for me," I implore, and he relents. I lean him against the wall as I move furniture and prepare everything for him. The guards work quickly, assembling the bed and bedding, and I add a side table with his medication and some drinks before turning on the record player. A soothing song fills the air as I help him into bed, smoothing the covers around him.

"Join me," he orders, reaching for me.

"In a bit. I'm going to cook you something." His eyebrows rise and his eyes widen, since we both know I can't cook for shit. "Okay, I'm going to watch while Helena cooks you something, and then you will eat and sleep or I'll take you back to the hospital."

"Such a mean nurse." He sighs as he settles in, closing his eyes despite his words. I leave him to nap, and when I come back with food, I help him sit up and hand feed him every bite. When he's done, I carefully read the instruction leaflet for his medication and administer that before settling him back, then I climb in next to him, curling into his side.

"The world wants answers," he starts.

"The world can wait," I snap. "They will get us when we're ready, not before. Just rest, it's my turn to look after you now."

We spend the entire week sleeping, eating, and relaxing. We don't speak of what happened or anything going on outside. I avoid the news and my phone, instead just spending time with him. I know this can't last forever, but we deserve it, and Elijah agrees, keeping everyone away as much as he can. When the doctor for Kage's daily checkup leaves, Elijah fidgets nervously in the doorway.

"What is it?" I ask, my eyes going back to Kage as he pulls his shirt down. He'll have three wicked scars, but we both know it will only make me want him more.

Yes, I've kept my rule—no fucking—though it is hard. I wake with him feeling me up or his hands shoved into my underwear nearly every morning. I have the will of a fucking saint to resist his constant teasing and pressure, but I won't let him hurt himself, not even if I'm craving him as badly as he craves me.

I'm not an animal, I can go without, or so I tell myself, but I know I'm eyeing him like he's a piece of meat, and he smirks when he catches me. "Come touch instead of staring."

Jerking my gaze from him, I narrow my eyes on Elijah. "Well?" He gets the brunt of my sexual frustration, though he doesn't say anything about it.

"The police are here. I've been putting them off for the last two weeks, but they are insisting they need to speak to both of you." He shifts uncomfortably. "What should I do?"

I glance at Kage before sighing and getting to my feet. "Let them into the kitchen. We'll be there in a minute." Heading over to Kage, I cup his face. "Let's get this over with. We both knew they would be here sooner or later." Taking his hand, I let him lead me to the kitchen, where two detectives sit.

They stand as we enter, and I gesture for them to sit as we take the chairs opposite them. "My assistant tells me you need to speak to us."

"We want to keep you both informed about the investigation. We're thankful for all the evidence you collected. It's been a big help. We're not the only agency working on this now, and I have no doubt it will only continue to snowball, but we wanted you to know there will be no escape from this. The evidence is damning, and those names you gave us? They stand no chance. It might not be tomorrow or in a month, but they will get their comeuppance, and you'll have your justice. We thought it was important to tell you that. Their money and power can't protect them now."

"Too late for Evelyn or Lennie," I reply, even though it isn't their fault. "Thank you for telling us. I can't wait to watch this unfold and for justice to be served."

"And on behalf of everyone in our field, we want to apologize for our failures thus far. It won't happen again." They both nod to me as they stand. "If you find anything else or need anything, please don't hesitate to contact us. We'll try not to bother you, since we know how busy you are." The one on the left grins. "We're all big fans."

I can't help but smile. "Thank you, it means a lot. Elijah will see you out."

I watch them go, and I realize there's something I need to do—something important.

I sneak out while Kage is napping, something he says he doesn't need but continues to do every day. It's adorable, actually, watching him fight it. I take guards with me, and we manage to get away from the paparazzi fairly easily, so when we pull up at the cemetery, we're left in peace.

I don't know why, but I knew she would be here. Leaving my guards at the car, I clutch the flowers I brought and head her way. She smiles when she sees me, and I crouch, laying the flowers on the grave.

"I'm sure you heard, but the world remembers you now. They know your story, and you'll have your justice for what they did to you," I tell Lennie and her mother, Mrs. Miller. When I stand and step back, her mother takes my hand.

"All thanks to you," she murmurs. "Thank you, Fallon."

"Thank you for trusting me with your daughter's story and legacy." We both lapse into silence, staring at the grave that has been her mother's jail.

"Will you be okay?" I murmur. She has spent years fighting for justice, for her daughter's memory, and now that it's over, what will she have left to keep her going? Her whole life is frozen in time, so when it begins to thaw, what will remain?

"In time," she replies.

"What will you do now?" I ask, glancing at her.

"I think I'll move. This city holds nothing but bad memories, and I think it's time. I can finally think about my daughter without feeling guilty. You gave me that. You gave me a second chance. I'll never forget what happened, but I want to live my remaining years as happy as I can for her, in her name."

We share a sad smile, both of us wishing her daughter were here to live it with her. "Will you check on her from time to time for me?" she asks sadly, glancing back at her daughter. "I don't want her to be lonely here."

"Absolutely," I promise, squeezing her hand. "She'll be happy you're finally moving on. I know I would be. She's lucky to have a mother like you."

She blushes. "I just did what any mother would."

"No, not any mother. Just because you gave birth to her doesn't mean you had to do all this. Some wouldn't. Most, in fact, but you did. You are a wonderful mother, and she was very lucky. I would have done anything to have a mother who loved me as deeply as you loved her."

"Then I'm sorry you never did. You are a wonderful person, Fallon. You deserve to be loved." She glances back at her daughter and smiles. "It's not goodbye forever, my angel, just for now."

"I'll see you soon," I promise. No matter how busy we get or where we are in the world, I will come back here and bring flowers for the girl who deserved to live.

Once we say our goodbyes, we linger for a moment. "Are you ready?" I ask her.

"I am." She looks at her daughter's grave once more before turning away and walking with me.

I hold her hand as we walk out of the cemetery and toward our futures, leaving the past where it lies, but we'll visit from time to time, if only to say hello to the ghosts that await us.

K F
Golden Love
I'll be with you.
I'll wait for you.
Golden Love
Can't you see
I'm your fool?

FORTY-SIX

KAGE

Three months later . . .

Our industry is still in anarchy after what Fallon did. Some record labels haven't been able to recover, while others are scrambling to slip into their empty spots and force bands who once might have sunk to swim.

One thing is very clear though—nothing will ever be the same after that fateful day, and Fallon loves it. She loves the fear and respect she demands now. She was so worried about how people would treat her, that they would look down on her for what she survived, but if anything, they love her that much more. Her fans have taken over the world, demanding justice in her name and pushing her to new heights.

Oh, and Hall Movies? Well, their CEO, Mr. Perrier, swiftly stepped down with an apology, but everyone knows they won't be able to recover from their bad image unless something drastic is done. I heard a rumor they brought in a wild card in his spot, an ex-actress with a mean streak, but I guess only time will tell.

Evelyn Mitchel's funeral was a huge affair, the outpouring of love like nothing I have ever seen. My girl spoke on that day of her strength and passion, and even from beyond the grave, her name and legacy will live on, helping those who need it.

As for us?

I've healed up nicely, and I have the signed paper in my back pocket to prove it, with all three hundred doctors' signatures on it. She might have been joking when she told me she wanted all the doctors to sign off on me, but I made it happen. She should know I don't joke when it comes to her. It wasn't easy either because some of them were in different countries on vacation, but Elijah helped make it happen. I patiently wait for her to finish in the recording studio. I'll give it to her tonight, along with my other surprise. For now, we have music to make.

She rushes in, handing coffees out to everyone in the booth before blowing me a kiss as she heads inside, settling in with her headphones on. My girl smiles more, and I love it. She seems so much freer since everything came out.

It's as if those ghosts that haunted her no longer have power. I know it's not the truth, since she will always bear the pain and scars of what she endured and she has nightmares every now and then, but they are far less frequent, and I'm proud of how hard she's fighting for her future.

We haven't given many interviews since everything happened, only one or two to keep the bloodhounds at bay, otherwise we have been busy healing and making music. Oh, and Fallon decided to start a foundation for survivors of childhood sexual abuse, mainly catering to those affected by the fallout of what they have dubbed "Electric Downfall." She's poured her heart into it and is helping so many people, giving them safety and security for the first time maybe ever, as well as opportunities within this industry if they want them.

They called her the ice queen, but staring at her now, I wonder how they ever could. She is nothing but a flowing river, filled with life and vibrancy.

She has that raw kind of beauty that makes others sit up taller and try harder, and when she starts to sing, all of that flows into her music, bringing people to tears.

Even me.

I made the king fall then I walked away.

Heartless, that's what they call me.

Well maybe I am, but the organ is yours.

All yours, my beautiful blue boy . . .

I can't help but grin as she sings our love song, her eyes on me.

Yes, Fallon is a legend, but it turns out, so am I for capturing the elusive ice queen and making her love me. Little do they know, it was my plan all along.

Now, I only have one more thing to do—make her mine forever.

FORTY-SEVEN

Fallon

Kage left the studio earlier since he had a meeting with the producers of our upcoming concert. It means I can continue recording, and when I'm satisfied and exhausted, I head home, hoping he will be there. I can't wait to crawl into bed with him and sleep, but when I get there, it's quiet.

Too quiet.

Opening the front door, I peer inside, frowning as his crooning voice fills the air, soft and loving. The lyrics and music are unfamiliar.

"Kage?" I call as I shut the door. I can't see the guards anywhere, which is strange. They have become a constant in our lives, something Kage won't compromise on. "Kage?" I call again as I head deeper into the house.

I freeze, gaping at the sight before me. Kage is wearing a suit, the deep V of the black, glittering jacket exposing his chest and a new tattoo I haven't seen before—a dahlia, if I'm not mistaken. His pants are perfectly pressed, and his hair is slicked back. He is surrounded by more dahlias than I have ever seen. They cover every surface, with candles and lanterns hanging from the ceiling, the flickering flames making everything extra romantic. When my eyes connect with his, he smiles, offering me his hand.

Stepping down the carefully created path between the flowers, I lay my hand in his. "What is this?" I ask softly as I look around, his voice crooning over the speakers.

"Fallon, you are the love of my life. You know that. I haven't made it a secret." I can't help but laugh, and he grins. "There is only one more thing to do so everyone, including you, knows I'm not going anywhere."

"Kage . . ." I frown, a feeling welling in my chest.

Adrenaline maybe?

"We're taking root, like these flowers, baby," he promises. "We'll keep growing together, keep loving and finding happiness." He drops to his knees. "I will stay here, on my knees for the rest of my life. It's yours, as am I. Fallon, my love, will you marry me? Will you make me yours?"

As I stare into his hopeful eyes, there is only one thing I can say, and the word rolls from my tongue before I can even think it. My usual perfect composure disappears in the face of his devotion. "Yes," I whisper.

His eyes widen as if he thought he would have to fight me, and honestly, I did too. He leaps to his feet and slides the biggest rock I have ever seen onto my finger. It's black with blue stones surrounding it and so beautiful I could cry. "No taking it off now," he says as he kisses me deeply. "You're going to be my wife, Fallon."

I swallow at that word, staring into his eyes as fear suddenly takes root. I don't want him to have regrets, so he needs to know.

"I don't want children." I say it as a passing comment, another excuse for him to change his mind before it's too late. I swallow and repeat it, filled with prideful hurt. "I don't ever want children."

He simply smiles. "I'm not marrying you for the children you could give me. I'm marrying you because I'm in love with you and can't imagine my life without you. It's your body, your choice. I don't need kids to be happy. I just need you."

"I can't do it, Kage," I whisper, my voice fearful but also filled with understanding.

"You don't owe me or anyone an explanation."

"But I want you to know why. I don't think I would be a good mother. I'm too cold, too filled with pain and anger to hold them softly. I might have my mother's insecure, quiet voice, never defending or loving them enough. I could have my father's anger and righteousness, meaning I might not speak to them with kindness or love. I don't want to pass on what they passed to me. It's my legacy, and it will die with me. A child or children would deserve better than me as a mother. I'm too broken to care for another, but Kage, if I would have kids with anyone, it would be with you."

Taking a deep breath, he cups my face and stares deep into my eyes, as if to make sure I hear him. "You never need to care for me, be gentle, or hold back your anger. I mean it, Fallon. Children or no children, I'm marrying you, but just know, you would be an amazing mother. You were born for more than making another generation though. Just because you have a womb doesn't mean you have to use it. I want to marry you because I love you, because I can't live without you. No other reason."

I search his eyes, seeing the truth there, and I almost slump in relief. I should have known better. Kage made his feelings for me very clear. He wants me however he can get me, and he would never try to tell me what to do or have expectations of me. Maybe that's unhealthy, but it's also a relief when all I have ever known is love with strings.

"I love you, my fiancé," I tell him, and he smiles, tugging me into his arms.

"I love you too, my beautiful fiancée." He kisses my head. "We're getting married as soon as possible. I can't have you overthinking it and changing your mind."

I giggle as he wraps me in his arms, and with his love song filling the air and the flowers spread around us, we rock to the music, our hearts beating in sync.

A smile I will never be rid of curves my lips as he sings along to his song in my ear, giving me my very own show.

We stay like that for a while, just rocking to the soft melody, our eyes and bodies locked together until he pulls back when the next song finishes.

"Oh, I forgot to give you this." He pulls out a piece of paper, and I burst into laughter as he holds me up, grinning.

I scan the words, my smile only growing. It's a signed document saying he is healthy and can resume normal activities, and there are more signatures than I have ever seen. When I glance at him, he wiggles his eyebrows as he leans in and kisses me. "That means that tonight and every night after, you're mine, Fallon."

Gripping his neck, I slide my hands up into his hair and mess it up as I grin. "No, it means you're mine," I purr as I lean in and kiss him.

The music continues to spill around the room, the candles flickering as we kiss. It's filled with love, both of us knowing we have all the time in the world now. His hands slide down my back as my own massage his shoulders, and he lays me down on the floor, right there in the dahlia petals.

Our lips never break apart. My air is his air.

We went from being two strangers to two people who mean the most to each other in the entire world.

Kage is willing to die for me, but most importantly, he was willing to live for me and stand before me when the nightmares came. He became my shield, my safe place, my lover, and now, my everything.

I never believed in true love, but he's making a believer out of me.

He swallows my moan, leisurely sliding his hands up my body. He's already memorized every inch, but every time he touches me, it's like the first time. He turns my head and presses soft kisses all over my cheeks and neck and then moves back up, kissing my nose and then my eyes so they shut.

"My beautiful fiancée, I have waited for you for so long," he whispers as my hands slide down his jacket and part it. "You're never getting away from me. We'll always be together."

"Together," I murmur as my eyes open, and I sit up. Our lips meet in a flurry again as we work to undo his jacket, never once breaking the kiss. He rips it off and tosses it away before standing. He undoes his slacks and slowly pushes them down. His hard erection springs free before he falls to his knees. Sliding his hands up my legs, he takes my dress with them, his lips trailing kisses over skin others scarred and abused.

His butterfly soft touches have me reaching for him. "I love you," I blurt, unable to stop myself.

His smile is slow and sexy. "I know, sweetheart. I've always known. Now let me show you how much I adore you, how much I love and cherish you."

Gripping my dress, he pulls it up and over my head. His eyes land on my white lace bra next. Reaching around, I unhook it and let it fall with the rest of our clothes. He hooks his fingers in my matching panties and pulls them from me so we're both bare.

We reach for each other, our lips crashing together as I fall back with him between my parted thighs where he belongs.

Our hands slide over each other's skin with soft, loving touches. Lifting my leg, he runs his hand down my thigh as I hook it over his hip, and when his length presses against my entrance, I whisper his name, knowing how he loves it when I do.

Groaning, he presses his forehead against mine, our eyes locked as he slowly presses inside me, stretching me around his cock. He fills me to the brim and slowly pulls out, then he pushes back in with a rolling thrust.

It isn't like normal. This isn't us fucking, this is making love, and I can't look away, can't pull myself from the darkness in his gaze.

It used to terrify me, but he's shown me the beauty inside it, and I let it consume me now as our bodies come together. We find our rhythm, moving like we have been together forever and know everything about one another.

Our hands interlace, and he brings them between us, the ring sparkling on my finger as he rolls his hips, making love to me with our promise held between us.

I belong to him, mind, body, and soul.

That would have terrified me before, but I know he will never abuse that. He will never seek to control or use me. He will stand at my side as I take over the world. Kage doesn't want to own me, he wants to love me, and I let him.

When we reach our ultimate end, I will take him with me so we can be together in the next life too. I don't want to spend another minute without him.

"I can't wait for your hair to turn gray and your skin to wrinkle because it means I will have loved you the entire time," he whispers.

"Even when I'm not young and beautiful anymore?" I joke, but it ends in a gasp as he drives into me harder.

"It isn't your face that makes you beautiful, Fallon. When will you see that? I will love you in every form and every way." Leaning down, he kisses me as I lift my hips to meet his thrusts.

Slow pleasure builds within me, commanded by him.

Before him, pleasure was a way to forget, but now it's a way to remember how we fit together and the way we are building a life.

His lips brush over mine. "Let's fall together, my love."

"I'm with you," I tell him, and I am.

As the music reaches its crescendo, so do we. We swallow each other's moans of pleasure as we tumble over the edge together.

When we come back down from that high, we kiss softly, our hands still joined. We are surrounded by the petals of the flowers that brought us together, and with his ring on my finger, I know I'll finally get my happily ever after—the one I have only ever sung about.

He makes those words real, showing me what they really mean.

He gives them meaning, and I will spend the rest of our lives singing them with him.

FORTY-EIGHT

KAGE

Standing on the dark stage, I grin as I soak in the fans chanting and screaming for us. They don't know we're already here, watching and waiting. We're the last acts to perform. Fallon and I prepared this concert, and all money raised will go to those affected by childhood sexual abuse. It's been a huge success. The music industry has called it the concert of the year, maybe even the century. With so many big names, we had to expand the venue to this one, the largest in the country.

There are the Dead Ringers, Reign Harrow, Will Rock, and so many more names, including the smaller bands we handpicked like Sanctuary and Willows. It's been a day of music and enjoying the sun, but now the moon is high in the sky and the anticipation is astronomical.

Looking over at Fallon, I smile, and she winks at me just as the lights come on.

The crowd goes wild, and Fallon's crooning voice fills the air as I watch her, awestruck just as I always am. She captivates the crowd of thousands here and the millions streaming from home. Her blue gown flows behind her as she walks farther onto the stage, performing one of our new songs, and when the guitar shreds, I lift my mic and sing with her. I catch up to her so we are side by side, staring at one another as we sing our wedding vows.

This is what this song is—our promise to love one another no matter what storm arises.

"Not even death could part us," we finish, both panting.

Licking her lips, she turns to the crowd. "Are we having a good time?" They go wild as she grins. "I know I am. We've had some incredible performances tonight, and as you know, it's all for a good cause. Tonight is for everyone who has been affected and for every voice that was silenced or stolen."

I step back as she stands before the mic, one single light falling on her, creating a halo as she performs her new song. "Sun Rising" is a raw ballad, one of struggles, hope, and suffering. It details hers and every survivor's battle, and when it ends, she isn't the only one crying.

I don't bother to wipe away my tears. I let everyone see them as she holds out her hand to me, and I stride forward to her side, gripping her hand as I kiss her cheek softly. I am prouder of her than I have ever been.

"How about one more song?" I call into the mic. "This one, well, it's a new one and not yet released. We know you're going to love it. It's our story. It's our love, our past, present, and future. It's also our protest to this world, our riot. We hope you like it."

We perform it just like that, our eyes on one another, filled with love. It might not be what my fans are used to, but I know they will adore it like I do because it's real, raw, and loving.

I take her hand, and the fans scream as our voices trail off. I lift our clasped hands into the air, showing off our matching wedding bands before I tug her into my arms and dip her in a dramatic kiss, tasting her happiness and laughter.

They didn't get to see our wedding. It was a private affair just for friends, a bohemian meets rock ceremony held behind our houses where we swore our love to one another forever. I wasn't joking when I said I wanted to marry her as quickly as possible, and she looked stunning in her hand-stitched dahlia gown I had made, matching my suit and the flowers overfilling our house and garden.

I know the pictures are up on the screen behind us, telling the world and our fans, and if the ear-shattering screams are any indication, then they are as happy as we are.

Pulling away slightly, I look into her bright eyes.

"My ice queen."

She grins. "My rock star."

Then, for the world to see, I kiss her once more, claiming my wife.

My Fallon.

My entire world.

FORTY-NINE

I can hear the TV from where I'm sitting, and for a moment, I focus on the words the news is spreading.

"The music industry is once again exploding today as one of the biggest tours to ever be announced sells out within seconds. Fallon and Kage have teamed up for a new album, and the world knows by now that you can't separate the iconic duo. Where one goes, the other follows. The newly wed pair are a match made in heaven, even if they are total opposites, and who can forget that moment when Kage took a blade meant for his love? Fallon and Kage are no strangers to press. Just this year alone, they have been the faces of the battle against those who abused so many children during the infamous rock parties in the 90s, and just recently, they won. Every single person involved has been charged, with companies crumbling and legacies ruined. The names of her father and his bandmates have been removed from the Rock and Roll Hall of Fame, replaced by Fallon's after she was given the woman of the year award. As for Westie, who you may remember attacked both Fallon and Kage, he is serving a life sentence. It seems justice has been served, and now Fallon and Kage are ready to claim the world. Can anyone top this unstoppable pair? We don't think so. Stay tuned for all your updates on the world's favorite coup—" It cuts out, and I smile as I run my fingers over the keys of my piano.

I recently moved it to the greenhouse Kage had built for me. It was his wedding present. It connects to the back of our house—yes, ours, because Kage decided to build another house between them and make it one giant mansion while we were on our honeymoon. Still, this is my favorite part. Glass surrounds me on every side, only interrupted by the black framing. Blue-and-purple stained-glass butterflies hang from the ceiling, dancing in the wind. Dahlias cover nearly every inch of it apart from my piano in the center.

Rain slides down the glass panes, the pattering relaxing my soul as I play and hum along to a new song I'm writing.

It's a love song.

All of them are like that now.

When I'm done, I feel him behind me, and he slides onto the bench next to me, his hand finding my back. He's always touching me and connecting in some way. He was bad before, but since we got married, there is no longer an inch of space between us, and I like it.

Ice yawns, stretching out on top of my piano as I grin and kiss her head before playing the keys.

"I like your new song," he murmurs. "It might be my new favorite."

"You say that about every song I write." I grin, sparing him a loving look as he scoots closer. "The news makes it sound like we're taking over the world," I comment.

"We are." He grins, laying his head on my shoulder. "As we should."

"Really? So what's next for us?" I ask him as my fingers dance over the last note.

"Now we enjoy the rest of our lives, our love," he replies, kissing my shoulder. "We do this for an eternity, playing music and loving one another. Wherever it takes us, we'll go together."

"It sounds like a plan." I grin, and he places his hands next to mine, my song intertwining with his in our house.

My previously empty, cold mansion is now filled with love and laughter, all thanks to him.

The ice queen melted, the king fell, and they lived happily ever after—as they should.

EPILOGUE

Pressing the red button to turn off the TV, I let the hotel room lapse into silence, the darkness surrounding me only interrupted by the snores of my bandmates. The rhythmic sound is as familiar as my own breathing, but it's not relaxing my troubled soul enough for me to sleep tonight.

My eyes land on the bed I should be sleeping in, one side of the covers pushed back and empty, the other wrapped tightly around him—the reason I can't sleep.

I stare at his unmoving frame, wishing he were as troubled as I was. I wish he understood why everything is changing yet staying the same all at once.

We are on our way to the top, finally getting our big break with this tour. The world knows our names, and all the tiny shows and empty audiences are finally worth it. All the hours driving in crappy vans across the country, promoting our music, are coming to fruition.

I can't help but miss that simplicity though.

The contract we signed today burns a hole in my bag, the words echoing in my head and heart, reminding me why I am so restless.

I can't have him.

I signed it. It didn't say it in so many words, but it might as well have.

Can I stop these urges and feelings?

I have to if we're going to make it to the top where we all want to be. Right now is our time, and I won't ruin that for us all because of this forbidden love inside me.

He isn't mine, and he can't be, so why do I wish he were?

Why do I wish he would look at me as more than a friend, a band-mate? It's a hopeless dream.

No, I must resist.

I have to.

ABOUT K.A. KNIGHT

K.A Knight is an USA Today bestselling indie author trying to get all of the stories and characters out of her head, writing the monsters that you love to hate. She loves reading and devours every book she can get her hands on, and she also has a worrying caffeine addiction.

She leads her double life in a sleepy English town, where she spends her days writing like a crazy person.

Read more at K.A Knight's website or join her Facebook Reader Group.

Sign up for exclusive content and my newsletter here
http://eepurl.com/drLLoj

OTHER BOOKS BY K.A. KNIGHT

CONTEMPORARY

LEGENDS AND LOVE *CONTEMPORARY RH*

Revolt

Rebel

Riot

PRETTY LIARS *CONTEMPORARY RH*

Unstoppable

Unbreakable

PINE VALLEY *CONTEMPORARY*

Racing Hearts

DEN OF VIPERS UNIVERSE STANDALONES

Scarlett Limerence *CONTEMPORARY*

Nadia's Salvation *CONTEMPORARY*

Alena's Revenge *CONTEMPORARY*

Den of Vipers *CONTEMPORARY RH*

Gangsters and Guns (Co-Write with Loxley Savage) *CONTEMPORARY RH*

FORBIDDEN READS *(STANDALONES)*

Daddy's Angel *CONTEMPORARY*

Stepbrothers' Darling *CONTEMPORARY RH*

STANDALONES

The Standby *CONTEMPORARY*

Diver's Heart *CONTEMPORARY RH*

DYSTOPIAN

THEIR CHAMPION SERIES *Dystopian RH*

The Wasteland

The Summit

The Cities

The Nations

Their Champion Coloring Book

Their Champion - the omnibus

The Forgotten

The Lost

The Damned

Their Champion Companion - the omnibus

PARANORMAL

THE LOST COVEN SERIES *PNR RH*

Aurora's Coven

Aurora's Betrayal

HER MONSTERS SERIES *PNR RH*

Rage

Hate

Book 3 - *coming soon..*

COURTS AND KINGS *PNR RH*

Court of Nightmares

Court of Death

Court of Beasts

Court of Heathens - coming soon..

THE FALLEN GODS SERIES *PNR*

Pretty Painful

Pretty Bloody

Pretty Stormy

Pretty Wild

Pretty Hot

Pretty Faces

Pretty Spelled

Fallen Gods - the omnibus 1

Fallen Gods - the omnibus 2

FORGOTTEN CITY *PNR*

Monstrous Lies

Monstrous Truths

Monstrous Ends

SCIENCE FICTION

DAWNBREAKER SERIES *SCI FI RH*

Voyage to Ayama

Dreaming of Ayama

STANDALONES

Crown of Stars *SCI FI RH*

SHARED WORLD PROJECTS

Blade of Iris - Mafia Wars *CONTEMPORARY RH*

CO-WRITES

CO-AUTHOR PROJECTS - *Erin O'Kane*

HER FREAKS SERIES *PNR Dystopian RH*

Circus Save Me

Taming The Ringmaster

Walking the Tightrope

Her Freaks Series - the omnibus

STANDALONES

The Hero Complex *PNR RH*

Dark Temptations *Collection of Short Stories, ft. One Night Only & Circus Saves Christmas*

THE WILD BOYS SERIES *CONTEMPORARY RH*

The Wild Interview

The Wild Tour

The Wild Finale

The Wild Boys - the omnibus

CO-AUTHOR PROJECTS - *Ivy Fox*

Deadly Love Series *CONTEMPORARY*

Deadly Affair

Deadly Match

Deadly Encounter

CO-AUTHOR PROJECTS - *Kendra Moreno*

STANDALONES

Stolen Trophy *CONTEMPORARY RH*

Fractured Shadows *PNR RH*

Shadowed Heart

Burn Me *PNR*

Cirque Obscurum *PNR RH*

CO-AUTHOR PROJECTS - *Loxley Savage*

THE FORSAKEN SERIES *SCI FI RH*

Capturing Carmen

Stealing Shiloh

Harboring Harlow

STANDALONES

Gangsters and Guns *CONTEMPORARY*, IN DEN OF VIPERS' UNIVERSE

OTHER CO-WRITES

Shipwreck Souls *(with Kendra Moreno & Poppy Woods)*

The Horror Emporium *(with Kendra Moreno & Poppy Woods)*

AUDIOBOOKS

The Wasteland

The Summit

The Cities

The Nations - *coming soon*

Rage

Hate

Den of Vipers *(From Podium Audio)*

Gangsters and Guns *(From Podium Audio)*

Daddy's Angel *(From Podium Audio)*

Stepbrothers' Darling *(From Podium Audio)*

Blade of Iris *(From Podium Audio)*

Deadly Affair *(From Podium Audio)*

Deadly Match *(From Podium Audio)*

Deadly Encounter *(From Podium Audio)*

Stolen Trophy *(From Podium Audio)*

Crown of Stars *(From Podium Audio)*

Monstrous Lies *(From Podium Audio)*

Monstrous Truth *(From Podium Audio)*

Monstrous Ends *(From Podium Audio)*

Court of Nightmares *(From Podium Audio)*

Court of Death *(From Podium Audio)*

Unstoppable *(From Podium Audio)*

Unbreakable *(From Podium Audio)*

Fractured Shadows *(From Podium Audio)*

Shadowed Heart *(From Podium Audio)*

Revolt *(From Podium Audio)*

Rebel *(From Podium Audio) - coming soon*

FIND AN ERROR?

Please email this information to thenuttyformatter1@gmail.com:

- *the author name*
- *title of the book*
- *screenshot of the error*
- *suggested correction*

Printed in Great Britain
by Amazon

46159712R00185